CREDO'S BANDIDOS

Book Seven in the Alex Wolfe Mysteries

ALISON NAOMI HOLT

CHAPTER 1

I sat at a round, red Formica table and nursed a hard lemonade. Not the sexiest drink around, but I don't like beer, and mixed drinks have a startlingly quick effect on my sobriety. The pub, affectionately named The Hairy Lime, had dark wooden walls reminiscent of an old English watering hole, with a matching, highly polished oak bar that ran the length of one side of the establishment.

About twenty swivel stools, each with an elaborately carved wooden fox curled in a ball to form their backrests, were bolted to the floor along the front edge of the bar. Contrasting light oak footrests circled the lower circumference, and that, along with a padded leather seat, made them very comfortable to sit in for long periods of time. I know because I've perched on them many, many times, both alone, whenever I've needed some me time away from the other detectives I work with at the Tucson Police Department, and during those occasions when I've come to blow off steam with a bunch of friends.

Today, however, I sat away from the bar and studied postcards embedded beneath a coat of shiny, clear epoxy on my tabletop, each card depicting one or more 1950 movie stars. So far, I'd identified Grace Kelly in her signature gold lamé gown, a laughing Fred MacMurray with a starlet on his lap, and what looked like a colorized card with Gene Kelly wearing a pink shirt and smiling his winning, Hollywood smile.

Laughter rose from one of two pool tables set slightly in front of me and to my right. I glanced up in time to watch a boujee kinda guy in pinstripe slacks and an open-collared shirt swing his pool cue around his back and hit the solid orange five-ball off the maroon seven, sending them both into their respective pockets. The man's matching suit coat hung on a coat rack behind him, and he clenched a thick stogie between straight, white teeth. An ostentatious gold watch adorned his left wrist, shouting, 'Look at me' to anyone interested enough to listen.

Out of all my skills, I consider reading people one of my best. This man belonged to a type that fascinated me. Outwardly assured, amiable and handsome, but on the inside...on the inside, I saw a man possibly from the middle class, but more probably from the lower classes, frantically running on a treadmill trying to be what he most admired, a member of high society. I guessed he studied all the high fashion magazines, Gentlemen's Quarterly, Vogue, Esquire—I'd seen them in the homes of all the men I'd met who fit this personality type.

He bought clothes he thought the wealthy wore, usually more than he could afford, often going without basic necessities to feed his need to blend in where he didn't belong. His expensive watch told me that. At one point, I'd investigated an embezzling scheme at a jewelry store, and although I wasn't close enough to know what brand the watch was, I guessed he'd saved several months', or possibly even years' wages to purchase it.

The other two men in the game didn't have the same need for ostentation. One wore a celery green suit bought off the rack at a mid-range department store. His jacket lay discarded on the seat of a wooden-backed chair, and he'd left the top three buttons of his custard yellow shirt unbuttoned to reveal a gold medallion displayed on his mat of curling brown hair.

The third man wore business casual; tan chinos, a blue button-down shirt, and a thin-lined, red-striped tie that he wore pulled loose at the knot. His brown oxfords sported a professional shine, and I caught a glimpse of indigo and black argyle socks when he rested his foot on the lower rung of the chair to wipe away a perceived mote of dust marring the side of the shoe.

When Boujee sank the eight ball with a flair, his mates groaned and good-naturedly raised their cues in surrender. He basked in their admiration, smiling around the unlit cigar.

The tinkle of the tiny bell on the front door caught my attention, and I watched as my ex-ranger friend, Jerry Dhotis, walked in. I wouldn't have thought it possible, but his rock-solid body seemed even more granitelike than the last time we'd met. He shrugged out of his leather bomber jacket and folded it over one massive arm. He studied the room, his no-nonsense eyes taking in every aspect of the bar, eventually landing on the guys good-naturedly throwing insults at one another at the pool table.

During his perusal, his gaze had traveled over me on the way to its final destination. Instead of greeting him as I normally would, I made sure to dismiss him as coldly as I'd dismissed any of a dozen people who'd come in over the course of the last hour.

According to a pre-arranged signal, I picked up my bottle of hard lemonade with my right hand using only two fingers and a thumb, indicating the man I was interested in sat on the far right side of the bar in the second barstool from the end.

Without skipping a beat, Jerry walked to the coatrack near the pool tables and dropped his heavy coat on top of Boujee's pin-striped suit coat.

I didn't know whether Boujee was actually trying for bourgeois chic, but he fit the bill entirely, albeit in a handsome, somewhat rugged sort of way. He ran a hand through his slicked back, salt and pepper hair, a matching complement to his meticulously groomed, seven or eight days growth of beard, and addressed Jerry in a slightly irritated tone. "You mind taking your coat off my jacket?" Contrary to his tone, he struck a casually unconcerned pose as he removed the cigar from between his teeth with one hand—the cap had already been cut—flicked a flame onto his gold lighter with the other, and expertly toasted the foot of the cigar until smoke drifted up toward the ceiling. Returning it to his mouth, he drew smoke onto his palate and seemed to weigh the consequences of blowing it into Jerry's face.

Not a good move. Jerry's bushy eyebrows pulled down low over the caveman protrusions that served as his brows and he tilted his head slightly to the left.

Apparently, Boujee understood the subtleties of man speak because he smiled before turning his head to the side and blowing a fragrant cloud of smoke in my general direction. "Please. I need to wear that to work the rest of the week, and I'd rather not have to take it to the cleaners again."

Jerry's deep voice rumbled through the bar. "No problem." He grabbed the bomber jacket by the sheepskin collar and moved it to a lower, empty arm of the rack. "How about I rotate in?"

The man in the green seersucker suit placed his stick in the rack. "Take my place. I need to get some shuteye."

Boujee said, "See ya around, Eddie."

Jerry nodded his thanks to the guy and then strode to the rack where he made his way through several cue sticks, holding them one-by-one and sighting down their shaft, checking the grips to find one that fit his beefy hand, and balancing each on his palm before finally finding one that met all his requirements.

In my humble opinion, Jerry rivaled Boujee in the looks department, with his weightlifter's neck, oversized, square-shaped head topped with a military crew cut, and a strong, clean-shaven, admirably tanned jawline. After picking his stick, he pulled the triangular rack from the peg on the wall and, while laying it on the table, looked over at the bar.

It was a casual move, utterly unremarkable except for the fact that I knew he was checking out the guy I'd indicated earlier. I wasn't the only woman in the place still admiring Jerry's biceps as he leaned over the table. Unlike many of the other men scattered around the pub, his arms were tastefully covered by a fitted shirt that neither shouted, "I got muscles" nor "I have absolutely no taste in clothing."

I returned my attention to my postcards, resuming my game of guess the fifties star or starlet. I heard the cue ball crack into the other fifteen balls on the table and guessed the battle had begun.

Boujee good-naturedly asked Jerry what he was drinking.

"Jack' n Coke."

The third player piped up. "Another Cosmo for me."

I smiled at what I knew Jerry's reaction would be to what he called a "foo-foo" drink.

Boujee called to the waitress, who was at that moment setting another hard lemonade in front of me. "Hey, Darlin'. Jack and Coke for my new friend here," he paused, and I guessed he was rolling his eyes at his other friend's choice, "and another cosmopolitan for Jess and a Four Roses Single Barrel neat for me."

Four Roses? Not a cheap drink, but then again, it was a given any self-respecting boujee would drink an expensive bourbon, was it not? I glanced down at my bottle of hard lemonade. Hardly something anyone would consider sophisticated, but that pretty much described me to a tee. I'm your garden variety five-foot-six-inch woman, weighing in at around one hundred twenty-five pounds. My brown hair is short and non-descript, and there's nothing special about my green-brown eyes.

The bell tinkled again, and I looked up as my partner, Casey Bowman, walked through the door. She waved when she saw me and then stepped over to the bar and ordered a beer. Even before the bartender handed her the bottle, I knew it would be an IPA. Don't ask me why, but she likes the bitter, hoppy taste that I so dislike even in the mildest of beers.

She brought it to my table and sat in the chair next to me. She leaned in and asked quietly, "Did Jerry see him?"

I nodded and pointed to a postcard. "I haven't been able to figure out who this is. Got any ideas?"

She turned a bit in her seat to get a better angle on the picture. "I think that's Cyd Charisse."

"Who?" I leaned over and squinted at the picture as though that would help me recognize the face.

"My momma loved her, and I remember watching her dance with Fred Astaire..." She pointed to a card on the left featuring the dancer, "...and Gene Kelly." She tapped the table with the edge of her beer, indicating the card with Kelly in the open-collared pink shirt. "In fact, I think she danced with Kelly in Singin' in the Rain." Pulling out her phone, she took a moment to look her up. "Yup, she wasn't one of the three main stars, but she was in that and a bunch of other big movies." A look of nostalgia crossed her features. "Momma knew every star in the fifties. She would have loved it here.

I'll bet she'd go from table to table pointing at all the postcards and calling out each name as she walked by."

Casey's soft spot for her family showed on her face whenever she mentioned them. She pushed a strand of her short blonde hair out of her eyes and sat back comfortably in her chair. Crossing her lean, muscular arms, she glanced over her shoulder at Jerry, who pretended not to notice.

In fact, nobody paid us any attention, which was perfectly fine with me. I never liked it much when I went out with my best friend, Megan, who attracted males the same way a mare in heat brings the geldings on the run.

Leaning forward again, Casey said quietly, "How long do you think he'll stay?"

I shrugged, "Probably until I leave."

She sat back again. "When I'm walking or driving, I keep looking over my shoulder to see if somebody's following me, but I haven't caught anyone yet. You have any idea why this guy's been your shadow for the last few days?"

Shaking my head, I took a long drink from my bottle and watched the man stand and stretch. This was the first time I'd had a good look at his face, since the other times he'd followed me, he'd either been driving in a car behind me or standing in the shadows across the street from my house. That's the incident that had really brought him to my attention and made me want to know who he was and what he wanted with me.

The previous night, I'd let my dogs, Tessa and Jynx, out into the front yard, and just like I knew he would, little Jynx, a tri-colored Pappiwawa, began barking at the tree where I'd seen the guy minutes before. Staying in the shadows, the man had run around the side of the house, and before I could grab Jynx and give chase, he'd disappeared.

Looking at him now, I realized he wasn't a big man by any means. He looked to be in his mid-to-late forties, about my height and maybe forty pounds heavier than me. He had kind of an urban cowboy or rustic suburbanite look about him. Somewhat muscular but not nearly on a par with Jerry, he wore a collarless button-fronted shirt beneath a casual, blue sport coat, dark jeans, and really nice-looking cowboy boots. He certainly didn't look threatening. His grey hair was neatly cut on the sides and slightly longer on top, where he spiked it up with gel or mousse.

Today, when I'd gotten off work, I'd driven to the Hairy Lime, keeping an eye on his car as the driver tried to inconspicuously follow me—not an easy task when the person you're following is a cop. Once inside, I'd watched through the window as he'd parked, then took my seat and studied the postcards as he'd come in to claim his barstool. I'd already arranged for Jerry to meet me in the pub and was confident he'd have all the intel I needed on the guy by the time I sat down for lunch the following day.

Speaking of Jerry, he'd apparently won the first game, making it his turn to buy the next round. Instead of yelling across the room to the waitress as Boujee had done, he casually walked over to where she was clearing a table to give her his order. When she nodded, he returned to the pool table where the third guy, Jess, had already re-racked the balls and was leaning over the top rail, stick in hand, preparing his opening break.

When the man who'd been following me headed for the bathroom, I overheard Jerry tell his newfound friends, "I need to hit the head. Be right back."

Since guys are quicker than women in the bathroom department, both men were back to their respective places in less time than it took me to identify the last starlet on my table. I'd taken a picture of the woman and then texted the shot to my mother, who had immediately texted back, "Joan Taylor."

Casey shook her head. "Never heard of her."

"Me neither." My phone dinged again with a follow-up text from my mom. "Why can't you wear beautiful clothes like that? And her hair. You could at least try." Translated, my mother was desperate for me to marry and have kids—further translated, grandkids—and my lack of success in that area was a deep disappointment to her well-ordered view of how my world should work. Oh well.

We'd had a long day, and after casually chatting about some of the open cases sitting on our desks back at the station, both Casey and I were ready to head home. I left a good tip on the table, and the two of us walked out to the parking lot. I didn't particularly care if the guy followed me now because I knew Jerry had other people waiting outside to follow him, following me home. I also knew Jerry's guys wouldn't get made like this nimrod had done.

I'd asked Jerry not to contact the man until we had at least some intelligence on him. The guy had been trailing me for three days now. He'd never tried to make contact, but so far, I'd caught glimpses of him in a coffee shop near a crime scene, across the street from my house, and now actually following me into the Hairy Lime. And I'd lost count of how many times I'd seen his older blue sedan somewhere in my vicinity as I made my way across town.

When I got home, Tessa and Jynx were anxiously waiting for me to grab their leashes and take them for their evening walk. I hadn't seen anyone tailing me, and as I walked the pups around the block, dusk settled on the houses and surrounding trees. I kept an eye on every shadow, hoping to see the guy again, but didn't have any luck. We returned to the house after a good two-mile walk. I fed them, watched a little T.V., and fell asleep on the couch.

CHAPTER 2

A phone call the following morning brought me out of a sound sleep, and I groped between the cushions trying to find my cellphone. I knew my answering machine would pick up on the fifth ring and managed to punch the send button at four and a half. "Mornin' Jerry. I didn't expect to hear from you this early on a Saturday morning."

"I think you might want to head over to the K9 Academy; check out Megan's class."

"What?" I checked the time on my phone. Nine o'clock. "What are you talking about? Why would I want to go watch one of her classes?" Megan, my red-headed best friend since our diaper days, ran a dog training school where she taught everything from obedience, agility, and behavior modification to search and rescue classes for the local Search and Rescue.

When he wasn't working, Jerry was a fun guy to be around, gregarious even, but when he was on a job, he morphed into a highly focused contractor who hired out as a private investigator and/or bodyguard; the kind who didn't mess around with any type of polite chitchat. Traffic roared in the background, and I knew he must be sitting next to a busy street. He confirmed that when he said, "I'm here now. I'll wait for you."

I started to reply but having had him hang up on me mid-sentence on prior occasions, I checked my phone. Sure enough, he'd disconnected.

He'd parked his black truck across the street in a mini-mart parking lot, so I pulled into a spot outside Meg's academy. Since I didn't know whether I was being followed, I took out my cell phone and gave him a call.

Without preamble, such as the typical 'hi how are you' usually practiced among friends, he said, "You need to go in."

"Why?"

"Just go in and check out the class."

Exasperated, I growled, "Fine." First things first, though. I crossed the street and went into the minimart, poured myself a coffee, grabbed a chocolate doughnut, and headed back across the street, where I let myself in through her front door. I walked in on a class of about six or seven dogs running through various individual exercises.

Megan looked up from where she knelt on the floor next to an eager-looking black and white Boston Terrier. The terrier also looked my way, and I saw excitement and a glint of mischief in her eye.

Megan redirected the dog's attention to a set of weave poles lined up in the middle of the room. As soon as the dog focused, Megan released the collar and shouted "Poles" with an over-exuberant tone of voice. The dog's little legs churned as she sped into the first weave. She enthusiastically ran through the first three poles before noticing another dog disappear into a multi-colored tunnel in another part of the room. Probably thinking that looked like a lot more fun than the poles, she bounded off towards a possible new playmate.

"Peanut." Megan's shouted command left no room for doubt that she meant business.

Little Peanut stopped and turned to face Megan, her tongue flopped to the side of her muzzle and playful mischief exuding from every pore in her body. She bowed low, her forelegs flat on the ground and her butt stuck straight in the air and began weaving in place with her front legs bouncing back and forth in an invitation to play.

Megan growled low in her throat when she said, "Come."

Reluctant but obedient, little Peanut trotted over to where Megan waited.

This obviously hadn't been why Jerry had wanted me to come this morning, so I took a sip of coffee and glanced around the room. I nearly choked taking in a startled breath. Coffee went down the wrong pipe and started a coughing fit I had difficulty controlling.

Megan laughingly called over to me, "You gonna live, Alex?"

Nodding, I wiped the tears from my eyes. I tried not to look at the only student not dressed in jeans, sneakers, and a t-shirt or blouse—the only one wearing medium gray, highly pressed slacks and a light blue, button-down shirt sporting a tiny alligator embroidered on the left side of his chest. A braided brown leather belt, Gucci loafers, and a gold wristwatch rounded out the outfit. In short, Boujee.

A German shepherd sat by his side, muscles bunched and ready as he anxiously lined up in front of a make-believe window. He was a handsome dog, not typical of the American version with low slung hips that cause them no end of trouble. This dog had a strong, straight back and markings atypical of most black and tan shepherds. Deep black covered his head and body with a light brown undercoat showing through in places. His face matched the rest of his body, giving him what I thought of as a very serious mien.

When Boujee pointed, the dog instantly took two steps and leapt through the fake window, landing gracefully on the other side. He looked back at his owner for instructions, and with a flick of his wrist, the man brought him back to his side.

I didn't want Boujee to know I'd seen him, so I walked over to Peanut and her owner and started a conversation, all the while keeping a discreet eye on the other pair. "Her name's Peanut? She's quite a character."

Her owner smiled. "She is. She's still young and full of herself, but what a competitor. I couldn't ask for a better dog."

"You compete in agility?" Even as she answered, I watched Boujee walk over to another student and, with a quiet word, put his dog into a down. That dog certainly knew what he was about. I would have guessed this man would hire a high-end trainer rather than dirty his clothes in a small operation like the one Megan ran.

"Some agility. Mostly flyball."

That brought my attention back to Peanut, who was bored and had started chewing on her leash. "Flyball?"

"Yeah, it's mostly flat out running, something Peanut is exceptionally good at." She reached down and grabbed the leash next to Peanut's mouth. "Drop it." The little Boston terrier gave the leash a tug and a shake before letting the leash go and smiling up at her owner.

"I'll bet." I smiled at her and then found Megan working with another high-energy dog. I strolled over and asked, "What kind of dog's that?" I nodded a quick hello to a college-aged young man holding the excited dog's collar.

Megan smiled down at me from where she sat straddled atop an inverted V-shaped contraption. "Russel Terrier. You wouldn't believe the energy of this guy. If I had even this much of his speed and strength and stamina," She held up her pinkie finger to show me how little she'd need, "I'd be able to conquer the world."

The dog's owner bobbed his head in agreement. "He'd play frisbee with me all day if I had the time." He knelt to pet his pup. "Wouldn't you, boy?"

I jerked my head indicating I needed to speak to Megan in private.

She climbed down off her perch and said to the young man, "Why don't you go work on some obedience? That's his weak point right now."

Nodding, the young man and his playmate wandered to an empty corner and started on some basic obedience commands.

I steered Megan away from Boujee and turned my back to him. "When did the guy in the gray slacks and light blue shirt show up?"

She shrugged, "Last week. Why?"

"How many classes has he come to?"

She tilted her head. "He's kinda cute, isn't he?"

I squinted at her. "He's a little old for you, don't you think?" Megan and I were both in our early thirties, and if the salt in the guy's pepper hair was any indication, he was probably in his early fifties. "He must have a good fifteen years on you."

"Since when has that ever stopped me?"

Sighing, I said, "Just answer the question."

"What was the question, again?"

"How many classes has he been to?"

"Three, I think."

"Three in a week?"

She shrugged. "Yeah."

"It doesn't look to me like that dog needs any kind of training."

Glancing over at the shepherd, she nodded, "Yeah, but did it ever occur to you that consistently taking the dog to classes is why Gastro is so well-trained?"

"Gastro?"

She grinned, "Anyway, why are you asking?"

"I don't know. I'll let you know when I do. See ya." I started for the door and watched Boujee put the dog in a stay position. He walked away, and on a hunch, I veered over to the dog and used the down command Buck Paris used for Bear, his police K9. The command wasn't an English word, and very few dogs, other than those in the police world, would understand what I'd said. Seemingly more out of habit than obedience to me, the dog immediately lay down. He cocked his head and looked up curiously before Boujee called him to his side.

With a knowing smile, I met Boujee's gaze, which held an equal amount of amusement, and then I left the building. I took out my cell and called Jerry. "What the hell's he doing at Meg's place?"

"I'm not sure."

"Can you put someone on him?"

"I'm on him."

"Listen, I know I don't need to say it, but keep Megan safe. We have no clue what these guys are up to, and until we do, I don't want to take any chances with her safety." Megan was often a thorn in my side, a clown, and someone who continuously got me into trouble with my sergeant, Kate Brannigan, but I knew I wouldn't survive something lethal happening to her because of me.

"Yeah. You want the info on these guys?"

"You think maybe it's just a coincidence this guy was at the bar last night and at Megan's place this morning?"

"I don't do coincidences."

Neither did I, and as I got into my car, I stared at my best friend's business. "Maybe I should go back in." I started to slide out of my seat, but Jerry stopped me.

"I said I got this, Alex. I want to know what this guy's

doing here just as much as you." Some paper rustled in the background. "This guy here's name is George Ogilvie. Lives in Los Angeles, divorced, remarried now, lives with his second wife. The rest of his family lives there, too. Well, most of his family. His half-brother, who *coincidentally*," he emphasized the word, "is the other guy that's been following you has lived here for the last twenty years. I got one of my people getting all the info on him. I'll call you with it later."

I knew it would look weird to Boujee if I just sat in my car, so I backed out of the parking space and moved into traffic.

Jerry's bass monotone continued, "This guy lives large, as you could probably tell from his clothing and jewelry and stuff." Amusement crept into his voice. Jerry was a tough, former army ranger who probably didn't think much of a man wearing expensive jewelry. "I don't know how he can afford it because he's—"

I cut him off before he could say it. "A retired cop."

"You got it. Worked undercover mostly, but the last three years of his career—"

I supplied the answer again, "He was in the K9 unit."

The line was silent a moment before Jerry said, "You want to tell me the rest?"

I chuckled, "No, that's about all I know. His German Shepherd obeyed a command I've heard Buck Paris use, so I put two and two together. Do you think he's a P.I.?"

"He's not registered in Arizona if he is. He could be workin' for the feds. They tend to snap up retired U.C. guys like candy since the feds can't hide in a box of peanuts even if they wrapped themselves in a Mr. Peanut wrapper. I've got someone checking on that angle. He's coming out of Megan's place now. Like I said, I'll call ya later."

CHAPTER 3

I turned onto the street that runs in front of my house. I hadn't seen anyone following me, but then again, the guy knows where I live, so he wouldn't have any need to follow close behind. I thought Jerry was still on the line, so I jumped when my cell buzzed with Kate's distinctive siren ring. I clicked send and said, "Hey, Boss. What's up?" I definitely needed to talk to Jerry about proper phone etiquette.

"We've had another arson. Same M.O. I need you to meet us there." There'd been a series of arsons throughout the city in the last several months. Enough of them that our unit, Special Crimes, had been assigned to help out the arson guys, all two of them, with their investigations.

The department had had cutbacks recently, and they'd trimmed a few detective units down to the bare bones. Luckily, ours hadn't been affected in the first round of cuts, but we knew a second round wouldn't be far behind. The thought had us all on edge because we had one of the closest units in the department, thanks mainly to Kate's legendary leadership style.

Over the years, her reputation has grown to the point

where she has a waiting list of detectives wanting to get into the unit. The problem, if you could call it a problem, is none of us have any intention of moving on to a different team. There'd been a few times when Kate had tried to pawn me off on other sergeants, but that's another story altogether.

"Okay. I'm just getting home from visiting Megan. Can I grab some breakfast first?"

"No. Stop in a drive-through on the way if you have to, but don't waste any time."

Sighing, I quickly let Tessa and Jynx out, then walked over to my neighbor's house to ask him to spend some time with the pups while I was gone. Instead of going to the front door, which I knew he wouldn't answer, I skirted around a Mexican Bird of Paradise and knocked on one of his front plate glass windows.

Even though he was agoraphobic, Newton kept a watch on the neighborhood's comings and goings through openings at the edges of the thick curtains hanging from each of his many windows. I don't know if it was by design or chance, but he could keep an eye on all four sides of his house simply by moving from one window to another. Unless he'd been otherwise occupied, he'd known the instant I'd pulled into my driveway.

The curtain moved slightly, and I knew that was the only communication I'd have with him today. "Hey, Newt. I got called out this morning to go into work. Could you watch the dogs for a bit? I'm sure they're tired of being cooped up." It was a rare day that I didn't take them for a walk, but I still felt bad when I couldn't spend quality time with them during my days off.

A finger snaked into the open and pointed toward his backyard.

"Thanks, buddy. I'll pick you up a burger on my way home." Obviously, Newton didn't get out much, so I often brought him takeout and left it on his front porch on my way home.

The finger disappeared, and I called Tessa and Jynx over to me. Their tails wagged with joy when we walked around the side of his house and I opened the gate into Newt's backyard. The man must spoil them rotten on their visits because the two of them raced into the yard without a backward glance.

"Bye." Somewhat hurt by their lack of adoring devotion, I listened for Newt to join them with their toys before shutting the gate. I'd never actually been into the backyard, that would have been too much for him, but I had heard him stage whisper their names and call out "go get it" and "that's a girl" while he threw a couple of tennis balls for them. That's exactly what I heard as I returned to my front door to relock it before heading to the address Kate had texted me after she'd hung up.

I popped the remainder of my sausage, egg, and cheese sandwich in my mouth just as I pulled up to a one-story home on the southside of town. Or what was left of it anyway. One side of the structure had burned away. The roof on that section had collapsed, and water dripped into puddles that hadn't yet flowed out onto the street.

Kate stood in front of the mostly intact part of the home, talking to the arson investigators and their sergeant, Rick Longoria. Rick's barrel chest and big belly made him stand out at any crime scene. Add to that a booming voice and bright red, flyaway hair, and there was no way anyone would ever come up and ask, "Where's Rick?"

As soon as I stepped out of my car, his angry tirade thundered across the front yard as he wildly swung his arms in a circle to illustrate his point. "You know I don't have enough people for this! Two guys! I got two guys, and they're already tits deep in sorting out the last three fires. You think they'd give me more detectives, but no. What do they do? They reduce my unit by fifty percent! Fifty percent, Kate! Sometimes I don't think I'm gonna make it to retirement."

Used to his apoplectic temper, his two detectives, Garlan Fawley and Mitch Johnson stood off to the side waiting for him to ratchet down his anger and give them their assignments.

I didn't know Garlan very well. I'd only met him two cases ago when our unit had been seconded to help with these fires. Typically, homicide would have handled the assignment, but they'd had a spate of murders on the east side where a very influential city councilman lived, and there was no way the chief would pull them off those cases. Besides, our team was just as good as theirs, and we closed more cases than they did.

Mitch and I, on the other hand, go way back. We're both on the department's softball team that plays every year in the United States Police and Fire Games. Our team's okay, and we've made it to the regional competition a few times, but that's about it. Mitch is five foot eight, one hundred and eighty-five pounds of pure cop. He's been on the department about ten years longer than I have and has a reputation as someone you want on your team.

He had his arms crossed, and when he saw me walking in their direction, he raised his hand off his bicep to wave me away. Apparently, now wasn't the time to barge in on Rick's tirade, so I changed directions mid-stride and headed over to where Casey waited outside the front door. Miraculously, the doorframe had survived while everything around it had burned to a crisp. "That's weird." I pointed to where the actual door should be.

Casey nodded. "I know. The door burned, the walls around the frame burned, but the frame itself stayed intact. How do you think that happened?"

"Got me. We'll have to ask Mitch. We have a victim?"

"That's what the firefighters say. We haven't been allowed in yet. They're still checking for hot spots and any structural damage that might be a hazard. The fire captain said they should be done pretty soon, and then we can go in." She glanced at the crowd waiting outside the yellow police tape. "Did Jerry get any info on the guy following you?"

"No, but get this. You remember that boujee guy Jerry was playing pool with last night?"

"Boujee?"

"Yeah, you know. The guy smokin' a stogie in that super-smart looking tailored suit."

"What does boujee mean?"

"You've heard the word bourgeois? It's kind of a take-off on that."

She raised her eyebrows and scratched the side of her head. "Okay, so what about him?"

"This morning, Jerry told me to meet him at Megan's academy. Boujee was there with his dog. A German Shepherd. A really well-trained German Shepherd." I raised my eyebrows and cocked my head, waiting for her to figure things out.

"At Megan's? Does she know him?"

"He just started classes about a week ago, but Jerry's been tailing him and found out that he's step-brothers with the guy who's been following me. Pretty weird, huh?" Out of habit, I raised my cellphone and snapped some pictures of the looky-loos standing around. "We've got a pretty good crowd this morning. Seems like word's getting out."

The fire captain, a muscular woman with a squarish face and choppy brown hair, stepped through the doorframe. "You guys can go inside. Utilities are shut down, and most of the water has receded. As usual, watch out for the sharp ends of broken boards and screws and such. We used sniffers, and there's nothing toxic in the air. You're good to go." She shook her head. "It's pretty gruesome, just like the others. You guys gotta find the asshole doin' this. Even my own mother has moved in with us. She's scared to death."

"We're tryin', Captain." I looked at Casey's feet and realized she'd remembered the rubber boots we'd been given when we'd joined the task force. I'd left mine back in my trunk. "I'll see you inside. I need to get my boots." I made my way back to my car, popped my trunk, and rummaged around trying to locate both boots.

"Excuse me?" A timid voice behind me made me jump and spin around.

A black woman stood directly behind me. A bit frightened by my reaction, she took a step back and held up her hands in surrender. "I'm sorry. I didn't mean to scare you." Although her eyes were somewhat unsure, they held the glint of a smile, and I instantly took a liking to her.

To set her at ease, I held out my hand and introduced myself, something I rarely do when I'm on the job because shaking hands is a great way to get hurt. All the person has to do is hang onto your right hand while delivering a roundhouse punch with their left. I instinctively knew that wouldn't be the case with this woman. "I'm Detective Wolfe. No need to be sorry; you startled me, that's all. I should have been more aware of my surroundings."

A charming, almost impish smile lit up her dark features. Although a heavy woman, she wore her weight well. It suited her short five-foot-two-inch frame. I guessed she was in her early twenties. She wore her waist-length hair tightly braided into what looked like thirty or forty plaits that accentuated the roundness of her face.

She took my hand. "I'm Rosemarie, but everybody just calls me Babe," She playfully batted her eyes, exaggerating the movement by tilting her head and putting her hand to her face, "because I was just the cutest baby you ever did see."

I smiled back and privately thought she probably was adorable as a baby if the sparkle in her eyes was any indication. "What can I do for you, Rosemarie?"

"Babe." Her features took on a more serious tone. "I was just wondering, was there another senior in there? Just like the other four?"

I cocked my head and squinted at her, fervently hoping she wasn't a suspect. Many times, bad guys like to return to the crime scene, and arsonists especially enjoy watching the arson detectives do their thing. I had a suspect tell me once that he learned more about his craft by befriending arson detectives than by any other means. "It's early in the investigation, so I really can't say. What's your connection with it?"

Shrugging, she eyed the house with an angry intensity. "No connection. I saw the smoke and was worried maybe it was another one, you know, where somebody kills a senior citizen."

"I don't know if there's an old person in there or not. We just got here." I was interested in why she kept calling the victims' seniors' or 'senior citizens.' Most people just called them old and left it at that.

She shook her head. "If you'd spent as much time around them as I do, you'd know most of them aren't what we stereotypically call old. Their lives still have meaning, and they still want to be part of life." She looked a little sheepish. "Sorry for the lecture. Everyone in my family is either a doctor or a nurse or whatnot. I guess caring about people is just who we are."

"So, you're a nurse?"

"Naw," The smile came out again. "I just volunteer a couple days a week to visit seniors who need a little help with whatever."

"Do your parents live around here?" I was trying to interview her without actually interviewing her. I didn't want her to be a suspect, but I didn't want Kate asking me a bunch of questions I didn't have answers to either. I've worked with her long enough to know that majorly pisses her off.

"No. They all live in Pittsburgh. I'm just visiting a friend, well, I came to visit about two months ago and haven't left yet." A couple dimples appeared in her cheek, and I pulled out my notebook as unobtrusively as I could.

"You seem to know a lot about seniors." I emphasized the word, letting her know I'd been listening to what she had to say. "Can I get your contact information in case I have questions?"

"Rosemarie Holt." She gave me her phone number and the address of where she was staying. "The friend I'm staying with, her mother volunteers at the Armory Senior Center, and she got me involved."

"So, the only reason you're here is because you saw the smoke and hoped it wasn't another one of The Coward's victims?" The paper had started giving monikers to serial criminals but had decided instead of glorifying them, they'd rather shame them instead. This one had become "The Coward" since he or she preyed on old and helpless people in their homes. "Have you known any of the victims?"

She shook her head, "No, but I'm terrified that one day I'll read one of their names in the news and realize it's one of the people I visit."

Kate called over to me from the doorway. "Alex."

I quickly shut my notebook and grabbed my wellies from the trunk. "Gotta run. Nice to meet you, Babe. You take care."

She nodded and asked again. "So, is this another one?"

I shrugged, "Like I said, early days...oh..." On a whim, I dug in my pocket for one of my cards, hastily scribbled my number on it before handing it to her. I jogged over to Kate, who by that time had turned and was following Sergeant

Longoria into the crime scene. I stopped long enough to pull on the boots and then hurried after them. I didn't want to miss any of the briefing, and luckily Longoria had just started when I stepped up next to Casey.

The briefing consisted of Kate, Casey, two other detectives in our unit, Nate Drewery and Allen Brodie, plus Longoria and his two detectives, Garlan and Mitch. Garlan had been standing close to Casey, and when I edged my way in, he glanced down at me and lowered his chin in silent greeting.

I nodded back, absently wondering if he'd ever played college basketball. Like I mentioned earlier, I don't know him well and didn't want to stereotype this handsome, six-foot-five black man into a corner. I realized I'd been studying his profile instead of listening to the briefing, and when I turned to listen to Longoria, I found Kate staring at me. The muscle in her jaw twitched, and I knew she knew I had no idea what had been said up to this point.

I scrunched my eyebrows and zeroed in on Longoria's face to placate Kate, who sighed and shook her head.

Longoria pointed to a tarp the firefighters had set up to shield the body as best they could from external contamination, such as drips and falling debris. Since most of the front wall on that side of the house had been burned away in the fire, it also served to hide what was left of the bed and its contents from unwanted, prying eyes. "As I mentioned to you earlier, Kate, Mitch, and the fire investigators will handle the arson, and you and your team have the body." He opened his notebook and indicated Garlan with a lift of his chin. "Garlan and I are still sorting through the evidence of the other four fires. We'll be available if you need us, but we won't be spending much time on-scene. Any questions?"

Since we'd all just arrived, we didn't know enough about the scene or the crime to know what to ask.

He continued, "Kate, Garlan, and Mitch, let's go have a look at the body."

Kate nodded, "Right, Alex, you find out everything you can about the occupants of this house. Find out how many people live here, names, ages, everything. Find out if the victim had any family and if so, let me know so I can notify next-of-kin. Also, I want you to be Mitch's contact with our unit on this one.

"Casey, photographs. You know the drill: everything and anything. I want a pictorial grid of the entire home, burned-out areas, and non-burn areas. Brodie canvas the neighborhood and see if anyone saw anything suspicious, and Nate, hopefully, we'll get lucky on this one since only half of the home was burned. I'm sure that was a mistake on the part of the arsonist, and I mean to take full advantage of that fact. I want every surface possible fingerprinted. There may be too much smoke and water damage, but like I said, I'm hoping to get lucky. God knows we need a break on these murders." Having given us our marching orders, Kate and the other three disappeared into the house's more heavily burned area.

I silently sighed with relief. I really hated dead bodies, burned dead bodies in particular. A psychologist would probably say it has something to do with coming to grips with my own mortality. But honestly? There'd been too many times when someone had set a plate of food down in front of me that reminded me of something I'd seen on a dead body. For instance, several years earlier, I'd been on an arson where the victim's skin and muscle had been burned away from the woman's ribcage. I hadn't been able to eat a nice rack of ribs for about a year afterward.

I'd made it to what was left of the front door when Kate called out, "Alex."

I turned back. "Yeah, Boss?" By the time I'd turned, she'd

already ducked back behind the tarp, so I couldn't see what she wanted.

"There are some things here that might help you with your identification."

Damn. I reluctantly walked to the tarp and stepped around it. Luckily there was very little left of the body. Along with the characteristic smell of burned flesh, there was the distinctive smell of wet, burnt wood. This arsonist always made very sure there was very little of the body left intact. In the previous four fires, he'd poured accelerant down the midline of the body, making sure the fire destroyed almost all the flesh and organs. Occasionally there'd been a small amount of crispy skin and muscle left on the extremities and parts of the skull, but that was about it. I didn't have any reason to think he'd changed his M.O. on this one.

Not that I had anything to do with the arson part of these investigations. Arson investigation is a specialty, one where the investigators tend to spend their entire careers learning the intricate details associated with fire and arson, only to be snapped up by insurance companies when they retire.

Garlan was crouching by the side of the metal-framed bed with his head twisted around so he could look beneath it. The body lay on top of the metal springs; the only thing left of the twin mattress and box spring set. It was a good thing he was in excellent shape because he was balancing himself on his feet with his upper body parallel to the floor and holding a camera with one hand and a pointer with the other.

He held the pointy end to a mark on the floor—an accelerant pattern would be my guess—and clicked the camera each time he changed the pointer's position. He was describing the pattern to Longoria. "Same as last time. Suspect soaks something, probably crumpled papers, maybe cloth of some kind—I can't be sure until I do some more checking—in what I would guess is the same fuel oil and gasoline mixture he always uses and puts them beneath the bed."

Longoria agreed, "Yeah, and he doused the body too and used the candle in the eye as one of the ignition points. Plus, just like before, he has trailers leading to various points along the wall to make sure they burn as well." He glanced around the room, his bushy red eyebrows moving down low over his eyes as he focused on one point, then rising again as his attention moved elsewhere.

It made me wonder if he was near or far-sighted and needed the extra scrunch to get a better focus on his target. More probably, it was simply a force of habit whenever he needed a moment to think about what he was seeing. Longoria had a reputation around the country as an expert in his field. He'd been interpreting fires far longer than I'd been on the department and was well past where most people retire and begin their second career.

He continued his thoughts as though he hadn't just gone silent for a good minute or so. "He might have been interrupted because he didn't set a trailer to the other side of the house or around the perimeter. Like you said, Kate. We might get lucky on this one." He walked over and examined the one remaining hinge on the lower part of the doorframe leading into the bedroom. "Door was closed. Slowed down the burn." He shook his head, "Why the change in M.O? Our guy doesn't make these kinds of mistakes. Either he was interrupted, or he ran out of time. Maybe the victim delayed him somehow..."

I shrugged, "Or maybe we have a copycat."

Mitch, a clean-cut guy with short brown hair and hazel eyes, shook his head, "No, I don't think so. We've withheld certain pieces of information from the press, and those things we didn't mention are here, so I'm pretty certain we're dealing with the same guy." One of the reasons Mitch had survived the cut was because of his analytical personality. He was excellent with technology, and I guessed that even though he wasn't senior in the unit, Longoria couldn't or didn't want to do without his technological expertise.

Kate pointed to the floor beneath the victim on the side opposite Garlan. "This is what I was talking about, Alex. The chain melted enough to come free of the wrist."

I stepped around and saw a medic alert bracelet lying on the floor next to the bed. I pulled a small evidence bag from my back pocket and shook it open. "Has it been photographed?"

Shaking her head, Kate called out, "Casey."

Casey stuck her head around the tarp.

"I need this photographed." She looked at Garlan and his camera. "I know you're getting pictures, but I want a full set as well."

Casey came in, and both Kate and I stepped back to allow her access to the bracelet. She pulled a wooden ruler from her back pocket, laid it next to the chain to provide perspective for the diagram she'd draw up later, and took photos from several angles. When she'd finished, she lifted her chin in my direction. "All yours."

With gloved hands, I picked up the bracelet and dropped it into the evidence bag. It had begun to melt, but I could still make out a few letters, none of which looked like a person's name. I tried not to look at the corpse—skeleton really—but for some reason, my eyes betrayed me, and without any direction from my conscious mind, they snuck a quick look at the corpse's eye sockets. I couldn't see any wax, mostly because it had completely burned in the fire, but Longoria must have seen a telltale sign because he'd mentioned candles being used as one of the ignition points.

Longoria saw me looking at the eye sockets and took the time to explain, "Same as the other ones. This guy is getting his timing down because it's my guess he uses a delay device beneath the bed and times it to go off at the same time the candle burns down in the eye socket, igniting the accelerant both beneath and on top of the bed at the same time."

I waved away his words. "That's okay, Sarge. I don't need the details."

He snorted softly, "Neither do I. I'll never look at a candle again without seeing these eye sockets. But..." He looked me in the eyes, "whether you like dead bodies or not, Alex, every little detail, no matter how small or...disgusting, might help us catch this guy before he kills someone else.

Chagrined, I felt the pink rise into my cheeks. "I know, Sarge, sorry."

"No need to be sorry. Just don't miss some evidence because your breakfast is threatening to make a reappearance." He smiled at me before pointing to the skeleton's hip area. "And another thing. The house belongs to Norma Sandresin, but this is obviously not Norma."

Forgetting my natural aversion to anything related to death or dying, I moved closer and leaned over the metal bed frame to get a better view of the victim. I'd learned a few things from a forensic anthropologist on an earlier case, and I wanted to see whether what I'd learned could show me what sex the skeleton was.

Seeing my sudden interest, Longoria put on his instructor hat. "Males have bigger, thicker bones. Like here." He pointed to the femur, "And here." He followed the curve of the hip, keeping his index finger a few inches above the actual bone. Then he moved over the elbow. "The joint surface is larger for men and..." He moved his finger back to the hips. "...enough of the skin and muscle has burned away that you can see this sciatic notch is narrower than a woman's notch would be. Like I said, not Norma."

I hadn't worked much with Longoria, but when I had, I

always came away feeling like he respected me despite my various foibles. And I liked and respected him as well. He had a reputation of being an intelligent, fair supervisor. His detectives put up with his red-headed tirades because every single one of them wanted to grow up to be him someday. The best way to do that was to work in his unit for a good number of years. Not an easy task, especially now that they'd cut his squad down to two detectives.

The coroner had told us that the arsonist removed the eyes prior to burning—but post-mortem. It was a good guess he was keeping one or both as a souvenir. I glanced around to see if there was anything else that might give me a clue as to who the victim was, but the flame, at least in this room, must have burned super-hot because nothing that could possibly burn had been left to provide those types of clues. No pictures, books, address books. Nothing. The good news was, the arson detectives looked at the same room and rubbed their hands in glee because to them, the place was full of information they may not have had before.

I glanced at Kate, "Anything else?"

"Not here. Go check out the rest of the house."

Instead of going directly to the other part of the house, I detoured outside to deposit my bag of evidence in the trunk of my car.

And there he was, the urban cowboy from the bar. He was kneeling next to the neighbor's chain-link fence, trying to look like just another bystander as he petted the muzzle of a curly-haired dog through the triangular links of the fence.

Before shutting the hood of my car, I pulled out my phone and snapped a picture of the guy, edging the phone around the side of the trunk where he couldn't see what I was up to. Then I slammed my trunk and took off across the victim's front yard, running straight for the guy who'd been dogging my every move.

I don't know whether he saw the glint of anger in my eyes or the gleaming white of my bared teeth, but with fear in his eyes, he jumped to his feet and fled toward the alley behind the houses. The curly-haired dog matched his speed all the way to the back fence, excitedly barking his pleasure at their new game.

"Alex!" Kate had apparently followed me out and had seen me take off running through the yard, but from her angle, I doubted she'd seen the man I was chasing. I didn't have time to explain, but I heard her yell, "Casey," before I rounded the corner to the alley and pounded after the guy. I'd been hoping his cowboy boots would slow him down, but he was fast. We ran about two blocks before he cut down a side street. I slowed at the corner because my view was blocked by a six-foot wooden fence. I had no intention of being blindsided by the guy hiding in wait to take me out as I rounded the corner.

The sound of running feet and heavy breathing came up behind me, and I checked to make sure it was Casey before I fully stepped around the edge of the fence and saw the guy turning left onto another street. I pointed left and shouted, "That way, guy from the barstool…" before sprinting after the man. I knew Casey would split off to the left and try to cut him off from another angle, but I couldn't be sure she'd understood my hastily shouted and garbled description of the person I was chasing.

By the time I reached the corner, the road was empty. I ran a little way down the middle of the street, then bent over and braced my hands on my knees to catch my breath.

Casey ran up and did the same, and we both jumped when Kate's car came sliding around the corner.

She shouted out her window, "Which way and who am I looking for?"

I still hadn't fully caught my breath, but I gasped out, "I

don't know where he went. Urban cowboy, five-eight, one sixty-five, spiked grey hair, late-forties."

She motioned to both of us. "Get in."

I jumped in the front seat, and Casey took the seat behind Kate.

Kate began driving slowly, and as she did, she started with the questions. "Who is he?"

"I don't know." That was the truth. I didn't know just yet, other than the fact that he was the step-brother of another guy who was following me.

"So why are you chasing him?"

"Because he's pissing me off." I didn't want to tell her about him following me until I had something a little more concrete.

Turning and squinting at me, she said, "You'd better have a better reason than that for pulling us away from a major crime scene."

"It's nothing to do with the case. I didn't mean for you guys to follow me." I repeated, "It's nothing."

Casey said, "You need to tell her, Alex."

I glared over the seat at her. "No. I don't." I didn't need to go running to Kate every time something weird happened. That was why I'd gotten Jerry involved. He and I could handle this just fine on our own.

Kate pulled to the side of the road, put the car in park, and turned toward me, eyebrows raised. I was a pretty good poker player, so I met her quirked eyebrows and raised her glare with a stubborn set to my jaw. She countered with a narrowing of her eyes and a low, warning growl. "Alex."

Damn it. She always seemed to have the stronger hand. "Fine. I've noticed him following me around for a while. I'm taking care of it."

"Uh-huh. Like you took care of him this time? I'm only going to ask once more, Alex. Who is he?"

"I honestly don't know. But I'm working on finding out." I didn't want to mention Jerry if I didn't have to. He was doing me a favor, and I knew Kate wouldn't like the fact that I had a private eye checking into things for me.

"How?"

"How what?"

She glared at me. "What aren't you telling me, and why?" She looked back at Casey in the rearview mirror. "Casey?"

My partner wasn't very good at prevaricating when it came to our boss. "He... hasn't been following me." As if that would get her out of the loop without ratting me out.

I sighed and put my head back on the headrest. I didn't want to get her into hot water, so I let out a long breath and started in. "I've seen him at my house, I've seen him following me in a blue sedan a bunch of times, and he followed me into the Hairy Lime last night." I turned to look at her. "I'll catch him, Kate, and when I do, I'll let you know what's up."

"Do you think he has anything to do with the cases we're working on?"

I blinked at that. My gut told me, no, but I couldn't be sure the two men weren't involved somehow. "I don't think so, but..."

"But you don't know."

I shook my head.

Putting the car in gear, she pulled onto the street and headed back to the crime scene. "I want to know everything you know about this guy, Alex. I want a report on my desk by the end of the day."

I nodded. It was no use arguing. I'd just have to be judicious in exactly how I wrote up the report.

As we pulled in front of the house, the press, who knew Kate's work car on-site, gathered around and began firing questions at us as soon as we stepped out of the car.

"Has The Coward struck again, Sgt. Brannigan?"

"Was the man Detective Wolfe chased, The Coward?"

"Do you know who The Coward is, Detective Wolfe? Why were you chasing that man?"

Kate gave me an irritated look. "You two get back to work."

She didn't have to tell me twice. The media and I have always had a love-hate relationship—they love to harass me, and I hate to help them out. They're always sniffing around for a story about my Mafiosa friend, Gianina Angelino. For some reason, they think my friendship with her is newsworthy.

Before I'd started spending time with her, I'd never understood how awful it is for those people who are thrust into the public spotlight. Not reacting to the media's incessant rudeness is an art form I haven't quite mastered yet, and the fact that Kate was running interference for me meant a lot. Of course, she was mostly running interference for the department, but I like to think it was a little about me as well.

Casey and I returned to the kitchen, which had remained mostly intact. The flames had only begun to do their damage by the time the fire department arrived, and although the room was completely soaked and smoke-stained, I hoped I might find something in the drawers to help me make an identification.

Casey grabbed her camera off the countertop where she'd apparently dropped it when Kate had called her outside to help me. "I've finished in here, and Nate dusted for prints. You can go ahead and look around. There were some papers over there in those drawers. They're soaked, but maybe you can still get something off them."

"Thanks." I sounded distracted, even to my own ears, so when she turned and leaned on the countertop, arms crossed, I knew what she was going to say.

"Why don't you want to tell Kate about those two guys?"

I shrugged, "It's not that I don't want to tell her. It's just that there are times when I just want to blend in, you know? Maybe I don't want her to have to constantly be helping me or watching over my shoulder or worrying that I've gotten in over my head. Sometimes, I just want to be your normal, everyday detective who comes into work, does her job, and goes home, you know?"

I expected her to laugh or make fun of me by saying something like, "As if that'll ever happen," but instead, she crossed her arms and nodded. "Yeah, that's gotta be wearing for both of you. But you didn't do anything to make those guys follow you."

"As far as we know..." I sounded petulant, and I suppose I was, to some extent. She was right. I hadn't done anything, and yet here I was, in a situation where Kate had to step in and run interference with the media for me.

"Listen, Alex. Kate is our supervisor. Watching our backs is what she gets paid the big bucks for. Sure, you make her earn her money a hell of a lot more than the rest of us..." She grinned at the glare I shot her, "...but you are a damn good detective, and she knows it. If she didn't respect the kind of work you do, do you really think you'd still be in her unit?"

I snorted and grinned over at her, "She just can't get rid of me."

"Bullshit. If Kate really wanted you gone, you'd be gone. It's as simple as that. You need to give her credit. And you need to fill her in on what's going on with those two men. She's right. For all we know, they might have something to do with these cases. I mean, they didn't show up until we were seconded to the arson detail, right?"

That made a lot of sense. "Yeah, I guess so." Wanting to change the subject, I did a quick survey of the kitchen. "Used to be a nice, cozy home, I'll bet. A long time ago." At one time, many years previous, or possibly as long as a generation ago, someone with an eye for decorating had lovingly pasted wallpaper on the walls and had added a bumped-out bay window over the sink. The wallpaper had an off-white background and spaced evenly in angled lines were row after row of maroon cherries with light green stems and leaves. Dated ceramic tile covered the floor, and despite its age, no cracks ran through the tiles where the house had settled over the years. Someone who knew how to lay cement and tiles properly had spent time with this floor, and I glanced over my shoulder toward the bedroom where the skeleton lay on those sad box springs. "I wonder if he was in construction at some point."

"What makes you think it's a man's body?"

"Thick bones and a narrow sciatic notch."

Grinning over at me, she snorted her disbelief. "The sarge said it was a man, huh?"

I grinned back. "Yup." I moved to a short countertop, not more than two feet wide, where a phone had probably rested back when house phones were the norm. One long drawer was attached directly beneath the counter, and a set of three drawers held up the right side next to the oven. I pulled open the bottom drawer first, hoping it would have the least water damage.

Normally, I'd be surprised to find a city phone directory inside someone's home, but since we'd begun investigating the murders of elderly victims, it would have been more surprising not to find one. Most, it seemed, relied on good old-fashioned paper phonebooks and directories instead of the more modern contact list on their cellphones. That's assuming they even owned a cellphone.

Sure enough, a battered phonebook lay in the bottom drawer. It was only partially wet, as the two upper drawers had shielded it from most of the water.

I pulled it out and rifled through the pages, seeing occasional names or numbers circled in red. After digging my notepad out of my back pocket, I laid it on top of each page and wrote down the circled names and numbers, hoping that if I couldn't find the victim's identity in the usual way, someone at the other end of those phone numbers might be able to help me out.

Finished with that, I bagged and tagged the directory and moved up one drawer. Every house seems to have a junk drawer, and I'd just found one. I rummaged through screwdrivers, batteries, twist ties, stray keys, an assortment of screws, and a ton of other items that wouldn't help my investigation. The top drawer was also a disappointment, so I moved on to the fridge.

Refrigerators can tell you a lot about a person, and this one told me no one in the home did much grocery shopping. A small quart container of milk—half-empty—and a jar of olives, and a sixpack of beer were the only items on the shelves. Some half-rotten vegetables sat in the lower bin. I picked up a cucumber that looked like someone had recently cut off a portion, and I wondered if the victim was actually eating off the partially rotted piece that remained.

Moving to the pantry, I at least found a couple of boxes of cereal, probably what the milk was for, and two boxes of crackers, one opened and only half full. A can of sardines sat alone on the lower shelf, and oddly enough, there was a yellow post-it note with the word "Tuesday" written in a shaky hand. Curious, I went to the trash bin and pulled out old tissues and an empty can of beans. I saw an open sardine can down at the bottom, and beneath it was an identical sticky with the word "Thursday" scrawled across it.

"Damn."

Casey, who was scrolling back through her pictures to make sure she'd gotten everything, glanced at me. "What?"

"Well, the only real food around seems to be a box of

cereal and a carton of milk, some crackers, and two cans of sardines, one for Thursday and one for the following Tuesday. Wasn't anybody checking in to make sure this person had enough food?" I knew the answer and didn't expect her to reply. Both of us had been around long enough to know there were a ton of old people who slipped through the social services cracks. It happens to kids, and it happens to the elderly, and there wasn't much we could do to stop it.

That isn't to say that we don't both have our favorites that we help out on occasion. Most cops who give a damn do, but then we run into another sad case, and all we can do is report it to social services and hope someone has the time to follow up.

I checked the rest of the cupboards and drawers without any luck. Pointing through a door leading to another room, I asked, "Have you finished with the pictures in there yet?"

"Yeah, I just did."

I moved into what I suppose could be called a small office. The room looked to be about twelve-by-twelve square feet, with one window on the far wall giving the semi-dark room some extra light. I was surprised there wasn't an overhead light and maybe a fan in the center of the ceiling, but since the firefighters had turned off the electricity, it wouldn't have mattered anyway. Someone, probably Casey, had raised the cheap set of off-white plastic, louvered blinds, and the small amount of sunshine pouring in did little to add any type of cheer to the place.

An ancient, semi-rusty, two-drawer file cabinet sat on the floor next to a plastic folding table. A cardboard box rested on top of a milk crate next to the table. Rifling through the box, which contained old magazines, mostly western-themed, I wondered if the home's occupant used to be some kind of cowboy. Every little hint helps when trying to identify a home's occupants, so I pulled out copies of Western Horseman, another simply called Western, and several old Life Magazines. The address labels on the first nine or ten were missing. I could see the yellowed glue in the shape of a label, but obviously, the glue had lost its adhesion.

Western Horseman was by far the most popular, at least in this lot, and I flipped through all of them one-by-one. Each of their covers was decorated with vibrant paintings of horses or broncos doing their best to unseat their riders. After close to fifteen months' worth of magazines, I hit paydirt when I pulled out one that actually had the label still attached. I actually liked this cover, with its herd of cattle in the distance, a full moon overhead, and a lone cowpoke on his horse riding slowly through the grass playing his harmonica.

I groaned when I took a closer look at the mailing label. The magazine had been sent to the city's public library system, and I doubted I'd have any way to trace it. "Damn it."

Casey came over to take a look. "What's the matter?"

"I was hoping this would have the homeowner's name on it, or at least someone's name that would help me get a head start, but—" I stopped and thought a minute.

"But?"

I blinked, "Oh, sorry. But it was sent to the public library. But, I might have someone who could help me out." I pulled out my cellphone and called Kelly Bruster, a librarian who had helped me out on several previous cases.

She answered immediately, something that rarely happens. "Alex. Great to hear from you."

"Hi, Kelly. I was wondering if you could answer a question for me."

Kate walked in and saw me holding the magazine. She raised her eyebrows, silently asking if I had an identification for her yet.

I held up a finger and listened to Kelly say, "Shoot."

"I have a magazine from..." I found the date on the

bottom right-hand corner of the cover, "...1970. The library is listed on the label. Is there any way to know who checked it out? For that matter, do you even check out magazines?"

"We don't anymore. Is there a line through the label, maybe with a magic marker?"

"No."

"Look on the inside of the front cover. Is there a card envelope taped to the front?"

I flipped open the cover. "Nope."

"Okay, then look inside the back cover."

I turned the magazine over and checked. "Yup. Here it is."

"Can you read out the sixteen-digit number, please?"

Surprised that this might actually work, I read out the number.

"Okay, give me a bit. I'll call you back."

We disconnected, and I looked over at Kate, who wore a pleased expression for a change. "Not bad. Gather these family pictures, too." She indicated several framed photographs lined up along the back of the plastic table.

I nodded as she returned to the burned-out bedroom. The drawer to the file cabinet was stuck, maybe even rusted shut. I pulled and yanked on both drawers until the top one finally squealed open. More magazines littered the inside. I closed that drawer and tried the bottom one. With effort, I pulled it open as well.

This one at least held hanging files, and I rifled through a bunch of utility bills, the most recent having the name Knox Cailleach."

"Hey, Case. You remember in the academy, they mentioned that guy who murdered his wife and kids back in the eighties? Wasn't his name Knox? I mean, that's not a common name."

She pushed her blonde bangs out of her eyes. "I kind of remember. But not really. Why?"

I held up the bill. "This is addressed to him. A utility bill from about six months ago."

"Hm."

Further back in the drawer, someone had stuffed a manilla envelope into a green file folder. I pulled it out and found "Arizona Department of Corrections" typed in the top left corner and the words "Knox Cailleach" centered in the middle. Pushing up the two sides of the clasp, I opened it and discovered case files and parole paperwork referencing the 1984 case. He'd been granted parole nearly thirty years after butchering seven members of his family.

I wondered how his release from prison had gotten in under the radar. Usually, the press is all over that kind of parole hearing, but I hadn't heard a single word about it in the news. I found Kate standing outside the home talking to Mitch. I didn't see Longoria anywhere and assumed he'd gone back to the station to work on the other cases.

They'd had their heads together speaking quietly when I walked up, so I waited patiently for them to finish their conversation.

Kate finally turned to me. "What do you have, Alex?"

"Do you remember a man named Knox..." I wrestled with the last name and finally came up with "Cuhleach who—"

Apparently, Longoria hadn't left because he came up behind me and read over my shoulder, "Cailleach. It's Scottish and pronounced Kulach."

I didn't think I'd ever be able to make the guttural sound he just made, so I shrugged, "Yeah, him."

She grabbed my arm and directed me back inside the home. When we were out of sight of cameras and listening devices, she said, "Don't tell me this is him?"

I shrugged. "I don't know. The paperwork in the filing

cabinet belongs to him, but right now, there's no way to know if he's the skeleton." My phone rang. I handed Kate the paperwork, which she and Mitch immediately began going through, hit send and said, "Wolfe."

"Hi, Alex. You're never going to believe who checked out that magazine."

The excitement in her voice made me want to allow her this triumph, so I asked, "Who?"

"Knox Cailleach! Can you believe it? Do you remember him? I can't believe you found a magazine he checked out that long ago. I wonder if he took them into the prison with him. Where did you find it?"

I marveled at how well she'd actually pronounced his last name. "I can't exactly tell you that. But that's fantastic that you were able to find the name."

"I had to go into the archives, where we keep the old cards. A lot of them have been entered into the system and the physical files destroyed, but that far back, the boxes were still there."

"Could you hold onto the card for me, please? I'll stop by in the next few days to pick it up."

"Sure thing. Can I tell people what you found?"

"Not yet. Thanks again." I hung up and turned back to Kate. "The magazine was checked out to him, too." Holding open the flap of the Corrections file, I peered inside and said, "I'll go through this and see if I can find a parole officer for him." I pulled out a picture. "Hey, look. Here's his mugshot."

Kate took the photo and walked to the pictures on the desk that I hadn't collected yet. She held the mugshot next to them. "That's him all right. Standing with the wife he murdered and their six boys. That's pretty sick to have pictures of the family you butchered in frames on your desk."

There was a lot of information in the file, and it took me a moment to locate the blank line where the next-of-kin should have been listed. "It doesn't list anybody as next-of-kin, but it does have the parole officer...Jenson Levy, I know him. I've talked to him before." I pulled out my phone to make the call, but Kate stopped me.

"I'll make the call, Alex. You keep going through everything and bag and tag as you go along."

She probably wanted to keep a tight lid on the information we'd found until we could make a definite identification. I didn't care one way or the other. The day was wearing on, and I wanted to get home in time to take Tessa and Jynx out for a late afternoon walk.

I heard the wheels of a gurney bumping over the uneven cement walkway and absently thought that someone other than the original mason must have set the concrete since the walkway was cracked and had lifted up from the ground in several parts. It didn't take the techs from the coroner's office much time to bag the body, and before long, they were bumping their way back down the walkway.

When I'd finished with everything I needed to collect, I stepped onto the front walkway and once more took a picture of the hardcore people who'd stuck around until the gruesome end. At least most of the media had gone, and neither of my followers was anywhere to be seen.

Heaving a sigh of relief, I tossed all my bags in the trunk and drove to the station to enter everything into the evidence lockers. Once I'd finished, I headed home to my dogs.

CHAPTER 4

The next day was my day off, and I'd cleared it with Kate to leave the city for a day or two even though we were in the middle of these arsons. I needed a break, something she must have recognized because she'd granted my request readily enough, only telling me to keep my phone with me in case she needed me for some reason.

I piled Tessa and Jynx into my Jeep, and the three of us headed down to Sonoita to meet Gia and her great-niece, Shelley Greer, at their racehorse training stables. Every time I visit the little town about forty-five miles southeast of Tucson, I think of an African savannah and wish a herd of giraffes would gracefully top the grass-covered hills and pay me a visit. Tall yellow grass stretches as far as the eye can see, with mesquite and desert willows dotting the landscape.

As I topped the last rise, I pulled to a stop and admired Gia's compound. It's surrounded by nothing but high desert, and there isn't another homestead within a three hundred sixty-degree arc surrounding the place. The land's been divided into several areas expressly set aside for designated activities. To the east, several buildings are tucked into the side of a hill. The most prominent is an extensive barn facility with indoor/outdoor horse runs and grassy paddocks where the horses are turned out for a bit of relaxing downtime.

To the west, several jockeys were putting their million-dollar charges through their paces on a full-sized racetrack. Although I couldn't see any others, I imagined several were being ridden in the indoor arena directly north of the barn.

Further north and slightly west, away from the other buildings and out of sight from the hill I'd parked on, Gia's home is nestled beneath a stand of tall Cottonwood trees. I'm not sure how many homes she owns around the world, but this one is probably the smallest. She once told me she tired of the show-quality houses she needed to wine and dine the movers and shakers of the world. This is her retreat where no one but her closest friends come to visit.

And last but not least is what is referred to as "the barracks." This is a rectangular building large enough to house all of the jockeys and barn workers who live at the complex full-time. There was also a barracks-style room for Gia's bodyguards who travel with her wherever she happens to be—hence the building's nickname.

Oh, and I almost forgot, to the east of that is a three-bedroom home that houses the husband and wife team that trains Gia's stable of champion racehorses. To me, these two have the perfect life. They're provided an elegant home in a pastoral setting, a professional training facility that any horse person would drool over and, from the gossip I overheard one night as I was walking past the barracks, salaries that make my earnings as a cop look like chump change. Granted, they are world-renowned trainers who bring millions into Gia's coffers, but it would be nice to get even half of what one of them earns in a year.

Tessa and Jynx have accompanied me here on previous occasions, and they were anxious to get out to run and play.

Jynx barked and pounced on my legs, ordering me to get a move on, and Tessa was shaking so hard she seemed barely able to suppress the urge to jump out the window and run down to the stables. All the workers loved my two dogs, and I had a hard time keeping them from spoiling the pups rotten with treats, toys, and playtime.

"Okay, okay. I'm going." I drove downhill on a winding dirt road, one that took me over several bridges spanning dry washes—dirt expanses that flood during the monsoon season—and over which people would be unable to traverse during the roaring groundswell. Driving over them would be especially difficult with a horse trailer full of world-class horses. More tall cottonwood trees shaded this portion of the drive, making the traveler feel as though they'd left Arizona and had magically entered the forest surrounding Frodo's hobbit hole.

I parked in front of Gia's "little" house, a sprawling one-story, ranch-style affair. Built around an interior atrium, the resulting square held five bedrooms and one enormous kitchen with a dining area off to the side. There was a second, formal dining area, a living room, a comfortable den, and an office where Gia conducted business transactions she couldn't postpone during her visits. I reached across and opened the passenger door, letting the dogs jump out to join Shelley's dog, Muddy, in a playful romp around the property.

The front door opened—an ornate affair that had been carved by an Italian artist who'd been flown in to create a one-of-a-kind masterpiece—and Shelley, Gia's thirteen-year-old great-niece, ran out the door to greet me. I held my arms open wide, and she ran into me with such enthusiasm I almost ended up falling backward onto my bum. "I knew you'd come! Aunt Gia wasn't sure you could get away since you guys are working on another arson, but I told her you wouldn't miss my visit. I have so much to tell you about school and all my friends."

It didn't surprise me that Gia already knew about our latest victim. With her connections, she usually knew what cases I was working before I was even working them.

I hugged Shelley and lifted her off her feet, then set her back on the ground and held her at arm's length. "Damn, you must have grown a foot since I last saw you." I stood up straight and measured her height against mine. The last time I'd seen her, which had been several months earlier, the top of her head had come to about my eyes. Now, the top of her wavy black hair was even with my forehead. "You're not allowed to get taller than me, you know."

Gia had sent Shelley to an elite, international school located in rural Kentucky at my suggestion and prompting. It's for kids who are high-profile targets, which unfortunately pertains to Shelley. The families run the gamut of the wealthy one percent: politicians, celebrities, old and new money tycoons, and some who simply need a safe place to park their progeny while they get on with their lives.

A girl I didn't recognize, approximately Shelley's age, stood off to the side, arms crossed and looking extremely uncomfortable. When she realized I'd noticed her, her cheeks flamed pink, and she lowered her eyes, pointedly watching the dogs as they raced around the yard. Well, Tessa and Jynx raced while old Muddy ambled after them as best as his tired, arthritic legs would carry him.

Where Shelley had a dark, exotic beauty—dove-grey eyes and a cascading mass of jet-black hair—this new girl had plain, non-distinct features that might be described as leaning toward masculine; brown hair cut short on the sides and combed over on the top with a tattoo of a colorful peacock covering the entire right side of her neck. Expertly drawn and colored, the rendering could have been hung in a gallery if it hadn't been etched into this girl's skin.

Seeing me sizing up the girl, Shelley remembered her

manners and grabbed my hand, hauling me over to where the girl had stepped beneath the shadows of one of the majestic, white-barked cottonwood trees. Her crossed arms, sideways shuffle and lowered gaze suggested she wanted to hide, but Shelley was having none of that. She deposited me at the girl's feet and exclaimed, "I told you she'd come! This is Alex. Alex, meet my best friend, Jacqueline."

The girl glanced out from under where she'd been hiding beneath her mousy-brown, nondescript bangs and whispered, "Jack."

Shelley shook her head and, in her usual non-judgmental, matter-of-fact way, said, "Oh yeah, sorry. I keep forgetting. Jack's in the middle of transitioning. She was Jacqueline when I first met, but she—" She stuttered and shook her head, "Sorry again, *he* just started the process of becoming Jack." Shelley had been through so much during her short life, starting out as a child of a prostitute and then moving to live beneath the tunnels of Tucson with a schizophrenic bag lady. She'd finally come to stay with Gia, a great-aunt she never knew existed, and I'm sure having her best friend transition from a girl to a boy barely made her blink. One of her many traits that I've always loved and admired.

I held out my hand. "I'm pleased to meet you, Jack."

His face lit up with the beginnings of a smile, and he took my hand and shook it with an unexpectedly firm grip. "You, too."

I guessed from his initial hesitation at meeting me he hadn't had the most favorable of reactions from new adults he's met along the way, so I added, "And may I say, that is the most incredible tattoo I've ever seen. It's really a work of art. If you come to Tucson, we're gonna have to show it to my friend, Maddie."

The boy stood a bit straighter and his face lit in surprised delight.

Shelley crowed to him, "I told you she's not normal. Alex is the best. She's not like most people. It's who you are that matters to her, not who your parents are and not what people say you should be." She turned to me, "His parents are big muckety mucks, and they think he should be—"

Jack's face had gone completely red, and Gia suddenly appeared in the front door, "Shelley, that's enough for now."

The woman who stood in the door turned her incredible grey eyes on me. Relaxed, with one hand resting near her head on the doorframe, even in her mid-fifties she had more presence than any runway model anywhere in the world. The tabloids use all types of adjectives when attempting to describe her: radiant, sensual, vibrant, powerful, but sometimes I think the simplest words say the most. Gia is elegant, poised, and graceful, a woman people naturally follow with their eyes when she walks into a room.

I walked over and gave her a big hug, something I've learned only a very few people are allowed to do.

She hugged me back and said, "I thought maybe you'd bring Megan with you. She always enjoys it out here."

"She wanted to come, but she'd already scheduled extra classes with some clients for today, and she needs the money, so she didn't want to reschedule."

"Well, you arrived just in time. The girls—" Now it was her turn to shake her head, "I'm sorry, Jack. It takes a bit of getting used to the change in pronouns...Shelley and Jack, and I were headed over to the racetrack to watch Credo's Hope and Credo's Legacy do their morning gallop. Join us." She reached inside the door and grabbed a light jacket. As she started for the track, I admired how her English riding breeches followed her body's curves to perfection. Her black paddock boots sparkled in the early morning sunshine, and I wondered whether out here, at the compound, she shined her own boots. She pulled the tailored, navy blue riding coat over her cotton blouse, and I quickened my pace until we were walking companionably side-by-side.

The track was a good quarter-mile from the house, and as we approached, I heard the thundering of hooves as several horses made their way around the track. "Are we too late?"

Shelley, who'd put her arm through mine as we walked, shook her head. "No, they always wait for us to get there before they run Hope and Legacy. We have other horses here that need to be run as well; some old ones that aren't racing anymore but still need the exercise, and some newer ones who aren't old enough to race yet."

"Well, haven't you become quite the expert on racehorses? When did you learn all this? Don't tell me it was while you were away at school?"

With a matter-of-fact lift of her shoulders, she said, "Aunt Gia says that someday I'll be running the racing business, so I've been reading up on it during my free time at school. I really like it there. I asked the principal whether he would order books on the horse racing industry, you know, to put in the library and all, and he gave me an entire set as a gift!"

Knowing it was probably Gia who'd sent the books, I glanced her way and saw the telltale crinkling at the sides of her eyes that told me I'd been right on the mark.

Shelley hadn't stopped talking, however, and I tuned back into her monologue. "Aunt Gia said that she learned from the ground up, cleaning out the stables..." she leaned across me and sent Gia a mischievous look. "... I don't really believe that because I don't think Gianina Angelino would ever scoop poop, but she says that's where I'm going to start. And I don't really mind. I love spending time with the horses. Aunt Gia sent a hunter jumper to my school, and I've been learning how to ride and jump. I love it! I named him Mansfield Park. We call him, Parksey. Know why I named him that?"

I covered the hand she had resting on my bicep, "I

imagine it's to honor Anya. I know she'd be super proud of how well you're doing now." Anya had been a homeless schizophrenic bag lady who, at one time, happened to have been a professor of literature at the University of Berkley. She'd developed her illness when she was in her mid-to-late forties and had ended up living in the tunnels beneath the streets of Tucson. She'd taken Shelley in when the girl had run away from an abusive foster home situation and she'd educated her as best she could. One of the ways she'd done that was by making her memorize portions of the only book she still owned, Mansfield Park, by Jane Austen. Hence, the horse's name.

Jack walked behind us, and I wondered whether he was naturally quiet or if he'd just decided to be reserved because I was here. It didn't matter to me one way or the other. I figured if he wanted to be friendly, he would be, and when he got to know me better, being open and conversational would come easier to him.

Like with the rest of the compound, Gia hadn't spared any money when it came to building the racetrack. Or actually, it might have been her father who'd built the entire facility. Shelley had said that Gia had taken over the racing business. I wondered if Gia's father, Tancredo, had moved his racing empire from Illinois to Arizona when he'd relocated his family. He'd transferred the entire clan, his business enterprise, and everything associated with their life in Chicago after a rival mafia family had murdered his namesake and only son. I suppose, given all that, if he'd owned racehorses in Chicago, it wouldn't have been too far of a stretch for him to move an entire racing syndicate west, also.

The actual racetrack is a quarter-mile oval surrounded by a waist-high, metal three-rail fence. On the near side, an outdoor viewing area takes up half the length of the track. Four levels of bleachers stair-step backward away from the fence. These are exposed to the bright sunshine, but for the days when the Arizona sun gets too hot, an air-conditioned, second-story viewing enclosure overlooks the track.

I'd visited the facility a dozen times since Gia had gifted Shelley and me a racehorse, and I'd become quite comfortable watching the horses from inside the building. The ranch hands jokingly call it the grandstand, but from my perspective, it isn't a joke. To me, it's an actual, scaled-down version of the grandstands at the Rillito Racetrack, sans the betting booths and carnival atmosphere.

I followed Gia into the elevator that would take us to the viewing booth while Shelley and Jack hurried off to watch from the saddling paddocks. We emerged into a carpeted room with three floor-to-ceiling glassed-in walls. Two leather sofas faced the windows, allowing for a perfect view of the track. In addition to the sofas, several comfortably padded armchairs were placed in strategic locations around the room. A wooden-topped bar ran the length of the back wall, and behind it, several shelves were stacked three bottles deep with every type of spirits you could imagine.

A tall, lanky waiter in white slacks, button-down shirt, and jacket had just entered the room through a swinging door to the right of the bar. His Germanic ancestry was evident in the way his sinewy muscles stretched over a slender frame. He had the blonde hair and blue eyes Hitler had so admired in his followers, and there was a fullness to his cheeks and lower jaw that gave his face a bit of unexpected puffiness, something you wouldn't expect in a man with his particular build.

A burly bartender, who doubled as a bodyguard when Gabe wasn't in the room, wore all black and stood behind the bar polishing wood that already shone with the perfection of a star on a moonless night. Both men stiffened to attention as Gia entered the room.

Without acknowledging either, she walked to her favorite upholstered, high-backed wingchair while I stepped to the front window to watch the latest horses rounding the back turn. I'd noticed that while she always treats her employees with polite respect, she never crosses the line into friendly.

The waiter picked up a silver tray—when I say silver, I mean silver—and approached Gia. He balanced the tray on the palm of one hand and respectfully placed his other on the small of his back. He gave a slight bow and said, "Madame?"

"My usual, thanks, Tom."

"Of course." Instead of looking over at me and asking what I wanted, he stepped behind me and cleared his throat. I turned, and he gave me the same abbreviated bow of respect he'd given Gia.

The first time this happened, it had startled me so much that I'd laughed out loud. Back then, Tom had blinked at my reaction and then had stood at attention and waited for me to give him my order. Unsure of what he wanted, I'd looked to Gia for some hint about what I was supposed to do. She'd glanced up at the ceiling and, although I don't remember what she'd said, I do remember the slight chuckle that accompanied her words.

This time I had it down pat. "A dram of Glenlivet, two rocks, please."

"Very good."

"Oh, and two banana pancakes, heavy on the maple syrup, some bacon, and an egg over easy."

"Right away."

He bowed and had just made his turn when I added, "And a cinnamon roll, and you know what? I forgot how early it is. I'll save the Glenlivet for later and just have a glass of milk and a cup of hazelnut coffee, please. Six hazelnut creamers and six packets of sweetener."

Turning once again to face me, he waited to see if I'd finished.

I glanced back at Gia, who was holding her cigar next to her face and watching me with a twofold mixture of forbearance and amusement in her eyes. The thing is, when her smile reaches her eyes, I feel good all over. Like everything is right with the world. That look is so rare when she's in Tucson. The stress on her when she has to deal with politicians and businessmen always takes its toll.

I smiled at Tom. "That's all for me. And thank Marla for me, will you? She always makes the pancakes exactly the way I like them. The bananas are never overcooked, and she puts a ton of walnuts in the batter. Nobody makes banana pancakes the way she does."

Marla is Tom's wife, and although I don't think he's technically allowed to smile, I did see the side of his mouth lift just a bit. "Of course. I'll pass along your appreciation."

With Gia's arrival, Credo's Hope, a reddish-gold chestnut with a muscular chest and hindquarters, and my horse, Credo's Legacy, an all-black gelding, were saddled and brought to the track. They had a set of starting gates at one end, but since this was only a morning exercise, the jockeys mounted and were immediately led onto the track.

I mostly watched Legacy because he was the first and only horse I'd ever owned. The jockeys started them out with a slow jog and then gradually increased the pace until they were running in a comfortable canter. They were neither racing nor being timed, and I was able to watch without the usual rush of adrenaline that accompanies a full-out gallop.

"He's magnificent," I said to nobody in particular.

Gia stopped writing in the small notebook she had resting in her lap. She was a hands-on owner who discussed the horses and their performances with her trainers whenever she found the time to enjoy the facilities. The notes documented various points she wanted to bring up when the time came for their meeting after the morning runs. "They both are. Hope will be running in the Wood Memorial Stakes on the third, and Legacy will be entered in the Ashland Stakes on the same day."

"How many races will Legacy run this year?"

"I'm only putting him in fifteen, and that's assuming he stays healthy." At my startled gasp, she smiled, "And I have no reason to think he won't. Look at him. He has strong, muscular legs. That's something I do differently than a lot of breeders. I don't believe in breeding out the soundness of the bones to maybe get a slight edge as far as speed goes. When a breeder does that, they only have a horse for a few years before their bones and ligament break down. But most of them don't care. They have plenty of horses in their stables, and if one fractures a leg, they move on to the next. No, Legacy will run for a few more years, and then, who knows, maybe you'll be a competent enough rider by then to take him on pleasure rides."

I put my forefinger on my chest. "Me?"

"Shelley is determined you're going to learn to ride, and you know as well as I do when she makes up her mind about something, there's no arguing with her." She watched the horses while she spoke, occasionally jotting down her thoughts for future reference. "Hope is still going strong, too, but I'm a little concerned about that slight movement in his right forehoof. Do you see it?"

Try as I might, all I saw was a great-looking horse. "He looks fine to me."

"It could simply be that he's a bit tight this morning, or he could be starting an abscess in that hoof. Hopefully, it's nothing. If I have to pull him from the Wood Memorial, I will. I never run a horse that's not one hundred percent."

Our breakfast arrived, and Tom set everything on the

small dining table nestled up against the window on the room's left side. The chairs were set so that neither Gia nor I had to miss any of the activity on the track. As I settled myself with a napkin in my lap, I looked up to see Hope and Legacy being led from the track.

To my utter surprise, Shelley and Jack, mounted on a bay and a palomino, respectively, took to the track. Shelley turned in her saddle and waved up at the grandstand, and although I knew she probably couldn't see me, I swung my arm back and forth over my head in acknowledgment. "Are those retired racehorses?"

With a piece of sour cream herring on her fork, Gia glanced at the kids and then shook her head. "No. While Shelley likes to think she's an expert because she can jump two and a half foot fences, she's only been riding for a year and a half and hasn't developed the natural balance a seasoned rider possesses."

The herring disappeared into her mouth, and a moment later, she continued, "Jack, on the other hand, was carried on a horse from infancy. His grandmother competed in hunter-jumper trials at the international level, and I believe she earned a silver medal in the Olympics. His father is the master of a hunt club in England."

"In England?" We watched the boy as he walked his horse next to Shelley's. "What kind of saddle is that? It's different from what the jockeys use. Why England?"

"His father is British. Although I don't know what it is, he has a title and is referred to as Lord Capell. He married up when he wed Jack's mother. She is Danish nobility, and I've only met her once." The amusement in her voice told me everything. "I won't be encouraging that relationship any time soon. She's a spoiled harridan with a capital H."

"I'll bet they're thrilled Jaqueline is transitioning to Jack."

"He's the third of three painfully neglected children, so

apparently what happens to him is of little consequence to either one, but yes, the parents aren't pleased. They did sign the medical permission papers, though, but only after Jack's second suicide attempt."

"He tried to kill himself twice?" I thought about that as I popped a piece of banana pancake into my mouth. "Even so, I can't imagine either parent paying for anything like that."

"They aren't."

"Well then, who is?"

"His maternal grandmother. Now that's a woman whom I enjoy spending time with. She's the one who forced Jack's parents to sign the medical papers for her...I mean him. Money talks. Apparently, she still holds the purse strings for her side of the family. She's down-to-earth, still rides horses in her seventies, and most importantly, knows her Glenlivet." She popped another herring into her mouth. "She moves back and forth between Devon, England, and Kentucky and spends as much time with Jack as she can fit in. Honestly, without her, Jack would have no familial love. Even his siblings treat him like a pariah."

She finished with the herring, and Tom removed the now empty plate. This time the tray held a platter with tiny pancakes covered with some other strange concoction I didn't recognize.

"What is that stuff?" I wrinkled my nose and then remembered Gia had once said that particular expression made me look like an angry walrus. Relaxing my face, I picked up a piece of bacon with my fingers and took a bite.

Gia, who always cut her bacon with a fork and knife, scratched her forehead with a perfectly manicured fingernail, "They are blintzes covered in a blend of crème Fraiche with slices of salmon laid on top." Delicately placing some on the new plate Tom had set in front of her, she said, "Please bring Alex another plate, as well. I'm sure she'd love to try something new." Mischievous grey eyes met my own, boring brown ones.

I sat back, "What? No, she wouldn't. Fish? You're eating fish for breakfast. I mean, I've seen you eat herring in the mornings, which now that I think about is a fish, too, but..."

She motioned for Tom to carry out her orders, and it wasn't long before he returned with a small plate bearing one of her blintzes.

I poked it with my fork. "What's a blintz?" Tom offered me a second fork, and I waved mine at him. "I have one, thanks."

Gia accepted the fork for me and set it on the blintz plate. "You'll want to taste this without the extra flavors of banana and maple syrup."

"Oh." Taking my time, I picked up the new fork and once again wrinkled my nose. "I don't know, Gia..."

Instead of answering, she raised her eyebrows and dipped her chin in the direction of the plate.

Still not in any hurry, I carved off a piece of the blintz with the side of the fork and ever so slowly raised it to my mouth. I made the mistake of sniffing it first. It smelled of fish and whatever that crème Fraiche was. I didn't think the two odors should be mixed like that.

"Alex. You don't sniff your food in polite company." By this time, she'd put down her fork and was resting both hands on the arms of her chair, watching me.

Closing my eyes, I slipped the bite past my lips and pulled it off the fork with my teeth. My eyes flew open, and I sat up a little straighter in my seat. "Hey! That's good!" I took another bite. "That's really good!"

Chuckling, Gia retrieved her fork and resumed eating. "Have I ever led you wrong?"

"One word. Seaweed."

Who knew my bowels would object so strenuously to a

piece of a dried plant that grows on the bottom of the sea? She lifted a shoulder to acknowledge the fact that the one time I'd eaten seaweed, I'd had to make an emergency trip to her bathroom. "Other than that."

I'd forgotten about the kids, and when I looked down at the track, I was surprised to see Shelley cantering now. Watching the two kids, I could see what Gia meant about the difference in their riding abilities. I don't think Jack even needed a saddle; he was so attuned to the horse's every movement.

On the other hand, Shelley rode with a tenseness that belied her jaunty wave at the beginning of the ride. She did have a huge grin on her face, though, and she said something to Jack before kicking her horse into an even faster gait.

Gia tensed and put her hand on the table as though making to rise. She stopped when Jack pulled back his own horse, slowing it to a trot and forcing Shelley to slow down too if she wanted to continue riding side-by-side.

Speaking under her breath, Gia whispered, "Good girl."

"Boy."

"What?" She'd been distracted by Shelley's antics and hadn't understood what I meant.

"You said 'good girl.' I'm assuming you meant Jack, in which case you should say, 'good boy.'"

She put her fingers to her forehead and softly rapped on her temples. "Of course. I've known him as Jaqueline for a year and a half now, and I'm having a difficult time using the correct pronouns."

"Don't worry about it. From my first impression of him, as long as you're trying, it'll be just fine. Speaking of which, I haven't heard him speak much. Does he have an accent?"

"Yes. He's been at the Regency Academy on and off since the fifth grade. From what his grandmother tells me, he's always been different and, therefore, an embarrassment to his family. But she did make sure he had an excellent primary education prior to coming to the States."

"Why is he here instead of going to school in England?"

"Two reasons. First, His grandmother wanted to get him as far away from his family as she possibly could. They're bullies who try to force Jack into their version of what an upper-class snob should be. And second, Regency is better equipped to handle a depressed, suicidal child than the private school he attended previously. It really is a remarkable school, and I'll always be grateful to you for suggesting it for Shelley."

"Hmmm." The idea of a suicidal pre-teen wasn't a new one to me. I'd had to take a few calls where young kids had killed themselves, and I was just glad Jack hadn't succeeded on his first couple of tries. I decided to change that depressing subject. "So, what kind of saddles are those? They don't look like the ones the cowboys use in the movies, and they don't look like the other kind either."

"English."

"They're from England?"

"No, the other kind you're referring to is an English saddle. Those Shelley and Jack are using are Australian. They can be used for a variety of riding disciplines. Very versatile." That mischievous glint returned. "By the way, before we get off the subject of Jack's grandmother, she's coming to visit this weekend. She'll be arriving later today."

"What! No!"

She reached over and patted my hand. "It'll be good for you. Expand your horizons."

"No, it won't. I'll make a fool of myself. I'm not..." I groped around for the right word. "...trained."

If Gia's smile is rare, her laughter is pretty much non-existent. I must have caught her off guard because laughter bubbled up from that deep dark place where she keeps it under lock and key.

Both Tom and Andy, the bartender, or Andrew as Gia calls him, looked our way with startled expressions.

She covered her mouth with her napkin. "Alex. You and Shelley are the only two people in the world who can make me laugh."

Hearing her laughter made me smile, too. That is until I remembered grandma was coming to town. "Gia, I can't. I need to get back to Tucson, anyway."

"No, you don't. You had planned to stay until Tuesday morning, and I hope that's what you'll do."

"Gia. I don't even eat right. You just said I was using the wrong fork for the little pancake thingies."

"Blintzes and you weren't using the wrong fork. I simply wanted to make sure you had an unadulterated taste when trying something new for the first time. You'll do fine, Alex. Listen, there's no way I'd subject you to Jack's parents. They're snobs of the first order. Lady Allegra is another matter altogether. I think you two will get along just fine."

Something on the track caught her eye, and when I looked, I saw Shelley waving at us to come down.

Gia called out, "Thomas, please phone the track and let Shelley know Alex and I will meet them in the arena when we finish with our breakfast."

"Yes, ma'am."

We had mostly finished with breakfast anyway, and with my mind on all the horrible things that could happen while I spent time with someone from the Danish nobility, I half-heartedly followed Gia to the arena.

"You'll like her, Alex." Gia repeated as if she could convince me through sheer repetition.

"What's Kate gonna say if I cause some international incident or something? She'll blow her top."

She put her hand on my shoulder, "Not to worry, Alex. Shelley has something planned for us that will keep your mind off Jack's grandmother."

"What?"

"You'll see."

A guard in a pinstriped suit stood to the side of the door into the arena, and when we approached, he pulled it open for us. He dipped his chin to Gia and said, "Good morning, Ma'am." Gia graced him with a small nod before going inside.

When I passed him, he smiled and said, "Hey, Alex."

I stopped a moment. "Hey yourself. Where's Gabe? I haven't seen him all morning."

"He's doing something for Ms. Angelino. He'll be back later."

My feet crunched in the loose dirt covering the arena floor as I stepped through the door. Four horses stood saddled in the middle of the arena, and when I counted them and then counted us humans, I backed up a step.

Shelley waved me over with the enthusiasm of a flagman directing a jet to its parking space. "C'mon, Alex. We have a real gentle mare for you to ride." She walked over and gave a piece of carrot to a very muscular, brown horse that didn't look like any broken-down carthorse I'd ever seen. And that's precisely what she'd need if she ever thought she'd get me up on top of one of those things.

"No. That's okay. I'm good."

"C'mon, Alex. It's really safe. She's the first one I ever rode. She's twenty, and she never bucks, and she's real friendly. Just try it once. She's got a really long name, but the last one is Chopin, so we just call her Chops. Pleeeease." She drew out the last word, begging me to take my life in my hands and crawl five feet in the air to sit on the back of a wild animal.

Jack actually had a smile on his face. "C'mon, Ms. Wolfe.

I'll help you. I teach a lot of the newer kids at Regency how to ride."

Gia had already climbed on something that looked like a warhorse to me. Apparently leaving the begging to Shelley and Jack, she began circling the arena at a trot, putting the horse through its paces. I'd seen the same exercises on television where the horse moves diagonally and sideways and around in a circle. She made it look so easy that I sighed and decided to at least give it a try.

I walked up to the mare and shoved my hands in my pockets. "Does she bite?"

Shelley's brows drew together. "Why would she bite?"

"'Cuz she has huge teeth."

"Yeah, she's got big teeth, but she's not mean. She's really nice, Alex. Here." She dug in her pocket and pulled out another piece of carrot. The horse's ears immediately came forward. She watched me take the carrot out of Shelley's hand and sidled a bit closer, obviously wanting to be my friend now that I had the treat to offer.

I held the carrot pinched between my thumb and forefinger and inched it toward the horse's mouth.

Jack reached over and took it from me. "It's better if you hold your hand flat like this and put the carrot on your palm. That way, they can take it with their lips." He demonstrated, and the horse really did reach out with only her lips to take the treat. The teeth didn't enter into the equation until the hand was well out of the way.

Heartened that Jack still had all five fingers, I accepted another carrot, put it in the palm of my hand, and moved it forward one micrometer at a time. The mare repeated her gentle acceptance of the offering and happily munched while Jack began explaining how to mount.

"Have you ever been up on a horse?"

"No."

He took me step-by-step through the procedure and then led Chops over to a mounting block. One of the stable hands met me there with a helmet, which kinda worried me. "I thought you said she won't buck me off."

Shelley knocked on her helmet with her knuckles. "She won't, but Aunt Gia has a rule that everybody who rides has to wear one."

Somewhat dubious of a rule that assumed some people were going to land on their head at some point during their ride, I buckled on the helmet, climbed on the mounting block, and for the first time in my life swung my leg over the back of a horse. Nothing happened. I looked at Jack to make sure we were still good.

"Here. You hold the reins like this." He stepped up onto the mounting block and positioned my fingers around the reins. Then he climbed back down and pushed my sneaker into the stirrup. I tried to do the same on the other side, but the damn thing kept moving out of the way.

Thankfully, while all this was going on, Shelley mounted her own horse and went to join Gia. I only had Jack around to watch me make a complete fool of myself.

When Jack deemed me ready to rock and roll, he took hold of the mare's bridle and gently tugged her forward.

"Shit!" Slightly panicked when the mare moved to follow Jack's lead, I leaned forward and grabbed a double handful of mane.

Jack chuckled quietly and stared at the ground, hiding his face in his hand.

Chagrined, I sat back and took a breath. "Okay, okay. We're good. You just startled me, is all."

It took an entire walk around the arena before I was willing to allow Jack to let go of the reins. When I finally gave him permission, nothing happened. "Come on, Chops. Let's go, girl. You 'n me." Still, nothing happened, and I looked down at Jack, hoping for some kind of clue. "Is there a key I need to turn or something? A gas pedal?"

"Do you remember how to stop her?"

"Pull back on these." I pulled back on the reins and Chops quickly took several steps back. Since that was how I was supposed to stop her, I naturally pulled back some more. She stepped back even faster than before.

Jack's laughter edged up a notch. I couldn't blame him there as Chops and I were making our way across the arena backwards. He caught up to us and took hold of Chop's bridle. "Let go, Alex. Stop pulling back."

"You told me to pull back!" I released the reins and crossed my arms, angrily staring down at my thirteen-year-old tormenter. Jack flinched slightly, and I ratcheted down my automatic little kid response, took a big breath, and began again. "You said to pull back on the reins if I want her to stop."

"Only when she's moving forward. If you pull back when you're stopped, it means back-up."

"Well, you might have mentioned that little detail. Okay. Here we go again." Even though I could only drive in reverse thus far, I was beginning to feel like I was getting the hang of this thing. I picked up the reins again, expectantly waiting for Chops to move forward.

"Squeeze very lightly with your legs."

I did, and Chops moved out at a quick walk. "Whoa!" I pulled back on the reins, and she stopped so fast my butt came forward out of the saddle, and I had to brace my hands on her neck. I turned around, triumphant, "It worked!"

Jack raised a companionable fist and gave a rousing hoot of encouragement.

Chops and I made our way around the arena two or three steps at a time. Okay, sometimes four if I got really brave. I discovered that I barely needed to pull back to get her to stop, and she discovered that she could anticipate my need to stop and pull up before I tugged on her mouth.

Jack walked up beside us. "That's good, Alex. What she's feeling is you sitting back in the saddle when you decide you want to stop. When you sit back and move your feet forward a bit, she's trained to halt."

"I'm gonna go around again. I think I'm getting this!"

Gia chuckled behind me, and I turned to see her nod her agreement. "Yes, I think you are. Perhaps tomorrow we can go out to one of the paddocks, and you can see how different it feels to ride a horse out in the open. I'd love to be able to take you on a short ride with Lady Allegra before you have to leave."

"Oh hell no. You guys can go if you want, but Chops and I would just hold you back."

"Don't worry. I intend to send Shelley and Jack and her grandmother on ahead while you and I enjoy a nice stroll through the countryside. Nothing to be embarrassed about, Alex. We all had to start somewhere."

"Yeah, when you were two years old." I grumbled as I squeezed my legs to get Chops to move forward."

"Let her walk out a bit, Alex. I'll ride next to you if it makes you feel more secure."

I did as she said and was relieved when Chops didn't break into a trot or, worse, a canter. "Hey, this is all right. I think she likes me."

Gia reached over and stroked Chops' backside. "I've owned her since she was a filly. In fact, I bred her dam to one of my favorite sires to get her exact personality. She has patience in abundance, stamina, and a kind eye. She's carried quite a few novice riders in her time, and she's never thrown a single one."

I appreciated the fact that she cared enough to reassure me. I know she'd been watching my halting first trip around the arena and was worried I'd made a fool of myself in her eyes. Apparently not, or at least she had too much class to let me know about it if I had.

The door directly behind us opened, and Gabe stepped inside. Some kind of signal must have passed between him and Gia because she pulled her horse up short, turned, and began walking toward him.

I pulled Chops to a stop and called after her. "Hey!"

She pulled her horse around, "Sorry. I know I said I'd ride next to you, but I need to go speak with Gabe. Just turn Chops around and come with me."

I looked at my horse's head. "How exactly do I do that without making her do something I'm gonna regret."

"I have her, Ms. Angelino." Jack rode over and jumped off the palomino that was having a difficult time keeping all four feet on the ground. It danced in place like a hyperactive child. The horse had to be a foot taller than Chops, but Jack swung out of the saddle with the grace of a trapeze artist and landed close enough to take hold of my bridle while keeping control of his antsy ride as well.

Once again heading for Gabe, Gia called over her shoulder. "Thank you, Jack."

Jack watched her go with something akin to adoration in his eyes. "She's...fantastic. I can't believe Shelley and I are spending a whole month with her."

That was news to me. "You're staying the entire break? For some reason, I thought you two were only here for a week."

"That was the original plan, but we begged Ms. Angelino to let us stay longer, and she changed a few things around, and now we'll be here the whole month." He shook his head and sighed, "Shelley is so lucky to have her for her guardian."

I rolled his words around a bit, thinking about Shelley and Gia's relationship. I wasn't sure lucky was the right word. Gia was an emotionally distant person. She scheduled in family time and managed Shelley's learning like she'd manage any corporate undertaking. Not that Shelley was a business acquisition. Gia loved her fiercely, but she controlled vast empires, and the only way she understood to raise a child successfully was to model her parenting model after her business one. It's how life had shaped her personality, and at this stage of the game, I didn't see that changing a whole lot.

On the other hand, she had bent a little after Shelley came along. For example, inviting me out this weekend to ride and relax with the two of them. That would have never happened pre-Shelley. From what I'd gleaned around the campfire, so to speak, with the training facility's employees, before Shelley had come along, Gia's trips to the compound were one hundred percent work. She'd bring important people out to broker deals, and none of them would ever spend the night on the property. They'd stay in Sonoita or Elgin, but never as Gia's guests.

Now when she came, she scheduled rides with Shelley, and on one of my prior visits, the three of us actually went on a couple of picnics. Well, I say the three of us, but what I really mean is the three of us plus the bodyguards who are never more than a stone's throw away, plus the others who were assigned to watch the periphery of the property, and the occasional flyby of one of Gia's reconnaissance helicopters.

"Alex?"

I shook myself out of my musings and looked down at Jack. "Sorry, I was thinking about what you'd said. Yes, Shelley is very fortunate. And so are you."

"Me?" Jack put an incredulous finger to his chest.

"You. Very, very few people are allowed into Ms. Angelino's inner circle, and it looks to me like you just might be one of them."

He blinked several times and then beamed up at me with a huge grin on his face.

"Alex." The irritation in Gia's voice brought us both up short.

Jack blushed, "I forgot to tell you Gia was calling you while you were musing."

Glancing back at where Gia had dismounted next to Gabe, I held up a finger to ask Gia to wait a second and then said to Jack, "How do I turn this thing?"

"Don't worry, I've got her." He turned Chops in the right direction and led us over to where the two of them waited.

Gia motioned to the horse. "Dismount. Gabe has someone he wants us to meet."

That was a strange way to phrase things. For ordinary people, that would be a perfectly non-problematic sentence. But for Gabe to want us to do something was very unusual. Usually, he did Gia's bidding and rarely was it the other way around.

I remembered how Jack had practically leapt from the saddle and decided that wasn't going to happen. "How?"

Irritation flashed across Gia's face. Something had put her into business mode, and the amiable aunt had morphed into the take-charge Doña.

Jack hurried over to the portable mounting block, picked it up, and placed it next to Chops. He physically removed my foot from the left stirrup, and taking my cue from him, I removed the right. I swung my leg over Chops' broad back and slid down onto the block. Turning to Jack, I asked, "Do you have any carrots?"

Gia strode for the door. "There's no time for that, Alex."

I watched her a moment and then said, "There's always time to say thanks." Now, normal mortals never contradict Gia. Normal, intelligent people come to attention and salute when she gives an order. I've never subscribed to normal and wasn't about to start now. I held my hand out to Jack, who sent a nervous look in Gia's general direction.

I raised my eyebrow at Gia, who glared at me before nodding to Jack.

With noticeable relief, he dug in his back pocket and pulled out two carrots: one he handed to me to give to Chops, which I did, and the other he gave to his antsy charge. That accomplished, I joined Gia and Gabe, who hadn't waited for me but had instead left the building and were walking toward one of the black SUVs.

CHAPTER 5

Gabe nodded at a guard standing next to the passenger door.

The man opened the rear door and hauled a handcuffed, obviously terrorized person out into the sunlight. Now, it's a given that anyone who watches any news whatsoever will recognize Gia's face. She's a mover and shaker among movers and shakers. One well-known fact the news loves to shout to the heavens is that it's not healthy to irritate, or far worse, out-and-out anger her. Gia doesn't play to the media, and her people don't talk to them, so I'm not sure where the rumor came from, but there you have it. In this case, rumor or not, the sentiment was absolutely correct.

The man standing in front of the SUV blanched, not only when the light of recognition entered his eyes, but more specifically when he focused on the expression he saw on Gianina Angelino's face.

Curious, I stepped forward so I could see it as well.

Whoa. No wonder the blood that was supposed to be giving his face the normal color associated with robust health and pink-cheeked enthusiasm had deserted the man. I'd seen her steel grey eyes before, and if I was perfectly honest, they tended to scare the crap out of me whenever they appeared. Add to that her stiff, absolutely still posture, the slightly lowered chin, and the muscle jumping in her jaw, and I glanced down to make sure the man hadn't wet his blue jeans. This idiot had interrupted Gia's family time, and she was not a happy camper.

Never one for long explanations, Gabe simply said, "Found him spying on the compound. He says you know him." He glared at me as though I was the one who'd done something wrong

I knew the man alright. At least I knew who he was. I knew him as the second barstool on the right, as the man following me in the sedan, and as the jamoke I'd chased from our crime scene. "What do you mean I know you? I don't know you from Adam."

His eyes cut from Gia to me and back to Gia again. Squaring his shoulders so he looked more like the soldier he'd probably been at some previous time in his life—if his neat appearance and somewhat longish crewcut were any indication—he pulled in a deep breath and addressed Gia. "I didn't know this was your property, Ma'am. I had no idea, and I apologize for trespassing." He indicated me with a lift of his elbow since his hands were still bound behind his back. "I was following her, that's all."

If the tone of her voice were indicative of her mood, I should have seen a chilling fog rising off her words when she spoke. "You were following Detective Wolfe? Why?"

He swallowed and looked down at his grey cowboy boots.

The man standing next to him jammed his hand around the guy's throat. "Ms. Angelino asked you a question."

I couldn't help thinking how convenient it was to have Gabe and his goons getting the information I needed out of the guy, making it so that I didn't have to raise a finger. I mentally slapped myself as that unbidden thought rose to the fore. *No, bad girl. I shouldn't think like that. I am a cop. They are the mafia, and I'm a cop, and never the twain shall meet.* Yeah, good luck with that if the past few years were any indication. Unfortunately, this guy had forced the issue, so I sat back and let the cards land where they would.

The man took a step back to loosen the pressure on his throat. Since the blood that had drained from his face was now returning with a vengeance, my inner cop stepped in. "Let him go, Carmine." I'd gotten to know Carmine when gunshot wounds had landed Gabe in the hospital for an extended period of time. I liked him, and I like to think, despite his monosyllabic responses to me whenever we spoke, he liked me as well.

He let go with a shove and then resumed his menacing attack dog posture; back to the SUV, arms crossed over his impressive pecs, feet spread shoulder-width apart.

I returned my attention to the intruder. Finger marks stretched around a reddened neck, and I imagined if the man's hands had been free, he'd reach up to rub the pain away. Frightened but still maintaining his military bearing, he addressed Gia with a strange combination of polite obeisance and determined intent. "I can't answer you, Ma'am. But I'll tell her." He looked over at me and asked, "Can we go somewhere to talk?"

Gabe growled, "No," just as I answered, "Yes."

Well, this was awkward. Gabe had caught the man on Gia's land, so she had dibs on him there, but I wanted to know why he'd been following me, so my hand won on that account. I didn't usually ask Gia's permission for anything, but I thought it might be prudent in this instance. I stepped between Gia and the man so all he could see was my back and said quietly, "If you plan to kill him and throw his body down a mineshaft or beat the shit out of him for coming onto your land, in either case, I'd have to object and try to stop you. You either have to call the Sheriff and have him arrested for trespassing or let me talk to him."

Gia's lips thinned, but after a moment, she said, "Make it quick and then get him off of my land. Lady Allegra arrives after lunch, and if I see him anywhere near my family or me or my guests again..." She let the end of the sentence hang before turning and heading back to the barn where Shelley and Jack stood watching the whole situation unfold. She motioned for them to head inside and then followed them without a backward glance in our direction.

I hated that my work had possibly intruded on one of the few times Gia had taken to relax. I couldn't be sure this man and Boujee had anything to do with my work, but it was a logical conclusion. This facility was Gia's sanctuary, and I intended to let this guy know how very pissed I was for him having taken that away from her. I grabbed the upper sleeve of his jeans jacket and hauled him to the end of the barn.

Carmine followed us partway and took up a guard position far enough away to give us privacy but close enough to take care of the guy if he gave me any trouble.

"Okay. Who the hell are you, and what are you doing tailing me here on my day off? I know you've been trying to be sneaky following me around in your nondescript little sedan all over God's half-acre. You've followed me into one of my favorite bars and stood outside my home trying to conceal yourself beneath my neighbor's desert willow, and you had the gall to run from a crime scene, but you know what? All you've really done is be an obnoxious, irritating, reddened boil on my backside. And now? And now you have the balls to come onto Gianina Angelino's property, thinking you could sneak up on me to find out what's going on? What a fucking idiot."

The guy had the grace to look chagrined. "I didn't think you'd seen me in the bar, and you couldn't have seen my face clear enough from across the street from your house to recognize me." He sighed, "Look, can you take these off? I have a bum shoulder, and it's starting to hurt." He brought his cuffed wrists around to the side of his butt.

"No, Asshole, I can't. At least not until I find out who you are and what your game is because you know what? You have no idea what kind of a hornets' nest you just kicked, and if you're stupid enough to kick it once, you might just kick it again, and if you do, I'm going to have a hell of a time keeping your head on that achy little shoulder of yours, capisce?"

His Adam's apple bounced once when he glanced over his shoulder at Carmine. He nodded, "Capisce. Look, detective, my brother and I—"

"Your *step-brother*, you mean, the boujee guy playing pool in the bar."

He straightened and pulled his head back in startled surprise. "How..? You..?"

My irritation was mounting by the minute. I wanted this guy out of here so I could join Gia, Shelley, Jack, and Chops in the arena on my day off. My gaze hardened onto his, and I knew I needed to tamp down my impatience and growing irritation if I wanted to know what he was hoping to find by following me around. "Who are you, and who is your stepbrother?" Thanks to Jerry, I already knew the brother's name, but I never let on to suspects that I know anything about anything until I know what their endgame is. My anger had already let too much slip, and I knew I needed to momentarily remove my off-duty, relaxed persona and slip on my cop one.

A little boy's smile spread across his face. "Boujee?

The grin was kind of cute, and I had the feeling if I weren't so angry at the guy, I might actually get to like him. Maybe. "Your brother. That's what I call him."

Despite his current circumstances, he threw his head back and laughed. "Oh my God, he'd hate that. Wait 'till I tell him. Boujee. Whenever I call him DiNozzo, you know, after that agent, Tony, on NCIS, he growls about it for a week afterward." He puffed his chest out and mimicked his brother. "I'm not like him. No way. This is just who I am. I dress for who I am."

Despite the seriousness of the occasion, I couldn't help smiling at his antics. The guy was definitely growing on me. "Anyway...you were saying?"

That brought him back to the present, and he again checked out Carmine—probably to make sure my guard dog was still chained—before continuing. "Anyway, My name is Stephen Grate. Steve. And my brother is George Ogilvie."

"And?"

"And when we read about your cases..." he glanced over at the real dogs lying in the morning sun. "...we thought maybe we could help."

"Which case?"

"The Coward. The arson murders."

"And just how do you think you can help?"

He brought his attention back to me and shrugged. "That's what's been so frustrating. We don't know how. That's why we didn't contact you directly. George said without something concrete, you'd just laugh at us and send us on our way. So, we decided to follow you around, you know, see who you're talking to, maybe—" Color rose in his cheeks, and the thought occurred to me that this guy should probably leave the undercover business to George. He gave himself away in so many subtle ways it would be dangerous if he tried it around the wrong people.

"Maybe what?" When he didn't answer, I repeated myself with a little more heat. I had a pretty good idea what 'maybe' meant, but I wanted to hear it from him. "*Maybe what, Steve?*"

I had the impression that if his hands weren't cuffed, he would have flipped them out to his sides. "Maybe talk to some of the people you talk to. You know, witnesses and such."

I cocked my jaw to the side and narrowed my eyes. I spoke in a slow monotone, so there'd be no way he'd mistake my ire for friendly banter. "You followed me around and went back and re-interviewed the people I've been talking to?"

"No, no. It's not as bad as all that."

Again, if he could move, I guessed he'd be waving his hands in the air between us to try to erase some of the implications of what he'd just said. Interviewing someone with their hands cuffed behind their back can be somewhat problematic as far as reading body language is concerned. I called over to Carmine, "Do you have a handcuff key handy?"

Carmine dug in his pocket, produced a set of keys, and tossed them to me without a word.

I pointed to the ground and spun my finger in a circle, indicating Steve should turn in place.

Once free, he slowly turned to face me while rubbing the red indentations circling both wrists. I felt vindicated when he held his hands up between us, palms out—an abbreviation of the more emphatic waving I would have expected from him a moment ago. "It's not like we officially interviewed them or anything—nothing like that. We didn't say we were cops or anything. We just...happened to meet them somewhere, like when they were coming out of their house or going into a grocery store, and we...well, mostly George because he's better at it than I am, would chat them up."

"Again, why? What's your interest in my cases?"

He snorted, "Yeah, that's another thing. Cases. Plural. You have so many open cases that you work simultaneously, and it makes it really hard to know which one you're working when you go talk to someone." He absently shook his head, a pinch of irritation showing through. "A lot of unnecessary busywork for us, that's for sure."

"Well, excuse the heck out of me. Next time I'll be sure to phone whoever's tailing me to let them know which witness is which. Now, for the third and final time, what...is...your... interest in that case?"

He rubbed a stubbly, two-day growth of beard, one I'm sure he cultivated to give him that urban cowboy kind of look. "That's a long story, and I'd prefer George and I were together when we explain it." A hopeful smile touched the side of his lips. "Maybe over a beer or a game of pool? When you're back in Tucson, that is. I promise we'll stop following you. It was stupid, anyway. We're just two guys with too much time on our hands."

He hadn't answered my question, but then again, I didn't want this to turn into a full-fledged, potentially hours-long interview. And more importantly, I hadn't sensed anything sinister about either of the men. The little gnome who jumps up and down on my shoulder whenever something terrible is about to happen hadn't made an appearance. I called over to Carmine. "Do you have any paper and a pen?"

Without nodding or acknowledging I'd even spoken, he disappeared into the arena, probably heading for the office. He came back a short time later with the requested items.

I motioned to Steve's pockets. "You have any I.D?"

He pointed at Carmine. "They have it."

When I looked expectantly at him, all Carmine said was, "Gabe."

I often wondered how Gia had taught her people to say as little as possible whenever possible. "Wait here." I went in search of Gabe and found him exactly where I thought he'd be, standing just inside the door guarding Gia. "Carmine said you have the guy's stuff. Can I have it please?"

He reached into his inside coat pocket and pulled out a wallet and a cellphone, which he handed to me without comment. When I opened the wallet and pulled Steve's license, Gabe said, "I copied all his shit on the copy machine. The phone's fingerprint locked, but that ain't much of a problem."

I searched his face, and in response, he lifted an eyebrow. Even though I knew it wouldn't happen, I couldn't help picturing Gabe holding one of Steve's severed fingers to the phone to unlock its secrets. The lock screen at least had the time on it, and I realized, with regret, that Steve had taken up thirty minutes of riding time with Gia and Shelley. "Damn it. Look, can you arrange to have Steve transported," I held up a finger, "in one piece, back to wherever he left his car? I think he's harmless, and I don't want to deal with him right now."

When he nodded, I returned to Steve, took a quick jaunt through the contents of the wallet, and then handed it to him. I could get a more thorough look at everything later when I perused the copies Gabe had made.

He tucked it into his back pocket. Most people would want to check to make sure everything was still there, but it seemed like Steve didn't dare possibly insulting Gabe or Carmine in the process. Smart move.

I held up his phone. "Unlock it."

He hesitated, and just for effect, I leaned in and said, "Open it with or without your finger still attached." Okay, an idle threat, but fun to say all the same.

He blinked several times, probably trying to decide whether I was joking or not. He pressed his thumb to the screen, and his home screen appeared. There were several missed calls and texts from George and one from someone named Fiona.

I punched the settings icon, scrolled down to "phone," pressed it, and then wrote down his number. I suppose I could have simply asked him for it, but what was to say he wouldn't give me the wrong number and then disappear? Just as I handed him his phone, a guard I didn't know drove up in the SUV.

The pulse on the side of Steve's neck quickened, and I wondered if he thought I'd let them kill him and bury his body somewhere out in the vast Sonoran desert. I squinched my eyes at his implied insult and sighed. "Really?"

His nervous chuckle fell flat, and he turned it into a throat-clearing instead.

"They're going to take you back to your car. Do I need to tell you to leave this valley without stopping and to quit following me?"

With obvious relief, he shook his head.

"What branch of the military were you?"

"Army."

"Retired?"

"Yes."

"I'll call you Tuesday sometime. You and George have a lot of explaining to do. If I hear you've gone anywhere near anyone or anything associated with *any* of my cases, I'll throw the book at both of you. Understand?"

He nodded and made his way over to the SUV. Ever friendly, Tessa jogged over to him, wagging her tail and looking for a handout. I felt better about my decision when he took the time to kneel and accept some kisses from her, all the while stroking her sleek white coat. He looked back and grinned. "I always thought she looked nice whenever you took her out for your nightly walks." The guy actually had the nerve to tease me at a time like this.

I growled, "Get out of here, you moron," and watched as he climbed in one side of the back seat and Carmine climbed in the other. It took me a moment to regain my relaxed, friendly equilibrium before rejoining everyone in the arena. When I did, one of the hired hands brought Chops over to me and gestured to the mounting block, silently asking if I'd like to mount up and continue my lesson.

Across the arena, Gia was finishing a series of jumps with Shelley and Jack standing by as her cheering section. I was glad to see that the tight lines around her eyes and mouth had relaxed. She'd returned to the more laid-back woman who'd managed, if only for a few days, to leave her problems behind and get away from all the sycophants clamoring for her attention.

I climbed aboard Chops and managed to maneuver her to the center of the ring. Apparently, it was Jack's turn to take his horse over the jumps. Some were low enough that a horse would barely need to raise its front feet, while others—three in a row to be exact—were of a medium height, maybe three feet or a bit more.

There were also two final jumps, three poles high, that seemed too much for any horse to get over safely. Looking around at my companions, I was sure no one here would chance such a death-defying leap. Granted, people who know what they're doing probably jump that height every day, but to an ignorant peasant like me, the height looked horrifying.

Jack circled his horse a few times, and when he was ready, it seemed he didn't have to do more than release the brakes, and the horse was off

I glanced at Gia to make sure everything was okay and that the horse wasn't running away with the thirteen-year-old child left in her care. Apparently, all was well because she looked pleased as Jack took the first two low jumps as easily as a college hurdler would take a set of low practice hurdles.

Once clear of the easy jumps, Jack pointed the horse

toward the three-foot hurdles, all lined up in a row, which he took one right after the other without any hesitation or fear.

I was impressed and figured he was finished, but my jaw dropped when I realized he intended to take his mount over the last two hurdles. They had to be at least four feet high. Heart pounding, I shot another glance at Gia, fully expecting her to yell at Jack to pull up. Instead, she was sitting back in her saddle, loosely holding her reins. There was admiration in her eyes as she followed the horse's approach to the jump.

Since both of the teens rode and jumped at the Regency Academy, Shelley must have seen Jack do this many times before because she, too, looked relaxed, as though she had no doubt whatsoever that her friend would easily clear this jump as well.

As I watched in horrified fascination, I noticed from a purely neophyte's point of view that Jack adjusted something with the horse's gait, like the timing or the distance; I wasn't sure which.

In response to his urging, the horse changed its speed slightly and lifted its front feet high into the air. The muscles in its massive hindquarters bunched and flexed, and the animal soared over the poles, effortlessly landing on the other side with its ears forward, already looking for the next jump. The horse sped up and then leapt again, clearing the next hurdle with effortless grace. It looked for all the world like it wanted to go around again, and they did, two more times, before Jack slowed to a trot and then to a walk.

Jack made his way over to where all of us were congratulating him on an incredible ride. Well, it was incredible to me, but to everyone else, it was probably just a good training ride. He wore a satisfied smile, bringing out a feminine beauty I hoped would be preserved even after his full transition. I imagined it would be some time before people met him and automatically registered 'he' instead of 'she' or thought of him as a 'him' and not a 'her.'

I threw off my wool-gathering in time to hear Gia ask, "Well?"

Jack stroked the palomino's mane. Even though he'd jumped all the jumps several times in a row, the horse still had difficulty standing still. He jogged in place, moving this way and that, ears twitching back and forth and eager for Jack's next command. He wanted to move and didn't understand why Jack wanted to stand still.

Before he answered Gia, Jack tugged on the reins and ordered, "Stand." Jack apparently spoke horse because the palomino stopped fidgeting. Once again stroking the horse's neck, he said, "For the most part, he's excellent. His movement across the ground is good, he has a long canter and he folds his knees tightly over the fences..."

Even as he hesitated, I felt this was a completely different person than Shelley's shy friend, the one I'd first met in front of the house. This Jack sounded more like an experienced trainer than a thirteen-year-old middle schooler, making me wonder what kind of training he'd had up to this point. His British lilt suited him perfectly. Unpretentious yet still upper-class. At least to my untrained ears. It didn't sound anything like the lower-class cockney I'd occasionally hear on the British pay-per-view channels.

Gia prompted Jack to continue, sensing the same hesitation I'd noticed, "But? And please be candid, Jack. You know your grandmother will be."

Chuckling at a shared private joke, he said, "Yes, she will. My only hesitation is there." she pointed to the top of the horse's head. "Between the ears. He's fine over the jumps, and he keeps his concentration." He paused to figure out how to form his answer. "He's brave enough...and he likes to jump." He gave him a fond pat. "I always look for that."

Always? How many horses could Jack have gone through at his age?

Again, Gia prompted, "But?"

"It's not exactly a but. He's young and full of himself, and he might grow into having a calm personality. But then again, he might not. At the really big competitions, he needs to have focus. He needs to be able to ignore the crowd. This guy, I'm not so sure how he'll be in a few years, but I like him, and if Grandmama likes him..." He raised a shoulder. "We'll see."

"You'll see what?" The conversation was interesting, but I was a bit lost.

Jack had to turn around to answer me. "Well, some of the horses Ms. Angelino breeds aren't fast enough to be racehorses, so, instead of just selling them at auction like so many other breeders do, she has her trainers figure out what they're best at. Apollo here loves to jump, so she wanted to know whether I'd be interested in buying him. Well, whether Grandmama would like to buy him for me."

The two talked for a while longer, and since I was lost anyway, I glanced down at Chops, hoping I could get her moving in the right direction.

Shelley also wanted to ride more than listen, so she helped me get Chops pointed in the right direction, and the two of us walked around the edge of the arena. When she figured I could handle Chops on my own, she told me to keep going and then trotted off to practice weaving this way and that, moving in and around the jumps and generally finding her equilibrium on top of the horse.

After a bit, Gia called a halt to the morning's ride. Two of the stable hands came and took Chops and Gia's horse, Magma, but Gia told Shelley and Jack they needed to unsaddle their own horses and clean their stalls. We watched the two of them cheerfully ride out of the arena toward the barn.

Gia turned to me. "I have to make a few phone calls, Alex. Make yourself at home. Jack is staying in the yellow room, and Lady Allegra will be taking your usual one, but I've assigned you to the Modigliani."

"That's great, as long as that one painting of the guy with the weird eyes doesn't keep me up all night." There was a portrait of a man with a crooked face and crossed eyes hanging on the wall facing the bed. I'd hoped I'd never have to sleep with him staring at me, or worse, wake up from a sound sleep to find his tiny, pinched mouth and unbalanced eyes looming over me. There were other paintings in the room as well by the same painter, but that one had to be the strangest of them all.

Gia accepted a face towel from one of the stable hands. "I should hope not. Amadeo Modigliani was an artist who was part modernist with maybe a touch of surrealism, but an artist you can't put in any stylistic box. Although, he was influenced by other painting going on in Paris at the time. He was a fascinating man who captured the faces of the early nineteen hundreds."

Gia often takes the time to educate me on topics I know nothing about. She wiped her face and then continued, "He was also a troubled man, an unapologetic Jew who painted from deep within his soul. If you consider those things while studying his work, you may see more in the painting than simply a man with weird eyes. Remember, fascism was rearing its ugly head in Paris, where he lived. The man in the portrait was a fellow Jew. Perhaps he was making some kind of statement?"

I wasn't convinced. "Maybe I could hang my towel over it or something."

Gia stopped in the middle of the path and studied my face, trying to decide if I was kidding or not. "Alex. You know how the paintings hanging in my home in Tucson are reproductions of paintings I have out on loan to various museums?"

"Uh-huh."

"This is an original Modigliani, worth more than you will ever make in several lifetimes as a police officer. I assume you're joking?"

Grinning, I said, "Of course I'm kidding." When she turned to begin walking again, I added, "I'd make sure the towel was dry first."

Shaking her head slightly, she said, "Just so you know, if the painting moves even the slightest amount, bars will come down on all the windows and doors, an alarm will sound, and heavily armed men will surround the property, weapons drawn and at the ready. I would advise you to use your towel for its intended purpose."

"If you insist. But I'd think you'd want to put Grandmama in there, you know, to impress her."

"Lady Allegra isn't impressed by a person's art collection, Alex. She grew up surrounded by Monets and Jacques-Louis Davids, and Tussauds. She values the paintings, yes, but doesn't assign that value to the people who own them. That is an excellent lesson for you, by the way. One I think you would innately embrace without being conscious of the thought process that brought you to the understanding." We'd reached my car, and she stopped for a moment, "Now, we'll be dining sometime mid-afternoon. I assume you brought some formal clothes as I requested?"

I shrugged, "As formal as I have, which probably isn't formal enough for Lady Allegra. Not a dress or anything."

"I'm sure whatever you wear will be fine. In fact," Gia sized me up from my feet to my shoulders, "If you'd permit, I'll send Kathleen in with some of my blouses. Between the two of you, I'm sure you'll present a striking first impression." Kathleen travels everywhere with Gia. I suppose you could call her a valet, although I don't know if women have valets. She stays with the trainers in their home whenever she has to come to the compound and generally keeps out of the way except when needed.

At my nod, Gia continued, "If you're hungry in the meantime, help yourself in the kitchen, but I'd suggest treading lightly around the cook, Mrs. Foleni. I can personally attest to the fact that a whack with her wooden spoon is not something I would recommend to anyone."

"Oh, come on, nobody would dare whack you. Well," I shrugged. "and live."

She was in the process of lighting her cigar, and her dove-grey eyes met mine through the smoke drifting skyward. I read amusement there, but not a definitive answer to my implied question. I'd have to guess about the formidable Mrs. Foleni.

"Why Mrs. Foleni and not Marla?" Every other time I'd been here, it had been Marla doing the meals. In fact, Marla had been the one who'd made our perfect breakfast.

"Marla is an excellent cook. One of the best. However, Mrs. Foleni is a three-star Michelin chef. While Lady Allegra will not be impressed by my art, she will appreciate Mrs. Foleni's masterpieces."

About an hour later, Shelley came running into the house yelling at the top of her lungs. "Jack's grandmother's here! We can see her car coming down the hill! Alex! C'mon!"

I was hoping to hide in my room as long as possible, maybe not meeting Grandmama until I absolutely had to come out for dinner.

Shelley burst into my room and grabbed me by the hand, pulling me into the hall with such enthusiasm I banged my shoulder on the corner of the door as we maneuvered around it. "C'mon. You gotta meet her. I told her all about you. She comes to Regency all the time and takes Jack and me to lunch. She's really nice!"

Gia appeared at the door to the office. "Shelley. Calm down. Remember what I've told you about the proper way to greet our guests."

"But—"

"No buts. I expect you to introduce Lady Allegra to Detective Wolfe—"

"To Alex, you mean."

"No, I mean to Detective Wolfe. It will be up to Alex to grant the more familiar form of address."

"Okay." Shelley let out a long breath, pulled her shoulders back, and tucked her chin a bit, probably the way Gia had told her to stand when in polite company. I had to admit, she did look very proper, so I did the same and checked myself in the mirror. Not bad.

Gia led us to the front porch where we joined Jack, who was waiting while Gabe produced a step stool from the rear of the black SUV. The floorboard was higher than my knees, and the stool would make it easier and more ladylike, I'm sure, for Lady Allegra to disembark. I was surprised to see he and the other guards had changed into business suits and ties. When I looked down at my jeans and sneakers, I suddenly didn't feel so ready to meet the redoubtable Lady Allegra.

Gia slipped her arm through mine. "You'll be fine, Alex. Breathe."

I copied Shelley, pulling in a deep breath and letting it out slowly.

After placing the stepstool on the ground, Gabe opened the door and offered his hand to Jack's grandmother. The woman who emerged wasn't what I was expecting. In my mind, she should have been wearing a brightly colored floral tea dress or some kind of pleated frock. She'd be a bit overweight and frumpy and have permanent frown lines etched into her forehead.

Instead, a handsome, fit woman wearing grey denim jeans and a brown tweed blazer emerged. Beneath the coat, she wore a starched white blouse with a matching scarf wrapped several times around her neck and tied in a knot in front. Classy but down-to-earth. Just how Gia had described her.

Jack went to her, and the woman wrapped him in a bearhug. When they released each other, he led her to where Gia, Shelley, and I waited.

Gia let go of my arm, and the two of them air-kissed. I hoped they didn't expect me to do anything like that because it wasn't gonna happen.

Shelley followed, and the two of them hugged briefly, not nearly as effusive a hug as Lady Allegra had given Jack.

Then it was my turn. I straightened, or stiffened as the case may be, tucked my chin and listened as Shelley introduced us.

"Lady Allegra, may I introduce Al—uh, Detective Wolfe. Detective Wolfe, this is Lady Allegra."

Taking my cue from what Gia had mentioned earlier, I held out my hand and said, "I'm very pleased to meet you, Lady Allegra, and please, call me Alex."

I guess I sounded okay because the woman gave me a broad, somewhat toothy smile and gently took my hand. "I've heard so much about you, Alex. The pleasure is all mine."

Thankfully Gia stepped in and led Lady Allegra into the house. I say thankfully since I had no clue what to say next.

Shelley nudged me with her elbow. "Did I sound okay? That's the first time I've ever introduced somebody. I've practiced with Jack, and they give us lessons in that kind of thing at school, but…"

I saw real worry in her eyes, probably the same thing she saw in mine. I nodded, hoping to reassure her, "I think you were perfect. Now, if we can just get through the next day or so without creating an international incident, we'll be fine."

As I'd hoped, she giggled, which loosened the worry lines creasing her face. I knew she'd taken my words as a joke, but in reality, I wasn't joking. Spending time with Gia had undoubtedly opened my world up to new and exciting experiences, but it had also complicated a relatively straightforward life. I used to go to work, find the bad guys, arrest them, and go home to have pizza and a movie with my friends.

But I have to admit I like most of the changes. I enjoy meeting interesting people without having to interview them as victims or suspects. And I think I've opened Gia up to new experiences as well. We have kind of a symbiotic relationship that I hope will be around for a long time to come.

Jack walked up with Lady Allegra's luggage, and he and Shelley went inside while I went to my car to get my stuff. I didn't have the expensive-looking luggage that Lady Allegra had, but I liked mine just the same. When my grandfather died, my mother had passed along his old leather suitcase to me. There was nothing particularly fancy about it, but it was special to me because his initials, HWG, were stamped into the cinnamon-brown leather side panel. The entire bag was encased in a removable canvas cover that also bore his initials. My grandfather had been a very particular man who had treated his belongings with care. I don't own a lot of nice things, but having his suitcase means a lot to me.

As I made my way to my room, Lady Allegra was just coming out of her's. She happened to glance down at my suitcase, and by the way she stopped and blinked, I thought she'd try to hide the pity she must have felt for Gia's poorer friends.

Instead, her voice held a wistful tone when she said, "Oh my. My father used to have a case like that. It was so elegant, and he was so proud to take it with him when he traveled. Is it light tan or cinnamon beneath the canvas? They made these bags both ways, you know."

Pleased, I set the bag down and unzipped the cover. "It's the cinnamon color." I pointed to the raised letters, "And these are my grandfather's initials."

She ran her hand over the leather. "Wonderful. And how fortunate you are to have inherited such a treasure from your grandfather." She absently held two fingers to her lips. "I'll have to mount a search for my father's bags. There are several places they could be, but if I find them, I'll send you a photograph, shall I?"

I was definitely warming to this woman. "I'd love to see it. What color was your father's luggage?"

"His was a light tan. Do you have a matching second piece to complete the set?"

"Yes! It's a bigger version, for bigger trips, I guess. I just needed this one because I'm only staying a short time." I rezipped the canvas and stood, unsure whether I should move past her to my room or wait for her to go wherever she was headed.

She solved it for me by making her way to the great room. "We're taking a walk around the property if you'd care to join us."

I noticed Kathleen hovering in the background, and I figured she wanted to see what I planned to wear to dinner. "Uh, no, thank you. I need to hang some stuff up."

Even though the Modigliani room was small compared to the other bedrooms in the house, it was still bigger than mine back home. I set the suitcase on the bed, and as I guessed, Kathleen followed and knocked on the doorframe.

"Detective Wolfe? Ms. Angelino asked me to help you dress for dinner. Maybe we could start by going through the clothes you brought?"

Over the next hour, Kathleen decided my light grey tweed

slacks were acceptable but tsk-tsked over the two blouses I'd brought. Who knew picking out clothes could take more than two minutes, tops? Okay, I have to admit I'd bought the blouses somewhere around 2005 from Target or some similar high-end store, but I hadn't needed to dress up for the last several years. It was either chinos and a short-sleeved blue or white polo shirt with Tucson Police embroidered on the chest, or jeans and a casual shirt for my day's off.

She brought in some starched button-down shirts and several blazers that fit me as though someone had tailored them specifically for my body. By the time she'd finished, my outfit was more stylish than anything I've ever worn in my life. I guess with clothing, like whiskey, you need to pay more than ten dollars for the item if you want to look like a million bucks.

Kathleen asked if I'd brought high-heeled shoes or boots, and when I laughed in her face, she nodded and said, "Right." Luckily, she approved of the black loafers I'd brought, and in the end, the two of us stood staring at me as I posed in front of a free-standing, full-length mirror.

Smiling at my open-mouthed reaction, she reached out to straighten an already straight collar. "Now that's an outfit you could wear anywhere."

I thought about walking into The Backdoor, a gay bar where my friends Gus and Single worked, and grinned, "Not most of the anywheres I frequent, but I love it. It gives your self-confidence a boost when you look like this. Well, it does mine anyway. You probably always look great. Listen, thanks for taking the time to help me out. I really appreciate it."

"My pleasure. I hope we can do it again sometime."

By the time she left, the others were getting back from their tour of the property. Shelley stuck her head in my door. "Aunt Gia says we'll—" Shocked, she stopped mid-sentence and stared at me. "Wow."

I did a turn in front of the mirror and admired the way the jacket fit my curves. I usually didn't do curves, but this was nice. "You like?"

"Well, yeah. I've never seen you looking good, Alex."

"Hey!"

"Aw, you know what I mean. Anyway, I came in to tell you Aunt Gia says we're gonna eat in about forty minutes, so we need to get ready, but you're already dressed, so—" Her lips thinned a bit and her nose scrunched. "Maybe you should just sit in here and not move or anything."

That was probably good advice. "Yeah. Are Tessa and Jynx still outside?" I could just see a line of muddy pawprints snaking across the pants and jacket.

"They're in with Grandmama. That's what she said I should call her. Do you think that's okay? I mean, she's not really my grandmother, and I feel kinda strange calling her that, but I think Aunt Gia would say it's the polite thing to do since that's what she told me to call her. What do you think?"

"Well, so far, I like her, and if you did have a grandmother, she'd be a pretty cool one to have, and really, what's it gonna hurt? In fact, I doubt she has many people other than her real grandchildren call her that, so maybe just go with it."

Gia called out from another room. "Shelley."

"I gotta run." With that, she hurried out, yelling, "Coming."

So Jynx and Tessa had adopted Lady Allegra as their own. That said a lot since my dogs were fairly loyal to me. For the most part, anyway. That made me worry about heading into the dining room with the two of them around, so I pulled out my cell phone and called Gabe.

"What do you need, Alex?"

I whispered so no one else could hear. "Well, here's the thing. I look good. I mean really good."

He snorted into the phone.

Slightly insulted, I said a little louder, "I do."

"And?"

"And I'm worried about Jynx and Tessa jumping on me before I even get into the dining room. Do you think you could throw them outside before I come out?" There was silence on the other end, and when I looked at the phone, he'd hung up. "Thanks." I turned and squeaked when I saw him standing in my doorway.

He wasn't exactly smiling, but his dimple made an appearance. "You do look good." He paused long enough to get a good look and then disappeared around the corner. I knew he'd take care of the dogs.

I shut my door and sat down to wait. When I heard the clicking of the dog's toes on the tile floor, I listened for Gabe to take charge and usher them out. I stood at the window, and when I saw them chasing after a thrown ball, I figured the coast was clear.

When I walked into the dining room, Gia and Lady Allegra were standing next to the rock fireplace. Each of them held a whiskey glass in one hand—a Glencairn to be exact—and a cigar in the other.

Tom, the racetrack waiter, had changed into a more formal uniform, and he approached me holding a tray with a third Glencairn. I already knew it would be full of Glenlivet, and I thanked him as I took it off the tray.

Gia had once tried to explain the differences between the various whiskey glasses, telling me she preferred the Glencairn because it allowed for better swirling, which released more of the aroma. She glanced my way now, gave my outfit a once over, and winked.

I smiled back and shrugged. I was in a strange predicament. My nerves were shot because I didn't want to make a fool of myself, but the whiskey that would help relax me would also help me make a fool of myself. I settled for little sips, intending to make this first one last as long as I could.

Shelley and Jack arrived, followed by Mia and Liam, Gia's husband and wife team of horse trainers.

Dinner went better than I expected. I held my own with polite conversation and thankfully remembered all the manners my mother had taught me over the years. I hadn't been raised a complete Philistine, but it often seemed that my every day, commonplace manners were one step below Gia's level of etiquette. I was more than relieved when dessert was over, and everyone retired to their rooms for an early night.

I spent the following morning riding Chops and playing with the dogs. Lady Allegra and I visited some more during lunch, which wasn't nearly as formal as dinner the night before. She was an engaging woman who knew how to draw people out. I found myself discussing my work and describing Casey and Kate with far more detail than I would in a normal conversation. I felt as though she was interested in me, and when we spoke, she focused her entire attention on what I had to say.

"Your Kate seems quite a formidable woman. And Casey sounds down to earth and dependable." Lady Allegra turned to Gia. "Perhaps we can arrange a time to meet this coming week?"

It didn't seem that Gia was taken aback by the question, and before she could agree to an outing, I said, "I... don't know if Kate..." I didn't know how to politely say that although Kate respected Gia, there was no way in hell she'd go on a social outing with her.

Luckily Gia understood. "Kate is supervising a series of very serious cases this week, and I doubt she'll be able to make it. But perhaps Alex can arrange to meet with us again."

"What type of cases? Are you part of that investigative team, Alex?"

I sensed nothing more than polite inquiry, and I gave her the abbreviated public version. "We've had a series of arson fires where people have died during the event. I—" As if on cue, my cell rang with Kate's distinctive siren ring. I'd left my phone in my room, but like Pavlov's dogs, I would hear and respond to that sound anywhere. I knew it was probably rude to leave the table for a phone call, but I pushed back anyway and said, "Speak of the devil, that's Kate now. Excuse me."

Hurrying to my room, I grabbed my phone, hoping it hadn't already gone to voicemail. "Hey, Boss. What's up?"

"I know you're out at Sonoita for a few days, but I need you to come back early."

"Another fire?"

"Not exactly. How long before you can get to the station?"

I looked at the antique clock sitting on the mantel. "It'll take me an hour and a half, give or take a bit if I don't stop to change."

"Come straight to the office, then. I'll explain when you get here."

I quickly threw all my clothes into my suitcase and snapped it shut. It didn't take long to zip the canvas cover over it, and I carried the case out and left it by the front door. I returned to the dining room where Tom had just set out a platter of homemade pastries, gooey chocolate brownies, and caramel-cinnamon buns I was going to miss. I heard myself whisper, "Shit," before I could stop the word from flying out of my mouth.

Lady Allegra and Gia both chuckled, and I sighed. "I have to get back to Tucson. I'm sorry I'm leaving early Gia. It was very nice meeting you, Lady Allegra. I enjoyed our visit." I turned to Jack. "Since you're going to be here a month, Jack, I'm sure we'll be seeing each other again soon. See you later,

Shelley." I hoped that was enough as far as polite goodbyes go.

Gia excused herself and walked with me to the front door. "I hope this wasn't too dreadful for you."

"Actually, I had a lot of fun. You were right, I do like Lady Allegra, and if I can, I'd love to meet with you guys again this week, but in Tucson this time." I enveloped her in a big hug, mostly because I knew I was one of only a handful of people who ever showed her any real affection. "I'll call ya."

CHAPTER 6

It was three in the afternoon by the time I walked into the office. I work a four-ten shift, meaning I'm on the job four ten-hour days and have three days off. Saturday was supposed to have been one of those days, but the arson had taken care of that. That left Sunday and today, Monday, as the remainder of my weekend, but I had put in for Tuesday off just in case I could stay an extra night. I hadn't been too surprised to get Kate's call. She knew Gia had invited me down to her compound and had begrudgingly let me go with the caveat I'd be available should the need arise.

Our lieutenant, Jon Lake, was sitting in Kate's cubicle when I walked in. Casey sat in the second chair, and Mitch Johnson, the arson detective, leaned against the glass partition.

Kate motioned to me with a flick of her pen, "Oh good. You're here."

Lt. Lake stood. "I'll leave you to it, then." As far as lieutenants go, Lake wasn't so bad. He tended to stay out of our way and ran interference with the brass whenever needed.

I nodded to him as he passed. "Sir."

A tenseness, both unfamiliar and disquieting wrinkled his brow as he passed. He stopped me with a finger on my arm and spoke quietly. "We need to stop this man, Alex." He caught and held my gaze, "At all costs."

I blinked several times, unsure of his meaning. Or rather, sure of his meaning, but not sure I liked it.

Not expecting an answer, he headed out the door.

When he was gone, Kate motioned for me to sit in the now vacant chair. "There was another attempted arson this morning."

"Attempted?"

"A home nurse sedated the elderly woman who was the intended victim before we arrived, so we haven't gotten anything out of her. The nurse told me the woman has a heart condition, is severely traumatized, and this upset could very well trigger an episode. There was a young woman at the scene who's also extremely upset, and she said she wouldn't speak to anyone except you."

"Me?"

Casey pulled a card out of her sweatshirt pocket. "She had this."

I immediately recognized the card as one of mine. When I turned it over, I saw my cell number written in the haphazard, barely legible scrawl I use when I'm in a hurry. "Who is it?"

Kate tapped a paper on her desk. "We at least got a name out of her. Says she's Rosemarie Holt." She glanced to see whether the name rang any bells.

It didn't, and I shrugged.

Casey chimed in again. "She says you might recognize her as Babe."

"Oh yeah. Pretty woman with a nose ring?"

Kate nodded. "That's her. I recognized her from Saturday's crime scene. You spoke with her near your car. Anyway, she's frightened and won't tell us anything. We have her in the interview room."

"Okay. Can I get some background on what happened?"

"That's just it. We have a lot of questions but very few answers."

Mitch chimed in. "There is one other thing. We found a small stain on an area rug that we think might be an accelerant. Obviously, I didn't put my nose down to it, but the residual odor tells me it could be. We won't know until the lab comes back with the results." He hadn't shaved in a few days, and his patchy beard had a few spots of grey. The dark colors under his eyes told of all the late nights the arson guys had been putting in on these cases. I felt a bit guilty about the great time I'd had with Gia and Shelley.

He must have read my mind because his mouth quirked up in a grin. "I hope you got your beauty rest down in Sonoita while the rest of us jamokes have been working overtime."

"Beauty rest wouldn't help your ugly mug, anyway, Mitch, so you might as well be doing something productive."

He snorted, and I turned back to Kate. "Anything else I should know?"

"There's not much else I can tell you. Go interview her and see what you can find out. I'd like to see if she'll talk with Mitch sitting in too."

I patted his slightly protruding tummy. "If his fluffy dad bod doesn't put her at ease, nothing will." In actuality, he was still in pretty good shape for a man in his mid-forties. He'd played a lot of sports in his younger days, and as I said earlier, he and I play on the same team in the police and fire softball league.

I playfully ran into him on the way past, and he shoved me out of the cubicle.

Kate growled, "Stop it, you two."

We both grinned back at her as we headed for the interview room. I stopped at my desk first to drop off my briefcase, grab my tape recorder, a pen, and a yellow legal pad. Even though I'd record everything said during the interview, I often like to write down points I wanted to circle back to before we wrapped up the conversation. I'd found that if I didn't write it down, I'd often miss important information and would have to go back and talk to the person later when I remembered what I'd wanted to ask.

Babe was standing at the window looking out over the city when I walked in. The window ran the entire length of the upper half of the exterior wall. Unfortunately, all she could see directly in front of her was the main fire station's back wall and parking lot. To the left, the hundreds of spaces in the black-topped Community Center parking lot stood empty, and across the street to the right was the side of Saint Augustine's Cathedral.

She was wearing colorful leggings with orange, turquoise, yellow and blue feathers floating on a black background. Over that, a black hoodie with the face of a hawk embroidered on front stretched to the top of her thighs.

When she turned to see who had walked in, her red-rimmed eyes lit with recognition. "Detective Wolfe. They said you were out of town. I'm sorry you had to come back, but—" Her lip quivered, and her eyes filled with tears.

Normally, I'd never touch a witness, but she seemed so broken up I went over and put my arms around her. "Don't be sorry, Babe. I was way out of my social comfort zone down there anyway, and it didn't take much convincing to get me back here." I neglected to add that cops have very little choice in the matter when Kate orders them back to the station. "C'mon over here and sit down." I led her to the only sofa in the room. This room was different from the ones where we interview suspects. Those are only about five feet square, with a single table bolted to the floor and two hard plastic chairs set on either side.

On the other hand, we use this room for victims and witnesses, especially children who have been traumatized in some way and need a safe place to talk. It has a very comfortable sofa, two armchairs, and a coffee table. All of the furniture made for a tight fit, but it worked. Calming pastoral pictures of lambs and open, verdant valleys hung on the walls, and a box full of toys and stuffed animals took up one of the corners.

Mitch had remained standing in the door—an excellent move on his part. That way, Babe wouldn't feel pressured by too many people barging in on her.

When she noticed him, I jumped right in with the introductions. "I don't know if you two met earlier, but this is Detective Johnson. He's with the arson unit, and he's been working these cases from the beginning. I was hoping you wouldn't mind if he sat in while we chatted about what happened."

Mitch stepped into the room and grabbed a tissue from a box on the coffee table, which he handed to her. "Here you go." When she took it from him, he gave her a fatherly smile and reached back to close the door.

I sat next to her on the sofa. Even though I'd said I hoped she didn't mind Mitch's presence, I didn't want to give her the opportunity to say she didn't want him in the room. With that in mind, I started right in. "First, when we interview people, even if they're friends, we still need to record everything that's said." I set the recorder on the table while Mitch lowered himself into one of the armchairs. I pushed the record button, gave the date and time, and mentioned everyone in the room. "The last time we spoke, you said you prefer to be called Babe, so for the record, that's how I'll be referring to you during the interview, okay?"

She nodded.

I smiled to ease the tension that had crept into her shoulders at the mention of an interview. "The thing is, Babe, the recorder can't see you nod, so could you try to remember to answer out loud?"

Catching herself in the middle of her next nod, she smiled a bit and said, "Yes. I'll try to remember.

"I've come into this whole thing a little late, so can you start from the beginning and tell me what happened?"

Hesitating, Babe swallowed and flicked a nervous glance around the room. "He said I'm dead if I tell you anything."

"Who said that? You need to realize, I don't know what's going on, and you're going to need to paint me a full picture so I can get up to speed and help you." When she didn't continue, I said, "The last time we talked, you told me you were worried about your seniors, and so are we. Look, I know you're scared, but you might be the first real break we've had in these cases, and if you don't help us, we're right back to square one."

She pursed her lips, and even though she still had frightened worry lines around her eyes, she nodded with a determination I'd often seen in the eyes of witnesses willing to brave the wrath of a suspect in order to stop them. "Well, this morning, I'd gone to the coffee shop early because I'd had a late night and needed some caffeine to get me going."

"Which coffee shop?" Every detail was important now, and I intended to learn everything I could while she was willing to talk.

"The Blue Goat. There's this hot guy I like who serves the coffee in the mornings." Thankfully, some of her previous sauciness returned at the mention of the cute barista. "I was in line, and my phone rang. It was Mrs. Holloway, but when I answered, she didn't say anything, and that really worried me, you know? Because of what's been happening."

She glanced over at Mitch, who nodded for her to continue.

I said, "Who's Mrs. Holloway?"

"You know my seniors?"

"Yes."

"She's one of the ladies I visit. Ninety-four-years-old going on twenty. She's wonderful and full of life, and if anything—" Her voice caught, and she swiped at her eyes with the tissue. After pulling in a breath, she continued, "Anyway, I couldn't hear anything, and that's really unusual because she never stops talking once she gets someone on the phone. Since she lives in the same general area as The Goat, I told Razi, that's the guy I like, I had to go, but I'd be back as soon as I could. When I got there, I started to knock, but...well, I raised my hand to knock—" She suddenly seemed unsure of herself. "Well, have you ever gotten that feeling, you know, back here?" She rubbed the back of her neck.

Mitch and I nodded in unison. "Oh yeah."

Relieved that we understood, Babe continued, "She keeps a key around back, so I decided to go back there..." She added sheepishly, "...I snuck under the windows cuz I was scared and kinda tiptoed. Anyway, I went looking for the key—"

Mitched asked, "Where does she keep the key?"

"Usually on top of the backdoor light. I always tell her that's the first place a burglar would look, but she's old school and said if her husband thought it was good enough—he's been dead twenty years now—if it was good enough for him, it was good enough for her. But it wasn't there. I turned the knob really slow, and the door was unlocked." Her eyes opened wide. "She *never* leaves her door unlocked."

Glancing over at the door, she said, "She keeps one of those little army shovels next to her door because she loves to garden—"

"Army shovels?" I had no idea what an army shovel was.

Mitch made a bending motion with his hands. "An entrenching tool. For digging foxholes. It's a three-piece folding shovel. It collapses down, so it's easy for a soldier to carry."

Babe shook her head. "Kind of, but this one only bent at the place between the handle and the head."

He nodded. "Like in World War II. I don't remember seeing one like that in her house."

Babe looked blank. "I have no idea what I did with it. Anyway, it's little, but it's all I could see to use if I needed to protect myself. I grabbed it; it wasn't folded because Mrs. Holloway has a hard time turning the collar to loosen the blade. Then I snuck inside. That door opens onto the kitchen, and nobody was in there, but I heard Mrs. Holloway kind of whimper, so I put the shovel on my shoulder like a bat and rushed into the living room."

I wanted to glance over at Mitch because I knew he was just as excited about what she'd say next. Maybe she'd gotten a good look at the guy. I made myself stay still and waited for the rest of the story.

"It was dark because he'd shut all the curtains and the only light on was the dim little lamp she has on her side table. She keeps a real dim bulb in it because bright light hurts her eyes. I couldn't see very well. Anyway, he had a paper bag over her head, and he was bending over her and I—" Her words came out in a rush. "—I didn't know what else to do, so I raised the shovel up like this and bashed him in the head!" She stood as though she was in Mrs. Holloway's living room, held her hands together gripping an imaginary shovel, and brought it down onto a make-believe head. "Like that. I would have hit him again, but he bellowed and turned my way and jammed his elbow into my stomach, and charged into me with his shoulder. I fell backward over the coffee table and then landed on a chair that flipped me over backward. I hit my head against the wall and jammed my head into my neck."

She reached up to rub the back of her neck.

Anxious to know whether she could identify the guy, I wanted to shout, "What did he look like?" Both Mitch and I were on the edge of our seats, but neither of us said anything since we wanted to hear the whole story before we went back for specific details. I took a breath and made myself relax. Sitting back on the sofa, I glanced at Mitch, who took his cue from me and did the same in his chair.

We waited for her to mentally come back into the room. When she sat again, she looked directly at me with a dark, angry glare. She indicated her plus-sized body with a wave of her hands. "Look at me. I'm not exactly Miss Gymnastics USA, and by the time I pushed up off the floor, he was gone." She shoved back into the cushions and crossed her arms. "I should have moved faster. If I hadn't been so slow, I would have seen his face, and you'd have him."

I shook my head, "No. You did everything you could to stop what was happening and save yourself and your friend. Things might not have ended so well for either you or Mrs. Holloway if you'd seen his face." That brought up something else I'd been wondering. "Do you know if Mrs. Holloway saw his face?"

"I don't think so. Like I said, there was a paper bag over her head when I came in. She was so upset when I took the bag off I had to untie a gag she had around her mouth, and once I got that off I couldn't get her to stop sobbing long enough to realize we were safe." She thought about that a second, "Well, I guess I didn't know we were safe, but I tried to convince her we were because of her bad heart. I thought she was going to cry herself into a heart attack; she was that upset. She was still crying when Gail got there. She got there before the police because she was visiting another patient about a block away—a bunch of seniors live in that neighborhood—and I called her after I called you guys." She glanced up at me. "Actually, I tried to call you, but I kept getting the wrong number."

I winced. "Sorry about that. I wrote the numbers so quickly that my nine ended up looking like a four. I'll give you a new card when we're done here. So, Gail is the nurse who gave her a sedative?"

"Yeah. She said her BP was sky high, and she needed to get it down." Tears welled in her eyes, and we waited while she worked to get her emotions under control.

I glanced at Mitch, who raised his eyebrows, asking what I wanted to do. I shrugged, silently letting him know he could do what he thought best.

It's sometimes difficult working with another detective who isn't your partner. A good team gets to know how the other one works, and they play off each other effortlessly. It helps when both interviewers are seasoned detectives. I had every confidence Mitch wouldn't intentionally do or ask anything that would stop Babe from talking.

Breaking the silence that had settled on the room, Mitch asked, "Would you recognize him if you saw him again?"

"I didn't see him, exactly. It was dark, and he had his back to me. Oh!" She sat forward as though she'd just remembered something important. "Here." She partially stood and reached over to grab a piece of paper off a bookshelf where we keep children's books and magazines. "I paint a lot, but I'm not good at faces, so a couple of years ago, my mom suggested I try silhouettes. I've gotten pretty good at them and...well, here."

She handed me a detailed sketch of a black silhouette surrounded by grey. "Like I said, it was dark and gloomy in the room," She pointed to the lighter part, "That's why I put in the grey. It's what I saw, and when I draw, I have to put in what I see, so I get the proportions of the silhouette right."

I set the picture on the coffee table. "Tell us about it."

Pointing to the head, she squinted and said, "I don't think he had much hair because I remember the shovel felt like it was banging against his skull and not hair. And I kind of remember seeing like wisps of white hair as the shovel came down on his head."

Mitch glanced up from the silhouette, "Was your impression that the wisps were like my hair or like yours?"

"You mean was it thick like mine?" She fingered one of the dozens of black braids that flowed past her chestnut-brown face and ended in the middle of her back. "No, he wasn't a brother. White or brown, but I didn't see him clearly enough to be sure." She ran a finger along the shoulder line. "This was kinda rounded."

I studied the picture. "Looks like he was slumping or had bad posture?"

"Exactly, but he had broad shoulders. Like I said, he was bending over her, but I got the feeling he wasn't very tall. When he swung around and slugged me in the stomach, I didn't think he was any taller than I am. Maybe shorter, even."

Mitch's brows drew together. "Shorter than you?" It was an important point because she stood about five-feet-three-inches tall, and a broad-shouldered short man would be pretty distinctive.

She shrugged, suddenly unsure of herself. "I think so... maybe." Her uncertainty grew, "Probably not. I can't say for sure because he never really stood up when I saw him. He was leaning over her, I bashed him, and he swung around and into me without straightening up. So probably not."

Smiling, Mitch waved his hands, trying to cancel out the

indecision he'd brought on. "Wait, wait, wait. It's okay if he was. I'm not doubting you. I just wanted to clarify, that's all."

Her eyebrows stayed low, and she gave a short shake of her head. "I know, but I can't say for sure. I wish I could."

I wanted her focus back on the picture. "What about his clothes?"

Her cheeks puffed when she blew out a breath. "I didn't notice. I'm sorry." Her frustrated look was one I'd seen on the faces of victims many times.

"Listen to me, Babe. It's perfectly normal when people are in life or death situations not to see many details. Their focus gets very sharp and narrow. If you can, close your eyes a minute and see the room as you saw it when you first came out of the kitchen." I waited for her to close her eyes and relax back into the sofa. "Now, I don't want you to look for what was normal. Look for things that maybe stood out as different or not the way Mrs. Holloway's house usually is."

Without hesitation, she gave a decisive nod. "Well, first off, I don't need to close my eyes for the first thing I noticed. That damn coffee table I fell backward over was in the wrong place. It's a square one, not long like most of them, and it sits right in front of her armchair. But he was standing where it usually sits, so he had to have moved it."

Another important point since we might get lucky and find fingerprints. I smiled at her. "Excellent. That's good, Babe. What else?"

Mitch also caught the significance of what she said and made a note of it on his pad.

"That stupid chair he pushed me into was from the kitchen. It shouldn't have been there either, and—" A far-off look came into her eyes as she tried to remember. "I think maybe there was something on the chair seat, I'm not sure, but..." Excited and gradually getting her confidence back, she said, "...there was! It was a bag or something because I remember falling with it partially beneath me. Then the chair tipped over onto my back 'cuz when I tipped over onto the floor, I landed on my stomach and shoulder and jammed the top of my head into the wall. I remember him grabbing my sweatshirt and kind of jerking me up to get it out from under me. He kind of hissed and said, 'You're dead, bitch.'"

Gripping an imaginary object in her fist, she held it across her chest, down near her opposite leg. Her voice rose with the intensity of her actions. "That scared the shit of me. I still had the shovel, so I swung it with my left hand," Her eyes jerked back and forth as she remembered, "I forgot this part, but I was kinda over my side, like this, and I swung it around. Like this!"

I jerked back when she nearly bashed me in the face in her enthusiasm. I don't think she even realized my nose was mere inches from her fist.

"My right arm was beneath me, so I had to use my left."

Once I got over the shock of just about having my nose rearranged, I asked, "Did that one connect? I mean, were you able to hit him a second time?"

"No, he'd moved back by then, and he was running...no... he was limping toward the kitchen door. Well, not a big limp, but I could tell he was definitely limping."

The human mind is a beautiful thing. Even though the person has absolutely no recall of an event, an item, or even a sound, something will happen to trigger it. Then whoosh, the memory comes rushing to the fore, playing out with intricate details that were lost moments before. I didn't want to jar her out of the memory, so I said as quietly as I could and still be heard, "Clothing?"

Once again, her head tilted to the left. She grabbed another piece of paper from the bookshelf, snatched up the pencil she'd used previously, and drew a pair of legs.

I watched as her pencil flew across the page, filling in the legs with a dark grey except for a squiggly line of darker black running the full length of the left pant leg.

"I don't know what color this dark part was, but it was definitely darker." Her hand moved to where the torso would be, hovering over the space with little jerks of indecision. After a few moments, she let out a frustrated sigh. "No, it's not there. I don't see his shirt."

Mitch leaned forward. His brows drew together, and from experience, I guessed he was trying to figure out a way to phrase his next question without asking a leading question. He began slowly, "Close your eyes again and look at him before he goes through the kitchen door. Back him up to right after you turned and swung the shovel. Watch him closely, Babe. As though you're watching a movie. Describe his movements."

Her words were hesitant as she watched the scene play out again. "He was limping." Her head and shoulders bobbed as though mimicking the man's movement. "He kind of dipped."

Mitch nodded as though expecting her answer. "Which direction?"

"To the left."

"Was the black stripe on the pants the whole time?"

Again, her head tilted almost down to her shoulder, and her brows drew together. "No, not before the dip, but definitely after." She opened her eyes and seemed a bit embarrassed. "I know you probably think I'm making this up because, I mean, who would notice something like that? But you gotta understand. I like to draw, and I see shades of greys and blacks on white when I look at things. It's just something my mind catches that I use when I go to draw later."

Mitch's eyes shone with approval, "I believe you, Babe. You just confirmed something very important for me. Thank you."

She lifted one shoulder in a shy acknowledgment of his words

"By the way, there was a wet spot on the rug. Do you remember anything about that?"

"No. I don't remember anything about the rug."

Mitch paused, and by the way he raised his eyebrows when he glanced my way, I guessed he didn't want me to think he was taking over my interview. He was an excellent interviewer, and he definitely wasn't stepping on my toes by asking pertinent questions. I prompted him to go on. "Anything else?"

He shook his head, "Not on that, but," He turned back to Babe, "you mentioned a bag that you fell on when you fell off the chair—"

"No, not exactly. I said I felt the bag on the chair when he shoved me onto it. The bag slid onto the floor when I crashed over; it wasn't already on the floor."

I shot Mitch an amused look. Babe was a fantastic witness who remembered details but didn't let any suggestions we made change her mind about what had happened. Well, except maybe for the guy's height, but we can't always expect perfection out of a rattled witness.

She noticed our exchange. "What? What's funny?"

I smiled. "Nothing's funny. I'm just so proud of what an excellent witness you've turned out to be. I'm pleased with you, that's all."

Mitch doubled down on his question about the bag. "What kind of bag was it? Could you tell? A paper bag or something else? Approximately how big?"

"No. I'm not sure, but not paper or plastic. Kinda like maybe a workout bag? Or a tool bag? I don't know. I didn't see it. I just felt it."

We sat for close to a minute, letting her process things. Once again, it was Mitch who broke the silence, something I was grateful for since he'd been to the crime scene and I hadn't.

He continued, "Okay, then what happened after he grabbed the bag?"

"He left, I guess. Like I said, by the time I'd swung at him a second time, he was running away. I picked myself up off the floor, and he was gone." She cocked her head, "I heard the kitchen door bang shut, though."

He followed up, "Did you hear anything outside after he ran out?"

Shaking her head, she said, "No. Like a car or a truck, you mean?" Damn, she was quick. "No, and there wasn't one in front of the house when I got there, either. I would have noticed that."

I looked back at some of the notes I'd taken while she'd been describing her experience. "Let's go back to when you hit him on the head. Did you see any blood? Did you hit him hard enough to draw blood?"

I was careful not to let my amusement show when she squinched her eyes shut. That happened pretty often when she was trying to recall events, and I'd was actually waiting for it this time. "I didn't see any. Now I wish I'd hit him with the side of the shovel, you know? Cracked his skull open, but I wasn't thinking like that at the time. I just wanted to get him away from Mrs. Holloway, and I ended up banging him with the flat part of the shovel."

"Still, that could draw blood. Are you sure you didn't see any red, anywhere?"

"I'm sure, but that doesn't mean there wasn't any. Just that I didn't see any. Like I said, he looked more like that to me..." She pointed to the silhouette. "...then like a real person. It was pretty dark."

Her head jerked to the right before she focused on Mitch again, an affectation that hadn't yet appeared consistently throughout the interview. Babe tended to think visually but looking right is usually associated with auditory memory. "Wait, I kicked something when I charged him. I heard a clank, but I didn't see anything."

Mitch nodded, "Close your eyes again, Babe. One more time, look at the room as you leave the kitchen. Do you see what you kicked over?"

She shook her head. "No, I'm sorry. I was completely focused on him bending over Mrs. Holloway."

He smiled, "Don't be sorry. You're an excellent witness, and as Detective Wolfe said, you did everything exactly right because both you and Mrs. Holloway came away alive."

Babe couldn't remember any other details, so Mitch and I went to brief Kate on what we'd learned.

It took a while to tell the story, and, apparently wondering what was happening, Babe wandered down the aisle that separated the Child Abuse Unit from ours.

Casey left her desk and intercepted her, probably letting her know what was going on and what would happen once we were through. It wasn't a good idea to have a witness listen when we compared notes or discussed an interview.

When Mitch and I finished filling Kate in, she nodded toward Casey and Babe. "She can go now. Do you have all of her contact info?"

Remembering I'd promised to give her a legible business card, I pulled one out of my card case and very carefully wrote down my cell number. I answered Kate's question as I wrote. "Yeah. She's been staying with a friend while she's in town, so she won't have to be alone after all this."

"She doesn't live here permanently?"

"No, she came to visit a few months ago and hasn't left yet."

"Find out whether she plans to leave town. It would make

things a whole lot easier if she stayed. That way, we can re-interview her in person if we need to."

Casey returned to her desk when I strode back to talk to Babe.

"We have all the information we need from you for now, but my sergeant is wondering whether you plan to return to Pittsburgh after everything that's happened?"

"Absolutely not. Mrs. Holloway needs me, and what if—"

The tears welled again, and I grabbed a tissue from Casey's desk. "Here. Will your friend be available for you? Is he or she someone you can talk to?"

"She's great. But I have cousins in town, too, and they've already called my mom and dad." She held up her cell phone. "Mom and dad called after you left the room, but I said I'd have to call them back. They're pretty worried, and they want me to come home, but I won't."

The picture showing on her phone was of a cheerful, Caucasian woman with a broad, loving smile. I indicated the phone with a lift of my chin. "Is that your mom?"

"Yeah, and here's my dad." She pulled up a picture of a handsome man, also white, with a balding pate and a smile that seemed to say he had a secret up his sleeve, and he'd give you three guesses to figure out what it was. I liked both her parents immediately. "Well, I'd say you look just like them, but..." I held out my hands, palms up.

Her cheerful chuckle was a relief. I was glad to see the Babe I'd first met reappear, if only for a quick moment. "They adopted my sister and me when we were babies. I'm lucky to have such a fun, loving family. Besides my sister, I have an older brother and sister who are both nurses, and my other sister is in college. My mom's a physician's assistant who doesn't practice anymore, but she does a lot of work through our church, and my dad's a doctor who provides healthcare for the underserved communities around Pittsburgh. I think that's why I'm so drawn to my seniors. And to answer your sergeant's question, no, I'm not going anywhere. They need me even more now than they did before."

Casey's phone rang. After listening for a few seconds, she put her hand over the receiver and called over her shoulder, "Front desk says her ride's here. He's waiting downstairs."

Curious, I asked Babe, "He?"

"My cousin, Nathaniel. He came to pick me up."

I escorted Babe down to the lobby where a handsome, bearded man in his mid-twenties walked down the row studying the antique badges and police paraphernalia displayed in shadow boxes along the south wall.

When he saw us, he hurried over. His worried expression spoke volumes, and before saying anything, he enveloped Babe in a big hug. "Are you okay?"

Not all our victims and witnesses come from such a loving family, and I was glad Babe would have the support she needed to get through the trauma she'd suffered. Handing her the new card with my legible phone number, I said, "I'm sorry you couldn't read the number on the other one. If you remember anything else, even small details you think might be insignificant, call me." I pulled her into a hug. I held onto her shoulders when I let go. "You not only saved Mrs. Holloway's life, but you also brought a ton of information we can use."

Worry lines creased her forehead.

I let go of her shoulders and asked, "What?"

Swallowing hard, she loosely crossed her arms over her chest. "I'm worried about Mrs. Holloway going back to her house once they release her from the hospital. He might come back to finish what he started."

Nathaniel spoke up. "She can come stay with me. I have extra bedrooms I rent out to short-term guests to help pay the mortgage. The guy doesn't know where I live, and she can stay until he gets caught." He looked at me with determination. "They can both stay with me if you want. I have room, and besides, I work from home. I'm an IT tech, and I think everybody is safer in numbers."

Babe beamed at him and enveloped him in an enormous hug. "That's perfect! I might not stay with you all the time because I have stuff to do at my place, but still."

Perfect wasn't the word I'd use, mostly because I didn't want another potential victim on my hands. Perpetrators—arsonists, murderers, and the like—don't hesitate to kill again simply because there might be collateral damage. I pulled out another card, wrote my cell number on the back, and handed it to him. "My name's Detective Wolfe. I'd rather you not play the hero. If you see anything that seems suspicious, call 911 first, and then give me a call too, okay?"

"Yeah, sure. I'll keep my eyes open." He pocketed the card and then put his arm around Babe's shoulders.

As I watched them walk out the door, I made a mental note to call the hospital to let them know I wanted to be notified when they released Mrs. Holloway. I had two reasons for wanting to be there when she got out. First, I wanted to make sure the arsonist didn't follow Nathaniel or Babe from the hospital to his house. Second, I wanted to see if I could spot the arsonist if he did follow either one of them home.

CHAPTER 7

Back in the office, Kate was holding an impromptu briefing with the detectives who were still working at their desks. I pushed in next to Mitch, who playfully elbowed me in the ribs.

Kate eyed us but pointed to a large map of Tucson hanging on the wall. She used her pen and touched a series of cardboard cutout houses stuck at various points around the map. "These are the houses that have been hit to date. All of them are single-story residences with no alarm system set up in the home. Every victim owned the house outright and had lived in the home for more than ten years. None of them had family who regularly checked up on them. The only exception is the latest woman who had a young woman who brought groceries and read to her." She moved aside and nodded to Casey, who stepped forward.

"I've checked every neighborhood for security cameras or doorbell cameras. These are poor neighborhoods, and I haven't found a single one yet. That might suggest the guy canvasses the neighborhood trying to spot any neighbors who might have one set up on their property. No one has reported seeing anyone suspicious roaming the streets prior to the arsons. Maybe the guy owns a delivery van or is possibly an employee of one of the delivery services and blends into the background."

Kate stepped back in. "Don't just think of the big three delivery firms either. That'll narrow your focus too much. Think about meal delivery, grocery, pizza. And don't forget, people get wine delivered, plants, that kind of thing."

I shook my head, "Probably not in these neighborhoods. Most of the people who live in the surrounding areas don't have two cents to rub together, let alone have their thunderbird delivered to their door."

Nodding, Kate said, "Good point. But if you do see a catering service that looks out of place for the socio-economic climate of the neighborhood, that should raise a red flag in your mind as well."

I shrugged, acknowledging her point.

Burney Macon, a long-time child abuse detective who'd been pulled into the case much the same as Casey and me, spoke up from where he was sitting at his desk a short way from the group. "Flower delivery. Sometimes old people get flowers."

Kate half-smiled at him. Burney was a loveable African American man, short, fat, and balding with a half-circle of hair running around the back of his head. "Care to join us, Burney?" He was notorious for doing a good portion of his work from behind his desk, and a few good-natured jibes rang out from our group.

"As if..."

"He'd have to actually get out of his chair..."

"His pants are glued to the chair. He'd have to come to the meeting in his underwear 'cuz he'd have to leave his pants behind."

His innate affability kicked in, and Burney grinned as he

held his hands up in surrender. "Yeah, yeah, yeah. You schmucks can't hold a candle to my legendary detecting ability." He looked at Kate, "I can hear ya fine from here, Sarge. No worries on that point."

Burney's skills as a child abuse detective *were* legendary. It was a lucky child who happened to get him assigned to their case, but a few of the group couldn't help but rib him some more.

"Legend in your own mind, you mean."

"Maybe a hundred years ago when you first got promoted."

Kate spoke louder than the others, "*Anyway*, that's a good point, Burney. Also, let's not forget utilities. Keep an eye out for meter readers. Nate." She gestured to the youngest detective in our unit, Nate Drewery, who straightened at the mention of his name.

"Yeah, Sarge?"

"Get in touch with the electric company. If there were any bucket trucks in any of these neighborhoods," she tapped the little houses again, "I want you to personally find the guys who ride in the cherry pickers and ask them if they remember anything that caught their eye. Let them know it doesn't matter how small a detail it is. And start with the latest victim and work backward. We'd have a better chance of them remembering something."

"Got it."

"Burney, how's it going tracking down sales of those chemicals Sgt. Longoria sent over?"

"Nothin' yet, boss. At least no one buyer has bought all three ingredients. By themselves, they're all normal stuff people buy all the time. It's just when you combine them, they become this accelerant the guy uses. I have the stores sending me invoices and credit card information, and I'm collating the names as I go along. I have a ton more places to call, though." He grinned at the group. "Yes, from my chair."

There were chuckles all around.

Kate ended the meeting by saying, "The chief has authorized unlimited overtime on this. If you have a lead you need to follow up on, you don't need to call me. Just do it and turn in your slip later."

Some of us returned to our desks while others grabbed their keys and headed out the door. The front of my desk butts up to the front of Casey's, making it convenient when we needed to talk. I pulled out my notebook, thought about contacting Stephen Grate alone, and then thought better of it. "Hey, Case. Do you have about an hour to come with me? I need to talk to someone and probably shouldn't do it alone."

"Sure. Someone to do with the arsons?"

"Not exactly."

Kate came up and leaned against the pillar next to my desk. "Casey, I know you're still working on the camera angle. What's your next step, Alex?"

"I need to go interview someone, and I was hoping Casey could come along as back-up."

"Who?"

"Remember that guy I chased at the crime scene?"

"You found him?"

"Ummm, not exactly."

"I just heard you say the same thing to Casey as I was walking up. Those words always worry me when coming from you, Alex. What *exactly* do you mean? Either you found him, or you didn't, and since you're going to interview him, I'm going with the former."

I sighed. "Gabe kinda found him."

She straightened, "What? You asked Gabe to look for the guy?"

Judging from the waves of anger flowing off her, I was

seriously glad I hadn't. "No! I'd never do that." Well, never say never, but still. "The idiot had the gall to follow me out to Gia's training place and..."

Casey leaned back in her chair. "Oh shit. Is the guy in the hospital? Is he even alive?"

"He's fine. I talked to him a little bit, got his number, dusted him off, and sent him on his way."

Kate crossed her arms, still not sounding pleased. "Who is he?"

"I don't know. That's what I'm going to find out."

"You let him go without finding out who he is and whether he has anything to do with our cases?"

"No...not exactly."

"Cut out the not exactly crap, Alex."

"Okay, well, I talked to him long enough to get a feeling for whether he's dangerous or not. I don't think he is. His name's," I checked my notebook, "Stephen Grate. I was just going to run him through the database when you walked over."

"Why is he following you?"

"He said he and his brother want to help with the Coward cases."

"How?"

"He doesn't know how, but he said his brother could explain things better than he can, and if I meet them, they'll let me know."

She looked from Casey to me. "And that doesn't sound strange to you."

"Of course, it sounds strange. The whole thing is strange. But what kind of a detective would I be if I didn't follow up? I realize arsonists love to come back and watch the fire department put out the fires and then jeer at us as we try to catch them. But I don't think these guys are the ones murdering people and lighting them on fire. If they have information they think might help us, I want to hear it, don't you?"

Her eyes narrowed on that last part, and I wished I'd left off the smartass part of that sentence.

"I asked Casey to come along. I'm being safe."

"Were you planning to tell me Gabe found this guy on Ms. Angelino's property?"

I knew I needed to say yes, but I hesitated a tich too long since the answer was really no.

She growled as she turned to go to her desk, barking orders over her shoulder while she walked, "Full, in-person report *today*, in my office, before you go home. Understand?"

"You got it, Boss."

Casey returned to the typing she'd been working on before I walked up. "Let me know when you're ready."

I set my notebook on the desk and pulled my chair up to my computer. I opened the window to the National Crime Information Center, generally referred to as the NCIC database, and typed in Stephen Grate. Several people with that name came up, and I narrowed the search by putting in his date of birth and social security number. What I found wasn't particularly jaw-dropping. No arsons or murders in his background. He didn't have a criminal record at all. His fingerprints were on file because of his military service, which might come in handy later on.

Just for fun, I ran him through Motor Vehicles and discovered several speeding tickets. Apparently, the guy liked speed since one was for going ninety-five down I-8 between Casa Grande and San Diego. I had to admit that stretch of Interstate is nothing but empty desert, and the quicker you get through that part, the better. Ninety-five's a bit much, but I get it.

I backed up a few screens and entered his brother, George Ogilvie. Nothing came up, but that didn't surprise me since a lot of cops petition to have their records blocked so no one can get their personal information. "Okay, then." I looked up the number for the L.A.P.D. A young-sounding officer Grant answered the phone, and he had to put me on hold when I introduced myself and asked about George Ogilvie.

A different person came on the line. This one sounded older, and I guessed he'd been around when George had been on the department. "This is Detective Moser. I understand you're asking about George Ogilvie?"

"Yes. I'm Detective Wolfe from the Tucson Police Department's Special Crimes Unit."

"Any way I can verify that?"

"Well, you can call the department and ask if I work here, or you can look up the phone number for our unit and..."

"Already done. Your number just came up as legit. What can I do for you, Detective?"

"I've run into Mr. Ogilvie in relation to one of my cases, not as a suspect, mind you, just as a person of interest. Are you familiar with him?"

"He and I were partners. Undercover. There's not a bent bone in his body, and I'd trust him with my life. Hell, if something happened to me and my wife, he'd be the one I'd want raising my kids." He paused a second, "Although they're all teens at the moment, and I'm not sure I'd foist them off on any of my friends. But if I did, he'd be the one I'd want them going to for advice. That good enough for ya?"

"Absolutely. After all that, I hesitate to ask the next question, but...has he ever been suspected of any type of crime?"

Suspicion crept into his voice. "I thought you said he wasn't a suspect."

"He's not, but if I didn't dot my I's and cross my T's, you know my sergeant would ask the question, and I wouldn't have the answer for her."

"Oh, yeah, I get that. The answer is no, never suspected

of a crime, never committed a crime. The department was sorry to see him go when he retired. Only, they put you out to pasture when you get older, and I couldn't see him working the front desk like I do now. My ego can take it; there's no way his could."

After working the often glamorous life of deep undercover, I can imagine sitting at a desk answering phones and talking to walk-ins would be a comedown for some people. I pictured Boujee at the pool table and understood exactly what Moser was saying. "Yeah, from the little I know of him, I can see how that might be hard."

"Anyway, like I said, my name's Moser, and if you need anything else, just let me know. And...ya gotta know I'll be calling him to let him know you're checking up on him."

"Listen, can you wait to make that call until this evening?"

"He's not a suspect?"

"No." I hoped not, anyway.

"Yeah, I get how timing can affect things. Have a good day, Detective."

And since he hadn't directly said he would wait, I knew he was probably on the phone to George by the time I picked up the phone to call Steve. I couldn't blame him, really. Partners stick together. That's just how it works. I glanced over at Casey, and when she looked up, I grinned.

"What?"

"Nothin'."

The phone went to voicemail, so I left a message asking him to call me back on my work phone. A lot of people don't answer the phone if they don't recognize the number, and I figured he'd call me back once he listened to his voicemail. Sure enough, my phone rang a minute later. "Tucson Police Department, Detective Wolfe."

"Detective Wolfe, this is Steve Grate. I'm returning your call. I didn't expect to hear from you until Tuesday. But I'm glad you called. George is here with me, and we're anxious to talk with you. Do you think we could meet somewhere?"

I checked my watch—six o'clock. Well, Kate had just okayed unlimited overtime, so I said, "Yeah, that's what I was calling you about. There's a coffee shop called the Sleepytime Café. Are you familiar with it?"

"Yes, we can be there in about twenty minutes."

"Great, I'll see you there."

CHAPTER 8

It took Casey and me about fifteen minutes to get to the café. When we walked in, the waitress, a crotchety older woman both of us were rather fond of, called out from across the restaurant, "Th' usual?"

Casey called back, "Yes, please, Maureen."

The men hadn't arrived yet, so we settled into our usual corner booth and waited for Maureen to bring my tea and Casey's coffee. She set the drinks down on the table and asked, "You guys eatin'?"

Casey ordered a burger and fries, and since I'd eaten lunch at Gia's place, I settled for a piece of hot apple pie. I kept an eye on the doors, and when the guys finally walked in, I waved them over to our table. I introduced them to Casey, who shook both of their hands before indicating they should take a seat.

Today, George had on a grey-blue silk shirt with three buttons opened down his chest. He wore a casual box plaid sport coat over the shirt with a silk pocket square tucked into the front pocket. And, of course, his dark blue chino pants broke perfectly over his brown loafers.

On the other hand, Steve wore his signature cowboy boots and jeans with a casual sport coat over a white button-down shirt. Nothing fancy there. Just good old down-to-earth urban cowboy.

The ever-pleasant Maureen strolled over, crossed her arms, and growled, "You guys cops too? Ain't never seen ya in here before."

George flashed her an ultra-white smile. "No, but we're hungry, and we hear you guys have the best food in town. I'll have whatever you think I'd like." Boy, was he smooth.

I rolled my eyes, but the first pleasant expression I've ever seen on Maureen's face appeared. I'd never realized she actually had a friendly face beneath the grumble. All I ever saw were the scowls and growls that came standard with every burger or pancake I'd ever ordered. I cocked my head. "You okay, Maureen?"

She lifted the side of her lip at me, kind of a new, scary look for her, and then leaned against the back of the booth and beamed at George. If I had to put a name to it, I'd say coquettish would fit the bill. Coquettish in a babushka baba yaga kind of way. "Ernie's special today is eggplant parmesan."

George flashed his megawatt smile again. "If that's what you suggest, then that's what I'll have."

I rested my temple on my fingers and watched the drama play out. "Oh, brother." Did that just slip out of my mouth?

It must have because Maureen turned to me and growled, "At least he tries new things. Not you two. You two never change, do ya? Coffee fer her, tea fer you. Two eggs an' bacon fer her in th' mornin' an' pancakes fer you. And don't you 'oh brother' him."

I held up my hands, "Sorry, it just slipped out."

She turned to Steve, who also smiled and said, "Since you think it's great, I'll have the same."

These two were definitely cut from the same cloth. Steve held up two fingers, "And two coffees, please."

Maureen had an extra swish in her hips as she made her way back to the kitchen. Who am I kidding? Extra? She'd never had any swish in the entire time I'd known her.

George looked at me and raised his eyebrows. "Boujee?"

I stared at him. I didn't know the guy and wasn't about to let him charm me the same way he'd charmed Maureen. "Look, let's get one thing straight. I don't appreciate the way you've been following me around. Playing pool in the bar and then taking classes from my friend, Megan. Who the hell do you think you are?"

I hadn't noticed that Maureen had returned with the two coffees. She set them down on the table and then stabbed at me with her finger. "You don't got no right talkin' to him that way. What'd he ever do to you anyway? I think you should treat him better'n that."

Her holier than thou tone irritated me. "'You don't got no right' is actually a double negative, which means I do have the right." Sometimes when I'm irritated, my forefinger taps on the table of its own accord, and right now, it was beating a staccato on the placemat. I didn't want any secret sauce beneath my apple pie, so I bit my tongue to keep myself from saying things I'd later regret.

Maureen and I weren't exactly besties. I ordered food from her, and she served it in her usual surly manner. We have a symbiotic relationship that works for both of us. Still, you'll never find us sitting around guzzling beers and eating pizza together.

Casey noticed my finger and decided to head me off at the pass, "Thanks for the coffee, Maureen. We have some business to discuss with these gentlemen, that's all. Alex didn't mean anything by it."

I slowly looked up at Boujee, who'd pulled a cigar out of his pocket.

Maureen cooed, "There's no smokin' in here, Hon. If you want t' smoke, just step outside that back door, an' there's a can for ya to put your butt in when you're finished."

He stuffed the cigar back into his pocket. "Sorry, darlin'. Force of habit. That's all." After she walked away, he turned back to me and got serious. "Look, Detective. I'm sorry. Both of us are sorry." He paused and blinked several times as though what I'd said had just sunk in. "I didn't think you'd seen me in the bar. I'm usually better at UC work than that."

Casey sipped her coffee. "Mr. Ogilvie, I don't know as much about you as Detective Wolfe. You worked undercover? Where?"

I hadn't stopped glaring at him. "Los Angeles. That is until he joined the K9 unit."

He nodded. "You've done your homework."

"But then you already knew that didn't you?" I had no doubt he'd already spoken to his ex-partner.

He lifted a shoulder as if to say, 'of course' and then turned to answer Casey. "I live in L.A. Steve read about the arson murders happening here. He called me, and I decided to drive out."

I sat back and crossed my arms. "Why?"

He grinned. "That's a very long story, and we have our whole meal in front of us. Wouldn't you rather we get to know each other first, and then when the food arrives, we can lay it out for you."

My first inclination was to say no, but Casey must have picked up on something I'd missed in my pique and said, "That's a good idea. Tell us about yourselves."

George drank his coffee black, but Steve seemed to be a man after my own heart. He poured four little containers of creamer into his coffee, then stacked four sweeteners together, tapped them on the table, tore off the tops, and poured them all in at once.

To no one's surprise, George spoke first. He was the more outgoing of the two, chattier. I remembered Steve wanting to wait until George was present to explain what they'd been doing, and now I could see why.

"Like I said, I'm from L.A. and worked for the L.A.P.D. for twenty-two years. I worked patrol, child abuse, undercover, and finally transferred into the K9 unit. As far as my personal life, I'm a gadget guy. I love checking out the newest technology, you know, things like smart wallets, the newest earbuds, high-end gaming computers—"

Steve chimed in, "Yeah, he has to have the best speakers, the coolest, newest drone, the most expensive Harley. You name it; he's got it."

George had worn an expensive watch that afternoon at the bar, and I wondered how he could afford that and the newest tech toys on a detective's retirement. "Are you independently wealthy, or what?"

George grinned and held up his left hand. "I married well. She's not only beautiful, but she started and runs her own tech marketing company. I'm pretty much a kept man."

His affability was winning me over, and I thought I'd try a little jab to see how he reacted. "That explains the boujee bit."

He laughed, "I'm not boujee. This is how I always dress."

"It's probably how you dressed for your undercover persona, and when you left UC, you just kept the persona."

Steve slapped him on the back. "Oh my God, does she have you pegged." Amusement sparkled in his eyes. "That's exactly what happened, Detective Wolfe. He went from being a jock who wore nothing but workout clothes pre-UC to what you see now."

"I did not." George stared at Steve and then shrugged

good-naturedly. "Okay, I did. But you try being someone twenty-four seven for several years and then have to turn off that persona just because you leave your assignment. I was deep undercover. Ended up costing me my first marriage." He lifted a shoulder. "I can't blame her for that. We're still friends, so that's good."

I turned to Steve. "What about you? You said you were in the Army?"

"I was an E9, retired three years ago."

"I don't know the ranks that way. What's an E9 in civilian speak?"

"I was a Sergeant Major. Army Intelligence."

I had no idea what Army Intelligence did, but I knew one thing. "I guess that doesn't include training in how to inconspicuously follow somebody."

He chuckled, "Ouch. No, my job was mostly analytical. I enjoy picking apart reports and filling in the pieces to a puzzle."

George added, "He was good at it too. Pretty specialized."

Our food arrived, and I had to admit, the eggplant parmesan smelled wonderful. I glanced at Casey. "Maybe we should broaden our horizons as far as what we eat here is concerned."

Maureen harrumphed. "What've I been tellin' ya for the last couple 'a years, huh? But no, you two gotta have yer routines, don'tcha?" She continued mumbling on her way to the next table, where I heard her say, "Eggplant parmesan. Smells good, don't it?"

After taking a bite of my pie, I waved my fork in George's general direction. "Okay, down to business. Why are you guys interested in the Coward cases?"

George swallowed, picked up his napkin, and wiped his mouth before beginning his explanation. "Like I said, Steve called me about three weeks ago. He'd been following the news about the murders. Well, at least what you guys have been feeding to the press, which isn't much. I can tell there's a hell of a lot more to the cases than what you're releasing."

He paused as if waiting for us to acknowledge the point. Neither Casey nor I had any inclination to do so. After waiting long enough to realize neither of us was going to fill in the blanks, George continued. "The murders were one thing. Every city has murders. And every city has arsons. But combine the two, and you begin to narrow down the specificity of the crimes." He indicated Steve with a quick hand gesture. "Our interest goes back to our childhood. My Dad married Steve's mother when we were both six-years-old."

Steve jumped in to correct his brother. "We were five. Almost six, but not quite." George might be the more outgoing, but Steve was the more analytic of the two. Precision was important to him, and we might be able to take advantage of that at some point.

This wasn't strictly an interview for Casey and me, per se. Neither man had committed any crime—that we were aware of anyway—and they weren't precisely witnesses either. So far, they'd been more of an irritant, an itch that needed to be scratched before it led to further problems down the road. With that in mind, we listened with only a minimal amount of prompts to keep the conversation going.

I did, however, want to keep this meeting as brief as possible, so I popped some more pie in my mouth and said, "So you were five, almost six, and..." What this had to do with the Coward cases was anyone's guess.

George took a couple more bites, wiped his mouth again, and continued, "We lived in Venice. That's a neighborhood on L.A.'s west side."

Steve swallowed quickly and added, "Some of Venice is nice, beachfront, that kind of thing. We didn't live in the nicer sections. Our dad was an electrician. Solid middle-class, and we lived in the lower-middle-class section of town."

I stared at him, again wondering what that had to do with anything.

He picked up on my questioning look and explained, "Believe it or not, that's important. The neighborhood is important to our story. It's probably why things happened in the first place."

Casey joined in, "What things? I'm not sure where you guys are going with this, and I don't mean to be rude, but we don't have all day."

Both men nodded, and George said, "You'll see why it's important in a minute. We talked about it, and we thought you'd understand why we're interested if we gave you some backstory. Anyway, when we were about seven, I guess we were in—"

"First grade." It was interesting how Steve filled in the blanks for George, but it seemed he was used to the interruptions because George didn't miss a beat.

"Yeah, first grade. We started hearing rumors about other kid's pets disappearing. This is why the type of neighborhood we lived in was important. The adults were more interested in earning enough money to put food in their kid's bellies than worrying about some animals disappearing. Nobody cared except maybe the kids whose pets disappeared."

Casey grumbled at that, but I know she understood what he was saying. Casey's pets were her kids and taking care of them was as important to her as a mother taking care of her human babies. Unfortunately, some pets who live in lower economic neighborhoods fend for themselves more often than other, more pampered pets. Fending for themselves means roaming the streets and back alleys, and when one disappears, it's not always noticed right away.

"Anyway," George continued, "Over a period of a few

months, a couple of animal bodies turned up. Burned. Steve and I had a rabbit that went missing from our backyard. We started looking around and found it in an old building. He'd been torched, but what was weird was we also found that someone had removed his eyes."

Steve chimed in. "They were just left off to the side. Well, a few weeks ago I was having coffee at a little corner shop, you know, outside at one of the tables. These two ladies were sitting at the table next to me, talking about some news story. Turns out they were journalists who were comparing notes. I don't think they noticed I was listening, and one of them said, 'I don't have any corroboration, but have you heard that the guy removes their eyes before he burns them?' That immediately got my attention. Unfortunately, the other woman hadn't heard about that, and they decided they couldn't run with that in the story because it was just an unsubstantiated rumor."

Casey muttered, "Since when has that ever stopped them?"

"That's why I called George. We never did know who was killing the neighborhood pets, but isn't it just a little coincidental if your guy is removing the eyes and burning his victims like the asshole in our old neighborhood? Besides," Steve blushed a bit, "I loved that rabbit. If there's any chance it's the same guy, I'd love to see him rotting behind bars."

Shy looked good on him. I watched him a moment while I thought about their story. Kate always pounded home that there is no such thing as coincidence. If something sounds coincidental, we investigate it until it becomes fact or until it turns out to be unrelated to whatever case we're working. I still wasn't convinced their story had anything to do with the current cases. "That was, what thirty-five or forty years ago in California? Sounds like you're grasping at straws just because you're interested in these cases."

George shook his head and sat forward. "But what if it *is* related? Can you tell us if this guy's taking out his victim's eyes? Because that's a pretty specific M.O. if you ask me. It's the whole reason I drove out here from L.A. If this guy has graduated to people, that's all the more reason we want to help."

Casey glanced at me before saying, "We can't release any information, Mr. Ogilvie. Do you know whether any of those pets were reported missing? Did the police get involved at all in the disappearances?"

"I'm not sure."

A lot of subtle communication had been happening between the brothers: brief eye contact, a lifted brow, pursed lips. Steve said, "You have to understand. We were just little kids. I don't remember much, and the disappearances didn't last all that long. I know our parents didn't report the rabbit. Our blue-collar dad would have been mortified telling a cop his son's bunny was missing. But George and I got to thinking. What if it was an older kid who's since graduated to people? Don't abusers start small as kids and grow into the monsters they become?"

Casey signaled Maureen for a refill of her coffee. "Sounds like your perp was already a monster. He or she didn't need to grow into anything."

"Did you know any of the older kids? I don't think any of your classmates were old enough to do that kind of thing." Even though I doubted there was a connection, I decided I wanted to hear a bit more of their story. George was right, it was a pretty specific M.O., and our guy *was* taking out the eyes before burning the victim. I thought it was worth doing a bit of research to see if we could find some tie-in. Who knows what small detail could blow this type of case wide open? If there was even a minuscule chance their information could lead us to the suspect, I was going to take it.

Both men thought about the question while they ate. Finally, Steve asked George, "What about Mike?"

"Who's Mike?" Apparently, Casey was having the same internal dialogue I was.

"Our older brother. He was four years older than us. He signed up for the Marines right out of high school and ended up dying in Iraq." Grief stole over Steve's features, but he quickly shrugged it off. "The point is, our mom died last year, and dad had gone five years before that, so George and I cleared out her house. You know, boxed everything up so we could sell up. She'd left his room just like it was when he left for the military, and I still have his boxes of yearbooks."

Huh. Now that was good thinking. Yearbooks would at least give us some names to work with, so I said, "Can you drop them off at the station sometime?"

George leaned forward, "Do you have any suspects? We can go through to see if any names match."

"I wish. So far, this guy hasn't given us much to go on." I hesitated to say more, but I didn't want these guys going behind our backs again if they thought we were cutting them out. "Look, let me think about how you guys can help, okay?"

"You can trust us to keep our traps shut, Detective Wolfe. I had twenty-two years on the job, and Steve's security clearance is still higher than any of ours will ever be." George didn't appreciate being treated like a regular citizen, and I didn't blame him.

"Just call me Alex. And, honestly, I think I agree with you. I'm not blowing smoke up your ass when I say I'll have to think about how you guys can help."

Casey caught my eye. "What about Babe?"

"What about..." I stopped when I realized what she meant. It surprised me enough that by-the-book Casey would suggest such a thing that I stared at her longer than I meant to.

She shrugged, "Never mind. I don't know why I suggested it."

"I think it's brilliant."

She focused on the ceiling, "Yeah, that worries me even more."

"Thanks a lot." I turned to the guys. "Look, there's a young woman who takes care of—" I realized we hadn't released the fact that the victims were senior citizens to the press. The information had leaked out, but we'd never confirmed it.

As always, Casey immediately knew what I was thinking. "Yeah, that's part of the problem."

I needed to make up my mind one way or the other. Either I was going to trust these guys, or I wasn't. Raising my eyebrows at Casey, I silently asked what she thought.

She answered by shrugging, which I took to mean she was leaning toward letting them help. I leaned in and spoke quietly, "Look, nothing we tell you can go anywhere, especially not to the press. Understand?"

"Understood." George relaxed a bit.

Steve looked me straight in the eyes. "I'll treat the information like I would any other kind of intelligence. It goes nowhere, and we'll do exactly as you guys tell us."

"Okay." I checked over both shoulders to make sure no one was sitting at any of the nearby tables. "Babe is a young woman who helps out with seniors. You know, takes them food, reads to them, and generally makes sure they're okay. One of the things we've kept from the press is that the victims are all over eighty. One was over ninety."

"And the eyes?" George was like a dog with a bone.

I stared at him, wondering why that one point was so important to him.

This time it was his turn to blush. "Okay. That stupid rabbit meant a lot to me, too. He used to follow us all over the house, and he slept in my bed with me, and seeing his eyes just lying there..." He sat back and crossed his arms. His jaw muscles worked overtime as he tried to hold in his temper. Childhood memories, especially traumatic ones, can have a powerful hold over us, even after we become old enough to have grandchildren of our own. I wasn't old enough yet for grandkids, but these two guys were.

Nodding, Casey said, "Yeah, I'd want to find the bastard, too. I get it. Yes, the Coward removes their eyes before burning them, but thankfully, he does it postmortem. This guy is sick and should be thrown in a hole and buried alive as far as I'm concerned." Casey hated nothing more than child abusers, animal abusers, and elder abusers. What she claimed were her wishes for the guy and what she really wanted to do to him were two different things. I remembered her saying she wanted to hang the guy up by his nipples and do all kinds of painful things to him while he hung there.

George harumphed under his breath, obviously agreeing with her. But then his easy smile returned. "Sorry, I just needed to know, that's all."

"That's okay." For confidentiality reasons, I couldn't tell them that Babe or Mrs. Holloway were victims, and I took a minute to figure out how to tell them what I needed. "So, I can't tell you why, but this woman, Babe, and another woman, Mrs. Holloway, might need protection for a while...followed to make sure nobody is following them."

It didn't take long for the light to go on for George. "Is Babe the African American woman you talked to at the last arson scene?"

I raised my eyes slowly and glared at him.

He grinned, "Ha! You didn't see me at that scene, did you? You just saw Steve." He grinned over at his brother. "I told ya they didn't see me. Pay up." He held out his hand.

Steve reluctantly pulled out his wallet and extracted a

five-dollar bill. "He's the reason you guys lost me. When he saw you go after me, he jumped in his car and picked me up before you came around the corner."

Casey pointed at George. "You drive a red beamer?"

"Yup."

"I saw you at the end of the street when I circled around. You were turning right off the street Alex ended up on."

George looked pretty pleased with himself. "That was us. I told Steve you didn't realize he was in the car, but he didn't believe me. Hence..." He snapped the bill taut in Steve's direction. "Told ya."

"Yeah, yeah. You were right for once."

"Once? I'm always right; you just can't accept my daunting superiority."

"More like a superiority complex, Boujee."

The two of them bickered like an old married couple, and I found myself smiling at their antics. When they'd been following me, I didn't for one moment think I'd come to like the two of them, but that's what was happening. Oh well, life can be weird like that sometimes. Despite my changing opinion, I decided to keep Jerry as an ace up my sleeve, just in case.

Putting the five into his wallet, George said, "Okay, so this Babe and Holloway. What do you need?"

"Mrs. Holloway is still in the hospital, but she'll probably be getting out soon. When they release her, I'll give you guys the heads up, and I'll want you to follow them home, specifically watching for anyone who might be following them. I'm going to follow them, too, but now that I have you guys to watch for the bad guy, I can be more obvious about it."

"You mean maybe draw him out into the open or make him careless if he thinks you're the only one following them. We do think it's a man, right?" George understood what I meant, and I couldn't help but think maybe these two could really help us keep Babe and Mrs. Holloway safe.

Understanding dawned on Steve once George spelled it out. It wasn't that Steve wasn't smart. Far from it. He just didn't have the same intuitive understanding of police work that his brother had.

I was still uncomfortable giving out information on the cases, but if he was going to be keeping the three of them safe, he should at least know the suspect's sex. "Yes, we're pretty sure it's a man. Babe actually bashed him in the head with a shovel. You know the kind. It collapses. Like what you guys use to dig foxholes and such."

His eyebrows rose at my description. "She hit him in the head with an entrenching tool? And he's still alive?"

"Yeah, she must have caught him a glancing blow. Anyway, it was her impression we're dealing with a man as well. They're going to Babe's cousin's house. He works in IT from home. I'm pretty sure they'll be safe there, but our suspect isn't going to know that's where she's going. Sometimes, these guys are single-minded. They pick out a victim and then fixate on that person until they can finish what they started."

I glanced sideways at Steve, "I think it might be best if you two ride together."

George laughed, "Translated, brother, that means she doesn't want to risk the amateur way you follow people."

With a good-natured grin, Steve acknowledged the point. "I have other talents, *brother*, that I'll bring to the table when the time comes."

Casey raised her coffee to her lips, but before taking a sip, she asked, "Such as?"

"I'm excellent with spreadsheets and organizing facts. I see patterns where other people don't, and as you found out, I'm a fast runner and have run marathons before."

George flicked his hand at Steve. "Yeah, and he forgot to

mention the most important thing."

"Which is?"

"He's a fourth-degree black belt in Taekwondo."

Looking at Steve in a slightly different light, I said, "I think I'm glad I didn't catch you when I chased you from the arson scene."

"I'd never hurt a cop."

"Glad to hear it. So, yes, I'd either like you two to follow us in the same car, or I may have some analytical stuff I could use help organizing. I'd like to introduce Steve to a friend of mine who works at the library. She's very good at finding information, and with the two of you working together, maybe we can get somewhere with those yearbooks."

"How?" Steve's interest sharpened.

"I have no idea. I think that's what you and Kelly are going to have to work out. I can't give you access to our database, so you'll have to be creative about how to connect the dots. Do you think you can meet me at the main library tomorrow morning with the box of yearbooks?"

"Absolutely."

I pulled out my cellphone and called Kelly. She'd worked for the library system for a long time and was relatively high up on the pecking order as far as answering phones was concerned. Unfortunately, this time I reached a young woman who'd given me trouble in the past. She was a committed gatekeeper when it came to people interrupting the librarians for personal business. After an irritating back and forth, I finally said, "Look, this is police business, and I need to speak to her. Now, please go tell her I'm on the phone or transfer me to your boss. We've been through this before, Annie. It's not your job to monitor who Kelly speaks to."

"It is my job to make sure she's not bothered by every Tom, Dick, and Harry who won't talk to anyone except her. She'd never get anything done otherwise. Why do you think she turns her cell off at work now? If you wait a minute, I'll go ask if she wishes to stop what she's doing to talk to you."

Finally. I loosely held the phone to my ear, far enough away that I didn't need to listen to the Musak playing in the background. It didn't take long to hear my friend's cheerful voice replace the pop song currently annoying the heck out of me.

"Alex! I hope Annie didn't give you too much trouble. She's a tad black and white, and we've been working on the shades of grey. We haven't found any yet, but we're hopeful! How can I help you?"

Her cheerful attitude was always a great pick-me-up. Kelly's life fulfillment came in the form of books. As long as there were more books in her world than people, then life was good. Not that she wasn't a people person. Far from it. She enjoyed hanging out with my friends as much as the next person, but when she walked into a person's home, it wasn't the kids or the pets she fixated on with a laser-like focus; it was the bookcase. I'd never taken her to Gia's home, but I know the floor-to-ceiling bookcases lining the walls of her den would have Kelly bouncing with delighted anticipation. She'd get the requisite pleasantries out of the way, ask permission to look through the books and then become lost in a corner, legs drawn up beneath her Indian style, head down and utterly oblivious to her surroundings.

"Hi, Kelly. I have a favor to ask."

"Ask away. You know I always make time for you. Is this case related? I hope it's about the Coward because I'd love to catch that bastard. Oops…" I pictured her covering her mouth with her hand and looking around to make sure no one overheard. "Pardon my French. That slipped out with a touch more vehemence than I intended."

Chuckling, I said, "That's okay. Most of Tucson is on edge, especially if they have an elderly relative or friend. I'd rather not discuss what I need over the phone. I have someone who can use your expertise and one of your private computer rooms. But he might need a good-sized table to spread out his things. Do you think you could reserve a room for tomorrow morning?"

"Pulling up the room schedule now. Okay, I have one booked for you. Will you be coming in with him as well?"

"I'll come in and help get you guys set up, but then I have other things I need to do. I'll see you tomorrow."

We rang off, and I turned to Steve. "Okay, all set. I'll meet you at the main library downtown at ten sharp."

When Maureen brought our bills, George grabbed them and magnanimously announced he was buying.

Casey plucked mine and hers out of his hand. "Sorry. Our boss has a policy that if we're at work, we pay our own way. It makes things cleaner that way."

George held up his hands, "Totally understand, but someday we'll meet you for real at the Hairy Lime and the first rounds on me."

With amused eyes looking out from beneath shag-cut brown bangs, Casey said, "For Alex and me, we only make it through the first round. Neither of us is a heavy drinker. Now Megan, on the other hand—"

George surprised me by interrupting her with a big laugh, "Megan, on the other hand, can really put 'em down."

"What?" I felt a shock wave travel down my spine as I stiffened.

He at least had the grace to look chagrined, "Well, I was trying to gather intel, and I'm partial to redheads, so I didn't mind taking her out for a drink."

I knew my glare had hardened to steel when I saw him wince.

He lifted his hands as a barrier between us. "Hey, easy, easy. I treated her like a lady the entire time. And you'll be happy to know that even though she puts 'em down, she keeps her wits about her. I kept trying to steer the conversation your way, and she kept redirecting me. We talked about everything except you and your cases. I like her a lot, and I like to think we've become friends."

I happened to know that's not always the case with Megan. There are times when the term "verbal diarrhea" comes to mind when she drinks too much. I leaned forward and spoke low and slow, growling out my words one at a time, "I'll only say this once." I punctuated my next words with a finger jabbed at his chest. "You leave Megan alone." The menace in my voice was obvious, and I felt Casey's toe on mine—her signal to back off a bit and think before I speak. I pulled in a deep breath, let it out, and made an effort to relax. "Look. Megan is my best friend, George, and I'm *very* protective of her. She's not a cop, and if I ever hear you've been pumping her for information again, you and Steve will be booted from helping us so fast you'll have skid marks on your butts." I tried for a friendly smile, but think I only managed an evil grimace.

George had a knack for reading people, and he said, "Understood. I apologize. Sometimes I have a difficult time reeling in the old UC persona. It won't happen again."

Satisfied I'd made my point, I stood, and the three of them followed suit. After paying the bills, the men followed us to the parking lot. I stopped them before they got in the Beemer. "George, I'll call you as soon as I hear they're releasing Mrs. Holloway. Steve, I'll see you tomorrow at ten."

After they drove out of the lot, Casey leaned against her car and crossed her arms. "I sure hope we're doing the right thing pulling them into the case like this. No scratch that. I'm sure we're not doing the right thing, but if it helps catch that bastard, I'm willing to skate on your thin line." She held up a finger, "This time."

CHAPTER 9

As I drove out of the lot, I told the little voice in my phone to call Megan.

"Do you want Megan Home, Megan Cell, or Megan Work?"

"Cell."

The phone rang enough times that I was about to tell the voice to hang up when Megan chirped, "Alex! Whattup?"

"What's up? I'll tell you what's up. You—"

"Uh oh. Gotta run." She pulled a typical Megan on me. She knew precisely why I was pissed and figured if she dodged me long enough, my temper would cool, and she'd get off scot-free.

Not this time, she wouldn't. I knew she was at work, so I made my way to the K9 academy, ready for battle. I pulled into the lot, and when I walked up to the door, I realized she'd outsmarted me.

Damn.

I pushed and pulled on the door to no avail. Locked. A note hastily scrawled in pink magic marker was taped to the door. "Class time changed. Call me for the updated time."

Having a friend who knows every tiny little thing about you is good most of the time, but other times it sucks. I tried her cell again, but of course, it went straight to voicemail.

"Fine."

We still didn't have a solid I.D. on the victim and wouldn't until the pathologist received dental records for Knox Cailleach from the Department of Corrections. Before I'd entered the medical alert bracelet Kate had found beneath the bed, or what was left of the bed, into property, I'd snapped a quick picture of both sides. I sat in Megan's parking lot and pulled up the images, enlarging them one at a time to study the remaining letters—those that hadn't melted—to try to make sense of what they said. I saw "d" and then melted squiggles and "tic." Diabetic?

Next, I could scarcely make out the letters P and R. I enlarged the picture, so I was looking at just those three letters. There was a barely legible C between the P and R. I played around with various vowels between the P and the C. Pucur, pucer, pancer, pecar. Nothing that sounded anything like a medical condition. I zoomed out again and noticed more space at the end of the word between the C and R than between the P and the C. Okay, I couldn't think of many words that began with Poc or Puc. When I stuck an A in there, though, I got it. Pace. Pacemaker.

Switching from the camera to the phone, I called Lisa Metzger, the pathologist scheduled to do the forensic autopsy. She answered on the first ring, so I must have caught her at a good time. "Medical Examiner's office, Dr. Metzger speaking." I'd always thought it strange she'd answer her own calls until I realized she'd given me her direct line after we'd worked closely together on a previous, complicated case.

"Hey, Doc. Alex Wolfe. You know the latest burn victim?"

"I haven't gotten to him yet, Alex. Sorry. I'm just really stacked up right now."

"No, that's okay. I wanted to let you know what I found on a medic alert bracelet at the scene. The bracelet was damaged in the fire, but I'm pretty sure it says diabetic and maybe pacemaker. I can only make out the P, C, and R, but I think it might mean pacemaker unless you can think of anything else that might fit."

"Great. Anything else?"

"Nothing legible. It's in pretty bad shape."

"All right. I've gotta run, Alex. I'll let you or Kate know what I find."

She disconnected just as I spotted Megan sneaking around the back of her building. She had a back door that opened onto the alley, and I jumped out of my car and sprinted after her. I got there just in time to jam my foot between the door and frame. I put my shoulder against the wood and shoved only to push against Megan, who was doing the same from the other side.

"I didn't tell him anything, Alex. He was cute, and I haven't had a date in a while, so I went out with him. No harm, no foul."

I stopped pushing. "Megan, we didn't know who he was. He could have been the Coward for all you knew. You can't go out with guys after I tell you they're somehow involved with my work."

She opened the door and ushered me inside. "I know. I'm sorry. It's just that he didn't give off bad guy vibes, so I went out with him. And like I said, he was cute."

"First of all, people said Ted Bundy was the nicest boy around. So just don't do it, okay? And second, do you remember if you told him anything about me or the case? He said you were pretty plastered."

"I was not. I asked Tina, you know, the redheaded waitress with the big hooters? I always wonder how she keeps them in her shirt, you know? I think more of them hangs out than stays in."

"You're one to talk."

"*Anyway*," She drew out the word. "I met her at the bathroom sink after we'd both tinkled, and I asked her to just give me coke when I ordered rum and coke."

I grinned. "You mean you outsmarted the ex-undercover cop?"

She returned my grin. "Yup."

"So, did you learn anything about him?"

"No, sorry. I just had a good time. He's happily married —honest about that, which I like—a good pool player, and he taught me a couple of smooth moves. I got pretty good toward the end of the night." She swung one arm behind her back, stuck out her tongue, and pretended to hit a cue ball.

Nuts come in all shapes and sizes, but Megan was my redheaded nut, and I wouldn't trade her for anyone in the world. But I would try to knock some sense into her. "Look, the next time I tell you some guy who's been following me is taking your dog training class, don't go out and date him, okay?"

"As if that's ever gonna happen again." She walked to the front door and pulled down her sign. After opening the door, she called out to a woman leading her Doberman back to the car. "Sorry, Stella. I forgot to take down the sign." The Doberman came running and practically jumped into her arms. "Saber! How's my buddy?"

Saber ran a huge tongue up the side of her cheek and then ran over to Sugar, Megan's Labrador retriever. The two began playing tug-of-war with a short rope. All was good in Megan's world again. She knew she'd been forgiven, not that my not forgiving her would stop her from doing something so stupid again, and she was ready to move on with life.

I called over my shoulder as I let myself out the front door, "See ya."

I'd almost forgotten that Kate wanted a full report on Steve and his visit to Gia's place, so I drove to the main station before heading home. A lot of the detectives were working late, including Casey. I nodded a greeting and then, for the next hour, dutifully typed out the report.

All of us had been working late the last couple of weeks, so I wasn't surprised to see Kate walk in and set her briefcase on the floor next to her desk. Her tiredness showed in the way she slowly lowered herself down to her chair, ran her fingers through her hair, and rested her elbow on the desk with her head in her hand.

When I finished, I printed out my report and laid it on her desk. It was nine o'clock by the time I said, "There ya go, Boss."

I turned to go back to my desk, and she said, "Take a seat, Alex."

Sighing, I reluctantly lowered myself into one of two uncomfortable chairs that sat at the front of her desk. I waited while she read the report, nervously tapping my foot and studying my phone while I pretended all was well with the world. I could learn a few things from Megan as far as feigning innocence was concerned.

When she finished, she slowly set the report down, leaned back, and propped her foot on the pulled-out bottom drawer. Her pen began tapping on her knee, and I was glad she was doing her breathing exercises before laying into me.

"You had a possible suspect following you to Ms. Angelino's, and you didn't think it would be a good idea to tell me about it?" Calm, cool, and collected. That was a good thing.

"I didn't consider him a possible suspect."

"Because...?"

I squirmed a bit. "I don't know why. I just didn't get

any hinky feelings about him." That included the fact that Jerry had done a thorough background check on him and found nothing that pointed to deranged arsonist/murderer. But I needed to keep Jerry's participation in the whole thing quiet because I knew Kate wouldn't look kindly on having him in on the case. I wasn't looking forward to filling her in on George either. Did I even need to tell her about George? Probably not. Not yet anyway.

"John Wayne Gacy was a shoe salesman who entertained children as a clown."

I tilted my head, wondering if Kate had some way to listen in on all my conversations. I'd just basically made the same argument to Megan. "It wasn't like I wasn't keeping an eye on him keeping an eye on me. The guy doesn't have a clue how to follow someone without being seen."

"He followed you to Gia's."

I blushed. "That was a mistake. I let my guard down because it was my day off. Plus, in the back of my mind, I knew nobody could get past her security. And he didn't."

"Mistakes like that can get you killed. How did you plan to identify him if Gabe hadn't brought him to you like a pheasant on a platter?"

"I'd decided to confront him when I chased him at that last crime scene, but he got away. And before that, I was curious to see how far he'd go to follow me. The guy walked into a bar five minutes after I did, for cripes sake."

The pen tapped twice more before she shoved in the drawer with her foot. I jumped at the resulting bang. Well, me plus about three other detectives scattered around the room. She leaned forward onto her elbows with her hands clasped together into one great big fist. "And you didn't think to call for back-up so you could talk to the guy right then and there?"

"Well, yeah. I'd arranged for Casey to meet me, you know, in case something happened."

"And you talked to him."

It was a statement rather than a question, so technically, it didn't need an answer. I raised my eyebrows and waited.

Apparently not what she wanted because her jaw jutted forward, and I heard a low growl.

"Not exactly?"

This time both hands slammed down as she stood to come around and lean against the front of her desk. She crossed her arms and stuck her foot on the front of my chair.

I wondered if she intended to send me flying ass over tea kettle if I didn't start dishing. "I wanted to find out more about him before confronting him. I didn't have any intel on him, and if I'd let him know his cover had been blown, I'd never have found out what he wanted. And I couldn't arrest or detain the guy just because he," I held my fingers up in quotation marks, "might have been following me."

"How did you plan to get more intel on him?"

"Well, his license plate for one. He doesn't have a front plate, so I hadn't seen that yet."

"And?"

Kate was getting to know me almost as well as Megan, and it was starting to irritate me in the same way. I am not that transparent. Really, I'm not. "And," I sighed, knowing I was going to have to spill the beans. "You know, it's funny, but you're never going to believe who walked in after I did."

"You mean besides a possible arson-murder suspect?"

I hoped my answering glare let her know she didn't look good with her sarcasm cape thrown over her shoulders.

"Casey walked in. You hadn't planned for her to come? You just said you arranged for her to meet you there."

"She did.

"And?"

"Kate. Can I have just a little bit of rope to hang myself every now and then? Can't we be like the old days when you didn't know or guess there's an 'and?'"

"No. Spill Alex. This is getting old fast."

"Jerry walked in."

Her eyes narrowed, and the jaw came forward again.

"Well, you know how he's a really good P.I.? I kind of asked him to see if he could follow the guy and find out who he was and what he wanted. I guess, kind of like an informant, you know?"

"I know all departmental informants need to go through the proper channels to be registered as one before we use them."

I nodded, "Yeah, there's that. But…" I thought I'd feel her out about how she felt about citizens doing research for us. "You don't mind when Kelly helps me with research on a case, and this is kind of like that. He was helping out. With research."

"By following a suspect?"

"Steve wasn't a suspect. He was a suspicious person, that's all. And it turned out I was right. He was following me for a whole other reason. He isn't the arsonist. He wants to help find the guy."

"You found that out when you spoke to him at Ms. Angelino's place?"

"Not—"

She whipped her finger in the air, stopping me before I could say 'exactly.'

"No." I debated telling her about our lunch meeting today and decided she needed to know. "I met with him at Sleepytime today."

Her voice dropped into the chilly range. "Alone?"

I stopped myself from saying 'not exactly.' It was a shame she'd taken that tool out of my toolbox. It covered a whole range of topics I didn't want to discuss. "No, but I'd rather not say who was with me."

She leaned forward so she could yell out of the cubicle opening. "Casey."

Oh yeah, I'd forgotten Kate had been there when I'd asked Casey to come with me to the café. Throughout this whole case, from the first arson to the latest attack on Babe and Mrs. Holloway, my anger and frustration had been steadily rising with each day that passed without any appreciable results. While we waited for Casey, I began to think about all the damage and pain the Coward had inflicted and how many more lives he could, and would, cut short if we didn't get better results than we'd gotten up to this point. It didn't matter that these people were at the tail end of their lives. Someone had to step up to protect them. That was our job. My job. I looked at my boss and shook my head. *Our* job. This case needed to get solved, and this man had to be stopped. "Kate."

Her tired eyes focused on mine. Sighing, she returned to her chair behind the desk.

Casey came and sat down next to me.

"This man has to be stopped." I looked into Kate's eyes, wanting to know she felt the same way I did.

Her lips drew together, and with her next words, I knew she understood exactly what I meant, "Within the confines of the law, Alex."

"Even the L.T. said—"

"I don't care what Lieutenant Lake said. Look at me."

At her words, I'd stubbornly turned my head to stare at the plexiglass because I was at that tipping point. Did the end justify the means? I mulled that over and made my decision. No. I wasn't willing to take that final step where evil justifies becoming the judge, jury, and executioner. I refocused on what she had to say.

"We need to stop this man *within the confines of the law*. Otherwise, we become him. I'm sure there are many people, both on the department and in the community, who want to see the absolute worst things possible done to this man. Who want to see him dead, and not just dead, but dying in a way that will make him know exactly what he's made these old, fragile people feel. But that's not up to you or me or anyone else working this case. We need to stop him, but not at the expense of our own humanity."

Kate often lectured, but I could tell this meant more to her than merely getting her point across. This was her sharing her core values with us. It was her attempt to make us not just understand what she was saying but to have us pull these values deep inside and embrace them as our own.

First, she held my gaze, and then she turned to Casey. "We all have parents and grandparents we're worried about. Who knows who his next victim will be if we can't stop him before he takes another life?" Her attention focused on me again, "But guard your humanity, Alex. It's cases like this where good people lose sight of who they are and what they're meant to do. The same goes for you, Casey. I've seen the look in your eyes when we walk into these crime scenes, and for the first time since I've known you, that look worries me."

I turned and looked at my partner. I mean really looked at her. I don't know how I'd missed the pent-up anger and hatred I saw in her now. She was wound tighter than I'd ever seen her before, which made me remember her words in the parking lot, "If it helps catch that bastard, I'm willing to skate on your thin line."

I rubbed my face with my hands and thought about what I wanted to say. "Then we need to skate super close to *our* side of that thin line, and we need to use every tool in our belt to stop him. You have to trust us to do that, Kate. You have to give us free rein—within the confines of the law—to stop him." I quirked my head to the side. "Maybe not within the confines of the department's rules and procedures. Maybe we step outside some of those at times?"

Kate sat back in her chair, crossed her arms, and studied us. "Only if you do it with my knowledge and permission."

Out of the corner of my eye, I saw Casey turn to look at me. I met her gaze and knew precisely what she was thinking. We needed to come clean with our plans. Turning back to Kate, I said, "Okay. You know we met with Steve Grate today at lunch. What you don't know is that his brother, George Ogilvie, was also there. He's been following me, too."

Kate narrowed her eyes but didn't say anything.

"We..." I tried to think of the right word. "...recruited them to help with the case." When she didn't come unglued at that, I continued. "George is a twenty-two-year veteran of the Los Angeles Police Department, and Steve retired from Army Intelligence as a Sergeant Major. They both have their strengths, and both Casey and I believe they can help. George worked U.C. for a big part of his career, and I asked him to make sure Babe and Mrs. Holloway are safe."

Being practical was one of Kate's strengths, and she knew we didn't have the manpower to assign someone to watch over the two of them twenty-four seven. She thought for a moment, nodded her head, and said, "Go on."

I went over their story of the burned pets and the missing eyeballs. "That's what made them want to help. There was too much of a coincidence between what happened to the pets in their neighborhood years ago and what's happening here. Steve has the yearbooks from his older brother's time in middle school and high school. His strength is analysis, so I arranged for him and Kelly to meet at the library tomorrow and see if they can come up with something using the names out of the yearbooks. I don't know what they're gonna do, but I think since that's where their strengths lie, we should leave them to figure it out."

Once Kate makes up her mind, she never...well, rarely hesitates. "I'll need to meet with both of them. If things go sideways, I want the blame to rest squarely on my shoulders. And both of you, look at me." When we did, she continued, "Don't for a minute think the brass will admit to telling you to catch him 'at all costs.' If you step outside of the law to stop this guy, they'll deny everything and will throw you under a bus in a heartbeat."

She checked her phone for the time. "It's late, and I need to get home to Thom. If anything happens, you *will*," she looked both of us straight in the eye, "call me before you go haring off on your own. Understood?"

I nodded. "You got it, Boss. When I spoke to the nurse in charge of Mrs. Holloway's care, she said they were keeping her tonight for observation. I intend to go home, eat some Chinese takeaway with Megan, and head to bed."

Boy, when I'm wrong, I sure know how to do it up right.

CHAPTER 10

I'm lucky in that when I sleep, I'm bracketed front and back with dogs. Jynx is usually curled up next to my tummy, and Tessa's back is butted up next to mine. I was in the middle of one of those dreams where I'm climbing to the top of a cliff and randomly decide it would be interesting to step off the ledge, you know, to see if I can fly, when I realized neither dog was in bed with me.

The double sensation of cliff and bed confused my subconscious enough to begin the torpid process of pulling me out of a deep slumber into semi-consciousness. I felt trapped between jumping off a cliff, knowing there weren't supposed to be dogs near the cliff, and lying in bed, knowing the dogs should be crowding me into a tiny corner of the mattress.

Tessa growled low in her throat, and I sat up, instantly awake. My ordinarily placid dog stood in the door to my bedroom, hackles raised and lip curled up to expose two rows of very sharp teeth. Even more strange was the fact that Jynx, who at night is typically either sleeping with me or barking his head off, was nowhere to be seen.

Since there are never any kids around when I sleep, I keep my Glock laying out on my nightstand, ready for instant access. When Tessa growled a second time, I grabbed it and slipped out of bed. When the temperatures dip into the cool zone, I sleep in a pair of sweatpants and a sweatshirt. My pants had fallen halfway down my butt, and I reached back with my free hand and pulled them up into position. I couldn't confront a bad guy with my pants falling off, so I set down the gun and pulled the drawstring tight, tying a knot in the end to keep them secure around my waist. It's the little things you remember after an incident, and this would be one of those habits I'd be grateful for later.

I padded to the side of the door, intending to peer around the frame into the other room.

Tessa had other ideas. As soon as she saw me approach, she bravely decided it was time to move further into the darkened living room.

I quietly hissed, "Tessa."

She stopped mid-stride but didn't look back. She never took her eyes off the kitchen window, which she could see from the living room since my house has a modified open-air design. When I say open-air, what I mean is my kitchen is separated from the living room by a low countertop on the right and a swinging door on the left.

I couldn't see anything from where I was peeking around my doorframe.

Every muscle in Tessa's body quivered with suppressed tension, the hunting dog in her rising to the fore. She stood with one paw raised, her head held straight out from her neck, perfectly aligned with her spine the way Springer Spaniels are portrayed in those hunting dog paintings hanging in the local pubs. That was a Tessa I'd only seen on a few other occasions.

But where was little Jynx? Usually, he'd be barking his

head off in a situation like this. I knelt and eased my head around the doorframe again to get a better look into the darkened room.

Nothing.

Staying low, I inched around the corner and crept through the living room to the door separating the kitchen from the living room.

I knelt again and peered into the kitchen.

Jynx crouched beneath one of the four wooden chairs surrounding the kitchen table I keep pushed up against the right side of the room. The door to my backyard—a half-door with a series of nine small windowpanes on top—is situated to the left of the table. To the left of that is my countertop. A second window above my sink looks out over my backyard.

Jynx's little lips were curled up to reveal a set of tiny, sharp teeth. His silence bothered me because he sounds off at the slightest provocation. He barks at cats who wander into our yard, at car doors shutting out on the street, and at the squeak of the loose piece of metal on my roof that moves whenever the wind blows.

I couldn't figure out why he wasn't barking until I saw a faint orange glow approaching the door. Little dogs have a lot of surprising powers. His super dog sniffer or maybe his oversized ears had alerted him to an atypical kind of danger. Instead of barking, he'd thought it prudent to come to the kitchen to check things out. Fire has always terrified him, and although he cowered beneath the chair, I was proud of the fierce way he growled at the door, refusing to leave his post.

Tessa crept up beside me, and I put a hand on her head and whispered, "Stay." I knew that wouldn't do a lot of good when she saw me move forward, but at least she stopped for the moment and, to my surprise, lowered herself into a down position. I guess the fact that she saw me, the pack leader, crouching meant she should do the same.

It's taking longer for me to explain what happened than for the events to actually unfold. When I saw the flickering orange light, I immediately understood I was in trouble. Someone, probably the Coward, was approaching with a Molotov cocktail or a lit torch, and I'd need to put it out or risk losing my home and my dogs to the asshole.

I had two choices. First, I could shoot him before he threw the flames. The problem with that was if my timing or aim was off and the fire made it into my kitchen while I was shooting, I'd lose the precious time needed to stop the inferno before it took hold and completely engulfed my home. The second option was to grab the fire extinguisher and put out the flames before they became a problem.

I decided on choice number two. Deal with the fire first and the arsonist second.

This is the part where the drawstring on my sweatpants comes in. Since I'd pulled it tight and had secured the ends with a knot, I was able to shove the Glock into the back of my waistband and have it stay put. I scurried forward on my hands and feet, probably looking like a drunken gorilla, and made it to the cabinet beneath the sink.

Ever since I'd taken an in-service training class on house fires where they'd accidentally caught the classroom on fire, I'd kept a decent-sized fire extinguisher beneath my sink. I grabbed it, pulled the pin, and decided on a preemptive strike. I planned to throw open the door and spray the guy before he could throw the flames.

Dumb move.

Luckily, I stood off to the side as I reached for the doorknob because a ball of flame crashed through the window and skidded across the top of my kitchen table.

Several things happened at once.

The best thing was that Jynx lost his nerve and ran into the living room. Otherwise, the stream of flaming accelerant that crossed the table and flowed over the edge might have flowed down onto him.

Next, his flight, plus the noise of breaking glass, panicked Tessa, who darted between my legs looking for the alpha to protect her.

The alpha tripped over her trusty sidekick and fell flat on her face. Luckily my gun safety had kicked in when I'd grab the extinguisher, and I hadn't yet put my fingers around the firing mechanism. I did, however, maintain my grip on the thing and was able to push to my knees and spray the table, chair, and floor in the back and forth motion they'd taught in the seminar.

All the while, the little gnome who jumps up and down on my shoulders was having a hissy fit because I had my back to the door and had no idea whether the arsonist had a gun ready to take my head off my shoulders.

God bless Tessa, who must have seen movement on the other side because she leapt at the broken window, barking and snarling enough to scare anyone away.

Little Jynx also had a resurgence of bravery when he heard Tessa's angry barks. He came to the door between the kitchen and living room, barking and bouncing up and down on his tiny front paws to lend support to his bigger friend, who was now scratching at the back door, desperate to get after the intruder.

The fire extinguisher made quick work of the fire. After checking to make sure the flames were completely out, I threw it to the side, grabbed the Glock out of my butt crack —okay, the knot in the drawstring only goes so far—and raced out the back door. My backyard is a dead-end for anyone trying to get away, so the arsonist's only path to freedom was to head around the side of the house toward my front yard.

He had a head start, and I skidded around the corner,

hoping to close the gap in the time it took me to reach the front yard.

Tessa and Jynx overtook me and streaked after a dark figure run-limping toward a four-door sedan.

"Stop! Police!" As I've mentioned before, that never works, but we're always supposed to yell it when we're chasing a subject. True to form, it didn't work. His limp gave me a slight edge in the speed department, but the sound of two dogs chasing him gave him enough of an adrenaline boost that he made it to his car and peeled out before I came within grabbing distance.

I regretted not snagging my car keys on the way out the door. I thought about trying to shoot out his tires—something that's frowned upon by the department—but Tessa and Jynx were chasing after his car and were subsequently in my line of fire.

He'd removed the license plate, so no help there, and when he turned to look at me through the rear window, all I saw was a ski mask covering his head and face.

"Tessa. Jynx. Get back here!" Running after the car for all they were worth, both dogs chased it around the corner and disappeared. I was torn between chasing them down or grabbing the phone to call in a sighting of the Coward. Knowing I could never actually catch the dogs, I compromised by continuing to shout out their names while running back into the house, tearing through the kitchen and living room to my bedroom, and grabbing my phone.

I threw open the front door and raced outside while calling 911 only to see the two dogs, who were extremely pleased with themselves, trotting up the road on their way back home. Their tongues hung from the sides of their mouths, and there was a bounce in their steps usually associated with the success they feel whenever they chase the package delivery guy away from the front door—after he's left the package, of course.

I gave the sedan's description to the 911 operator even though I knew he'd be long gone by the time patrol arrived. There was always the dimmest possibility he might be dumb enough to hang around, but I doubted it. Now that the adrenaline was leaving my bloodstream, I noticed a painful jabbing sensation as I walked bare-footed across the pavement. Everywhere I stepped, sharp rocks and tiny shards of glass stuck into the tender soles of my feet. I minced my way back to my front door, only to hear a strange clicking sound coming from Newton's house.

Both his front and backyards were habitually lit up like a drunken sailor on shore leave. That way, no one would ever be able to sneak up on him in the middle of the night. He'd pulled a small portion of the heavy curtain away from the edge of his picture window, and a disembodied hand was tapping something hard against the window.

Sighing, I made my way across my front yard, every so often lurching straight up when my aching footpad came down on something hard, sharp, or misshapen. "Hi, Newton. Did we wake you?"

The hand tapped again.

I leaned closer and peered at the tapping object, not recognizing it until the fingers held it flat against the window. Excitement surged when I realized he held a memory chip from a camera or phone. I glanced at his front door, remembering the security camera he'd had installed the previous year after some neighborhood kids had trashed the front of his house. "Is that from your security camera?"

The hand disappeared, letting the curtain fall back into place.

I wasn't sure whether that meant I should go to the front

door immediately or whether I should wait for him to put the chip outside on the porch.

He solved my dilemma by opening the door a crack and setting a white envelope on his welcome mat. I always wondered why an agoraphobic man would have a colorful, floral mat at his front door with neon green letters shouting, "Welcome!" It wasn't as if the mat was one his mother had bought before she'd passed on. If that were the case, you'd expect it to be faded and frayed around the edges. No, Newton ordered a new one every spring, like clockwork. Luckily for him, his parents had left him a very wealthy man. On top of his inherited wealth, he'd taken online courses and had become somewhat of an influencer in the high-tech world of gadgets. The man couldn't talk to you face-to-face, but one of my friends had discovered he was considered a guru in certain tech junkie circles.

There were two items in the envelope, a chip and a thumb drive. I definitely wasn't a techie, and I walked back to the window and tapped on it with a small rock. "Hey, Newton. Do these both have the same info on them?"

It took a minute, something I was familiar with when trying to communicate, but before long, the hand appeared holding a cellphone.

"Yeah, I get that the little one goes into a cellphone. But is one just a copy of the other?"

His index finger wagged back and forth before pointing straight in the air.

"One?" I guessed. "Look, never mind. I'm sure the techies at work will know."

The finger waggled back and forth again, then stuck straight up.

I could tell he wasn't going to let it go, so I dug the little square card out of the envelope and held it up.

He pointed to it and held the phone out again.

"Okay, so this one's from the phone." I grabbed the stick and held it up. "And this one?"

The finger pointed towards his front door.

"This one's from the security camera. Can I just plug it into my computer?"

The hand disappeared, and I took that as a yes. My cell phone rang with Kate's siren ring, so I waved my thanks at the window and answered. "Hey, boss."

"Are you okay?"

"Fine. I guess commo called you?"

"I assume calling me was the next thing on your list?"

I smiled. "Of course, it was. I'm heading back to my house now."

"What happened exactly? Patrol is really tied up, and the dispatcher asked if we could handle your case as a call-out, so Mitch, Casey, and I are headed your way."

"I was hoping patrol could get here fast enough to check out the neighborhood, but I guess that's not gonna happen?"

"Like I said, short-staffed, too many calls and not enough cops to answer them." I heard her husband saying something in the background. Her next words were muffled, and I assumed she'd covered the phone with her hand. After a moment, she said, "Okay, I'm back. Consider your place a crime scene until we get there. Give me the abbreviated version of what happened."

I gave her the highlights as I hobbled back over the sharp stones one more time.

Newton's lights didn't extend to my yard, so I had to wait a bit at the line between light and dark until my eyes adjusted. I finally made it into my living room, picked up a piece of pizza left out from the night before, and sat down on my sofa to wait.

CHAPTER 11

Headlights lit up my front window, and it wasn't long before a knock sounded at my door. That had to be Mitch, as I knew Casey wouldn't knock, and Kate hadn't had enough time to get to my house from her home on the east side of town. The dogs, already on high alert, started barking, and I ordered them back to the sofa and called out, "Come on in, Mitch. No need to stand on formalities."

The door opened, and Mitch stuck his head around the corner. "I'm not sure where the crime scene is, and I don't want to screw up any evidence."

I got up and indicated he should follow me to the kitchen. "It's in here. He threw a flaming...something through my window. I haven't gone back in there for the same reason. I didn't want to mess anything up until you got here."

The dogs would only get in the way, so I locked them in my bedroom before following Mitch into the kitchen. He stood in the doorway and took in the whole scene with the practiced eye of a trained arson detective. Like I said earlier, the arson guys see things the rest of us just pass on by.

"Smell that?" Mitch pulled in an exaggerated sniff and then turned concerned eyes on me.

Curious, I pulled in a deep breath. I hadn't noticed the smell from the living room, but now I detected the faint odor of an accelerant in the air. "Is that..?"

He nodded, "We won't know for sure until the lab does the analysis, but this..." He pointed to his nose, "tells me it's the same. Which means you were super lucky and really smart to grab your fire extinguisher."

"It was a toss-up between trying to go after him before he could throw the fire or go for the extinguisher."

"You made the right choice. If that accelerant had had any time to take hold and spread, you'd be without a house right about now."

If you simply looked at the left side of the kitchen, you'd never guess anything untoward had happened. But over by the backdoor and table was another matter altogether. Glass lay scattered across the floor and table. I'd already checked the dog's pads for cuts, and miraculously neither of them had a single laceration anywhere on their bodies. I'd been sure Tessa would have something based on the way she'd scratched at the door demanding to be let out, but she'd gotten lucky and came away without a scratch.

Okay, she probably hadn't been thinking that I had my back to the door while putting out the fire. Still, I like to pretend she has that kind of deductive reasoning inside that flighty little brain of hers. Tessa is more like Mickey Mouse's Pal, Goofy, than Rocky and Bullwinkle's brainiac friend, Mr. Peabody. But she'd once saved the life of a young friend of mine and was a much-loved part of my little family. I wouldn't trade her for a thousand Mr. Peabodies.

Jynx, on the other hand, *was* my Mr. Peabody. Despite having a tiny head that housed an even tinier brain, every one of his little gray cells fired to peak capacity. I like to say I'd taught him everything he knows, but in reality, it had been Megan who'd recognized the genius and put that pretty little head to work. I say Jynx was at least on par with Megan's dog, Sugar, although I have neither the time nor talent to give him the consistent training Sugar gets.

But I digress.

White powder from the extinguisher covered my table, a portion of the wall, and the floor. I was surprised to see I'd knocked over one of the chairs when Tessa had tripped me. I didn't remember doing that, and I took stock of my body, checking for any bruises I wasn't aware of. Sure enough, my upper left arm hurt when I ran my hand over it. I've never been shy about my body, and since I was in my own kitchen, I pulled my arm out of the sleeve to inspect the damage.

Kate chose that moment to walk through my front door. She cocked her head, then glanced over at Mitch, who was politely studying the kitchen floor instead of my body. Not that my boobs were exposed or anything. Not for long anyway. I'd pulled the bottom of the sweatshirt down and hooked it under one of the girls to keep it secured in place.

"Hi, Sarge."

Twisting my upper arm around to see the damage, I felt up and down its length to make sure the skin was still intact.

Kate stepped over to take a look.

"I thought you told the dispatcher you weren't injured."

"I'm not. Well, at least not bad enough to be seen by anybody. I didn't even realize I was hurt until I saw the overturned chair I'd fallen over when Tessa tripped me, and when I checked my body for bruises, I found this."

She looked down at my lower ribs and pointed to another bruise. "This one's pretty nasty too. You might want to go to your doctor to get checked out if it gets any worse."

"Yeah, okay." I didn't tell her I didn't have a regular doctor. Our insurance allows for a primary care doc, but I go so seldom I'd never taken the time to pick one out. I pulled my boob to the side to get a better look at my ribs. I think I've mentioned before that while Casey is a size A and proud of it, I'm more a thirty-four C who has to re-position if I want to see any part of my ribcage.

"Get dressed before Mitch turns any redder."

I glanced over at Mitch who'd turned his back, and sure enough, what I could see of his neck had turned a lovely shade of red. "Haven't you ever seen a woman's body before?"

He grinned over his shoulder. "I'm a healthy male of the species, Alex. And, like Kate says, I'd appreciate it if you'd put your clothes back on."

I motioned for him to turn his head away again and pulled my sweatshirt back into place. I used two hands to lift my boobs and said to Kate, "I'm gonna go find a bra."

She nodded sagely, "Good thinking."

On my way to the bedroom, I heard her ask Mitch, "What do we have?"

After a quick trip to find my bra and pull it on, I returned in time to welcome Casey as she strolled through the front door carrying a carton of four coffees and a bag of donuts beneath one arm. I groaned and said, "Bless you, my child."

When I reached for the nearest coffee, Casey stopped me, "Nope, yours is the one on the top right. Six creamers and six sweeteners."

I grabbed mine and took a sip, testing the waters in case the java was too hot to drink.

Kate and Mitch returned to the living room and followed suit, thanking Casey and grabbing the bag of donuts before they accidentally fell to the floor. There was no real hurry now that the Coward was gone, so we took the time to refuel and wake up before examining the "crime scene."

For some reason, I couldn't quite get my mind around the concept that a part of my house was now a crime scene.

Crime scenes happened to other people. In my mind, this was still "my house" and not "the crime scene."

Kate held the last of a sticky cruller to her mouth. Before popping it in, she said, "Okay, Alex. Run us through what happened. In detail this time."

I told them about waking up without the dogs next to me, how I went out to find them and saw an orange glow approaching the kitchen window.

Mitch interrupted me. "Describe the color in detail, please."

I turned my head to the side, trying to bring the moment into focus. "The most predominant color was orange, but I think I also saw some yellow." I didn't know what the colors meant, but I knew enough to know they were important to an arson investigator. "And I think when it hit the table, I saw a bit of blue?" I phrased it like a question because I wasn't positive about what I'd seen.

Cocking his jaw to the side, Mitch just nodded. "Okay."

I told them about sneaking in to grab the extinguisher and about how I'd thought about going for my Glock instead to try to shoot the guy before he threw the flames through the window. "I'm not sure what broke the glass or how the flame got to my table. Everything's kind of a blur once the glass broke."

Mitch spoke up, "I did a preliminary inspection of the crime scene."

I pursed my lips to keep myself from correcting him. Damnit, it was my home, not a crime scene.

"He used a mason jar filled with accelerant—" He interrupted himself to clarify a point to Kate, "I can't be sure, but I'm ninety-five percent positive it's the same accelerant as the other fires. He stuffed cloth into the mouth of the jar, which he lit. Alex saw two colors because one of the cloths was linen, which burns a bright yellow, and the other was probably some type of wool, which burns orange. We've never had any cloth leftover in the other Coward fires, so this is a good break. It's very unusual for an arsonist to use either material as a wick for a Molotov cocktail. Usually, they just use an old cotton t-shirt or something."

I listened closely because this type of forensics fascinated me. "So, where'd the blue come from? Assuming I did actually see blue. I'm not really sure on that point."

He nodded, "That's actually a critical observation and why I'm extremely glad you decided to grab the extinguisher and immediately douse the flame. Usually, unless you have a gas fire, the flames will go from a dull red to orange and then to a bright yellow as the fire heats up. The fact that you saw blue means he put something in the accelerant that burns very hot, very fast. Anyway, I didn't mean to hijack your story, Alex. Go ahead."

"So, the mason jar broke the middle panes but not the lower ones. Thank God because Tessa was scratching at the lower ones to make me open the door so she could chase him. When the jar broke the pane, she panicked and ran through my legs. That's why I tripped. I guess I fell over the chair, although I don't remember doing that. I got up and doused the flames. Then the dogs and I chased after the guy."

I looked at Kate. "Babe was right; the guy does kind of run with a limp. Not super pronounced, but..." I shrugged.

Both Kate and Casey wrote that down in their notebooks. Kate asked, "Did you get a look at his face? Commo said he covered his license plate?"

"No, he didn't cover it. He'd taken it off. And he was wearing a ski mask. He probably didn't wear a mask with Mrs. Holloway because he didn't intend for her to live long enough to identify him."

Casey shook her head, "No. Didn't Babe tell you he'd put a paper bag over Mrs. Holloway's head?"

Kate tapped her notebook with the end of her pen. "My guess is that was more to terrify his victim than to keep his anonymity. I went back to the hospital to talk with Mrs. Holloway before I went home last night. One of the first things the suspect did when he snuck up behind her was to hit her in the back of the head, so her glasses went flying. Without them, she's practically blind. Again, he intended to kill her, and there was no need to hide his identity from her. He knew that only being able to see blurry impressions would terrify her. Then, to increase that terror, he took that bit of control away with the paper bag over the head."

"Oh!" Talking about anonymity and identification reminded me of Newton's photo stick. "Newton downloaded video from his security camera onto this." I grabbed the envelope off my credenza and took it to the coffee table where I'd left my laptop. I moved the computer to the countertop between the living room and kitchen, plugged the stick into the USB, and we all gathered around to watch.

First, a dark sedan parked across the street from Newton's house. Unfortunately, the guy already had his ski mask on when he exited the car. He opened the trunk and grabbed the mason jar and another container. He set one jar on the pavement and poured liquid into it from the second jar.

Mitch leaned forward, "Hold on. Can you zoom into that other container? Can anyone tell what it's made of?"

I zoomed in on the hand but ended up going too close because everything blurred. I backed the zoom out a bit, and we all joined Mitch, who had his nose inches from the computer screen.

Casey said, "It looks like another mason jar to me. Why didn't he just take the lid off and stuff the rags down into that one?"

Mitch said, "He probably had too much in the original jar and couldn't risk spilling any on himself as he walked. The chemicals he uses for the accelerant aren't forgiving for a careless person, and we know this guy is anything but careless."

The man's limp wasn't visible when he walked, only when he tried to run or hurry. I wasn't sure what type of injury that pointed to, but it was another line of investigation. I stopped the video and pointed to Casey's notebook. "Can you write down that he doesn't have a limp when he walks, only when he runs?"

Casey nodded and did as I asked.

There wasn't much else to see except the guy walking around the corner of my house to my back yard, and then him run-limping as he returned to his car. It wasn't long before Tessa and Jynx came around the corner after him, and I followed soon after. I watched myself standing in the middle of the street yelling for the dogs.

Then something occurred to me. I rewound the video a bit and watched again as the man walked beneath the limb of my mesquite tree. "Look at that. He ducked just a little bit. I can easily walk beneath that branch, and he had to duck. I think Babe's impression of him being short was possibly colored by the fact that he was bending over the victim. After that, she only saw him running away. He could have been hunched over then, too. I'm five-foot-six and don't have to duck beneath that branch at all. That makes him a bit taller than me."

The way Kate rewound the video and watched it again told me she agreed. "Good catch, Alex. We need to update the description we put out to the media." She paused on me standing in the middle of the road, aiming my Glock at his retreating car. "I know why you didn't shoot, but I almost wish this was one of those times you disobeyed the rules."

I raised my eyebrows, "I didn't shoot because the dogs were in the way. If they hadn't been there..." I let them fill in the blank. Shooting at a fleeing car is generally frowned upon since it's too easy for the bullet to hit anything but the vehicle.

Kate started for the kitchen. "Okay, Mitch, you and I can look at the crime scene. Alex, get some shoes on, and you and Casey go outside and look to see if he dropped anything in his hurry to leave." She stopped and looked at me. "By the way. How did he know where you live? Did he follow you without you knowing?"

"Absolutely not. I was careful last night when I drove home. I took a lot of unnecessary turns so I could see if there was anyone on my tail. I even parked a couple of times and drove with my lights off to see if anybody followed. I'm absolutely positive no one followed me."

Kate got a far-off look in her eyes. "That presents a whole new can of worms, doesn't it?"

When I realized what she meant, I nodded slowly. If no one had followed me home, then how did the Coward know where I lived? Did we have a mole somewhere, and if so, who? I was pretty sure Babe didn't know where I lived. But what about Steve and George? I knew Steve had been to the house because I'd caught him standing in the shadows on the other side of the street.

And I was pretty sure George could have easily followed me without me seeing him if I wasn't aware of who he was, plus it was a given Steve would have told him my address. I turned those thoughts over in my mind while putting my shoes on and joining Casey out in the front yard.

I found her squatting by the side of the house. "You were barefooted, so it's a good bet these are his shoe prints. We need to make a cast and get it to the forensic folks to see what they can come up with. Good catch on the guy's height, by the way." She swiveled around on the balls of her feet to look at the tree. "Kind of reminds me of the way old Mrs.

Highland described her husband's height a few years ago, remember? She said he had to duck beneath that light on the porch."

I remembered all right. Mrs. Highland was well into her nineties, now, and was still just as sharp as the day I'd met her. "Have you seen her lately?"

Casey nodded. "As a matter of fact, Terri and I took her one of Terri's salmon dishes a few weeks ago. She and Reina, and Lupe are doing great. You ought to go visit sometime."

"I had to fix Mrs. Highland's cooler about two months ago, but yeah, I should go more often." I went to her trunk and brought all the tools and ingredients we'd need to cast a couple of the better prints. "Looks like a sneaker to me. That's odd. He's never left prints before. Do you think he's getting careless?"

"Yeah, or he's taunting us. You know, I don't think he just started doing this here in Tucson. He seems to know exactly what he's doing, starting from the very first case we investigated." She poured some dental stone into a pitcher, which I carried over to my hose.

I added about ten ounces of water and stirred the mixture for a good five minutes.

In the meantime, Casey placed a measuring stick next to the impressions and took several pictures from different angles.

When the mixture gelled the correct amount, I poured it around the outside perimeter of the prints and made sure the mixture completely filled the impression.

Kate came around the corner with her head down, following the prints from the kitchen.

Casey called out, "Watch it, Boss."

When she saw what we were doing, Kate stopped and carefully made her way over to where we squatted next to the drying dental powder. "He left prints?"

Casey nodded. "Yeah. We thought that was kind of strange, too. You think he's getting cocky?"

Kate raised her eyebrows. "I certainly hope so. Cocky means mistakes, like this one. If he keeps screwing up, we'll catch the S.O.B." She motioned back the way she'd come. "Mitch is picking up the rest of the broken mason jar. It'd be nice if we found prints on the glass, but I doubt it. The guy isn't that cocky."

Unless he'd touched the mason jar before he came. From the video, we knew for a fact he'd worn gloves when he'd poured the accelerant from one jar to the other and when he'd carried the Molotov Cocktail to my door.

Kate continued, "We're almost done here, Alex. I'll help you clean up the rest of the glass and the powder from the extinguisher. Do you have a second one around in case he returns?"

"I have the one in my work car. I'll bring it inside, but I doubt I'm gonna get much sleep. Do you think he'll come back?"

"Honestly? No, I don't. He obviously didn't know you had dogs because, judging by the panicked way he was running and looking over his shoulder, they scared him more than you did. I think you'll be all right. I also think your dogs will be listening for anything out of the ordinary now and will wake you instead of just going to the kitchen and listening."

It took the four of us about an hour to clean up and another half hour to pull the back off an old bookcase, which we used to cover the broken window on the kitchen door. It was three o'clock by the time I watched them drive away.

I was too awake to go back to bed, so I stretched out on the sofa, grabbed my Kindle, and forgot my worries in a good book.

CHAPTER 12

On my way to work the following day, I took Tessa and Jynx over to Megan's place because I didn't want to take the chance of the Coward returning and setting my house on fire with them inside. Don't get me wrong. Having my house burned down would be bad; having my dogs inside while it happened was something I didn't even want to consider.

Megan was all too happy to take the dogs and promised they'd have a wonderful time and maybe learn something new in the process.

I had a lot of paperwork to catch up on, so I went into the office and plowed through my inbox, and made a few phone calls. By the time 10 o'clock rolled around, I was ready for a break. Since the main library isn't that far from the police station, I walked the few blocks there and was glad to see Steve waiting for me near the library's front doors.

It just so happened that Kelly was the person who unlocked the doors, and she greeted us with a wide smile. "Hi, Alex. This must be the friend you were talking about. She held out her hand to Steve. "Hi. I'm Kelly."

Steve slipped the box under one arm and then returned the handshake. "Steve. I'm really looking forward to working with you. Alex says you're a research expert? So am I, and I think we're gonna have a lot of fun with all this." He lifted the box to indicate what "all this" meant.

The eagerness was evident in Kelly's eyes. "Well, helping people with their research is a big part of what I do all day. I love working on Alex's cases. In fact, I've gotten permission to work with you for the first half of the day so we can get set up." She led us upstairs and into one of the conference rooms.

The room was longer than wide, making the rectangular table in the middle an excellent place to spread out paperwork. Smaller tables were set up in two corners. One held a desktop computer, which Kelly immediately turned on. "You can set the yearbooks on either side of this main table. We'll have plenty of room to spread out once we get started."

Steve set the box on the table and pulled out eight yearbooks. "I decided to bring all of my brother's yearbooks and added my own, too. You know how people come and go, and I thought it would be better to have more than less."

Smiling, Kelly pulled the first book out of the box. "I like the way you think."

I explained to Kelly the bare-bones of what we were trying to do because I didn't want to influence their research. They were the intelligence-gathering experts, not me. They didn't even notice when I finally left about a half-hour later. They had their noses glued to the computer screen, setting up their databases and talking about exactly what data they wanted to capture.

The main library has a front patio that takes up almost as much real estate as the building itself. There's an extensive area of red brick with long, thin cement lines running through it. The architects had also incorporated good-sized, grassy areas where people can bring their books outside to lounge about and enjoy the Arizona sunshine. A bright red, abstract, metal sculpture sits in the middle of the area. It's maybe fifteen feet tall and ten feet wide, and it represents the artist's version of the Sonoran Desert. Honestly, I've never been able to figure it out, but that's just me.

I sat on one of the cement retaining walls next to the sculpture and called George to let him know I hadn't heard from the hospital yet.

He surprised me by saying, "Yeah, I came to the hospital to get a feeling for the layout and see how long it will be before Mrs. Holloway is released."

"You what?" I didn't like him ad-libbing on his own. "What if the Coward is watching her too? I don't want him to realize that you're involved in any way."

"You haven't done much U.C. work, have you, Alex?"

"Well, no, not exactly."

"Listen, I'm very good at what I do. There's no way that anyone would know that I'm interested in the victim. That young woman, Babe, you told me about, and her cousin arrived about an hour ago. They're waiting for the doctor to come around and release her. If you want to be here when they get out, you might head this way."

I stood and began walking back to the station where my car was still parked. "You didn't make contact with either of them, did you?"

He was quiet a moment before saying, "Alex, you're gonna have to trust me that I know what I'm doing, okay?"

I thought back to the conversation I'd had with his ex-partner. The guy had told me George was excellent at undercover work, so I guess I needed to trust him. "Yeah, you're right. I'm on my way back to the police station now. I'll grab my car and be waiting for the call."

It took about fifteen minutes to reach the station. Instead of going back to the office, I went directly to the underground garage, got my car, and called Kate. "I'm heading over to the hospital. They're waiting for the doc to come check out Mrs. Holloway. They're confident she'll be released this morning, and I want to be sure to be there when they leave with her."

"Sounds good. I have Casey following up on a few leads, and everybody else is out on other cases. I don't have anyone to help you follow them home. You're on your own."

I almost reminded her about George but then decided the less said, the better.

As usual, I underestimated her power of recall and the spooky way she had of reading my mind. "I haven't forgotten about George Ogilvie, Alex. I spoke to a commander at the L.A.P.D., who George used to work under. He assured me the guy was an excellent detective, and I've cleared it with Chief Sepe as far as him helping. I'm still worried about how The Coward found your house, though. I doubt it's this guy, George, but don't let your guard down completely, okay?"

"I won't, but I'm with you; my gut tells me it's not him. I'll call when we have the three of them settled in at Babe's cousin's house." I hung up and drove to the hospital, where I parked outside to wait. Normally I'd take more care not to be seen, but not this time. If we could draw the Coward out, we might catch another break. Sometimes, when criminals realize they're making mistakes, they begin to decompensate. All too often, they go underground for months or even years, and we lose track of them. I didn't want that to happen this time. I wanted to push him enough to keep him around, but not enough that he struck again or went silent.

I was confident that if he followed us, George would pick him out.

I didn't have long to wait. It was about 11:30 by the time Babe finally called. "Nathaniel just left to bring the car to the front of the hospital. The doctor released Mrs. Holloway and said she's going to be fine. He gave her some instructions as far as her blood pressure goes, so we'll be able to take care of that. She's excited to stay with Nathaniel and me. I think she's lonely most of the time."

"Does she understand what happened? Does she know it was the Coward who tried to hurt her?"

"She does, but she's pretty feisty. She's ready to take him on. Well, not really. She's scared but still feisty. She wants to stop by her house to pick up some things. What you think?"

"Absolutely not. Tell me what she needs, and I'll stop by and get it. But you tell her I said she is not to go back to her house for any reason until I say it's okay."

"Okay, hang on a second."

I could hear her talking to Mrs. Holloway, but I couldn't make out exactly what the old woman said in reply.

Babe came back online. "Do you have a pen and paper handy? She wants quite a few things."

"Yup, go ahead." I grabbed a pen and notepad out of my briefcase.

"She was wearing her nightgown when they brought her in, but she doesn't want to wear that one again. So, could you bring her a new one? She says it's in her top left-hand drawer. She needs new undies, some bras, two pairs of jeans, and three or four shirts that are hanging in her closet. All of her toiletries. There's a flowered toiletry bag underneath the sink in the bathroom. Just throw everything in there. Also, she has a knitting bag in the corner of the living room. Could you bring that too? Make sure knitting needles are in there and bring the Afghan that she's started. She says it's a teal color. I think that's about it. What's that?"

I waited while she got more information from Mrs. Holloway. Most of the old people I know are very particular about their clothing and their toiletries. I decided to wait until after work to go get the stuff so she'd have plenty of time to think about what she needed.

"There's a pair of sneakers in the closet she'd like you to bring."

"Tell her I'm not going until later this afternoon so she'll have plenty of time to make a list."

"We're coming out of the elevators now on the first floor, so I better go. I'll try not to look too nervous when we come out of the doors."

Nathaniel pulled his blue sedan into a parking slot in front of the hospital doors. He got out and opened the rear passenger door just as Babe pushed Mrs. Holloway out onto the sidewalk in a wheelchair.

Even though I had no clue what I was looking for, I scanned the lot on the off chance I might see a suspicious-looking person sitting in their car staring at the three of them —no such luck.

I waited until they turned north onto Campbell Avenue, let two or three cars go by, and then pulled in behind. It's a relatively easy road to navigate if you have to tail someone because it's a major north-south artery running through Tucson. The six lanes, three in each direction, give the tail plenty of maneuvering room to stay in sight of the target. The only possible obstacle was the number of traffic lights we had to go through. Still, I was able to keep close enough behind them by driving a couple of lanes over so that if they hit a yellow light, I'd be able to go through without having to stop on the red.

After a few miles, George called, "I've got them. Take a right at the next light. I want to check something out."

"Okay, I'm taking a right on Kleindale. I'll work my way around and pick up the trail coming off of Prince Road."

"Copy."

As luck would have it, they hit a red light at Prince, and

by the time I made it to Prince and Campbell, their light had only just turned green. When they moved through the intersection, I pulled in behind without a glitch.

George called again, and I realized I needed to give him his own ring so I'd know who was calling without having to look at my phone. "It doesn't look like anyone's following you or them. We're almost to their destination, right?"

"I'd say we're about 3 miles away."

"I think it's better if you break off completely. I'll follow them to the house and then take up surveillance from there."

I didn't like taking orders from him, so instead, I made a series of turns to corroborate his belief that I didn't have a tail. I sped up so that I arrived in Nathaniel's neighborhood before anyone else got there, parked two streets away, and waited.

Nathaniel's car drove through the intersection two blocks in front of me, and I watched in my rearview mirror until I saw George's car go by on the street behind me. I smiled at the fact that I could second-guess his route and then realized if I could do that, then the Coward could too.

I didn't think we'd been followed from the hospital, though. One of us would've picked up the tail. I wanted to see how George worked, so I drove around the neighborhood until I spotted his car on a side street. I parked several blocks away and approached on foot. George wasn't with the vehicle, so I slipped through back yards and down alleys, trying to spot his vantage point.

Believe it or not, I came around the corner just in time to see him shimmying up an elm tree several houses away from the target. The tree had a bird's eye view of both Nathaniel's front and back yards. I couldn't have picked a better vantage point myself. I suspected he'd scoped out the area prior to our arrival and nodded to myself. "Not bad."

On a whim, I returned to my car and retrieved the slingshot I kept in my trunk in case I needed to herd any errant cattle that might wander into the city. Yes, that really is a thing.

I slipped into a neighboring backyard and made my way around to the front corner of the house, where I could see part of George's leg amid the leaves of the tree. I fitted a fairly small stone into the sling, one that wouldn't hurt too much, and let it rip.

His leg jerked when it hit home, and a leaf moved to the side as he searched the surrounding area.

Before long, my phone buzzed. I pulled it out and smiled, "Hey, George."

I loved his single-word response, "Asshole."

There was a smile in his voice, and even though he couldn't see me, I smiled back.

My phone buzzed again as I returned to my car. I dug it out of my back pocket and said, "Hey, boss, what's up?"

"Are you with George Ogilvie?"

"Kind of." The line was quiet, so I decided to add, "He's watching Nathaniel's house, and I'm a couple streets away next to our cars."

"Where can we meet? I want to talk to him ASAP."

"No problem. I'll call and get him to come back to the cars, and you can meet us here."

I gave her the address, and she said she'd see me in about fifteen minutes.

When she pulled up, I was surprised to see another person riding shotgun. It wasn't until they began walking towards me that I recognized one of the commanders from the Pima County Sheriff's Department. "Captain Smith. It's good to see you again."

"Alex, it's been a while. I think the last time I saw you was when we beat your team in the division softball finals."

"Yeah, well, that's not gonna happen again." I looked at

Kate, hoping for an explanation as to why she'd brought someone from the Sheriff's Department along for the ride. She didn't feel an overwhelming urge to share, so I waited until George slipped between two houses on his way to meet us. When he arrived, I made the introductions. "Sgt. Kate Brannigan and Captain Myles Smith, this is George Ogilvie."

Once the handshaking was out of the way, Kate started right in, "Mr. Ogilvie, I understand you retired from the Los Angeles Police Department?"

"Yes, ma'am."

"Both the captain and I spoke with your previous command staff there, and they speak very highly of you."

George didn't reply; he simply nodded and waited for them to continue.

Kate gave him a smile that didn't quite reach her eyes. We were all on edge, and I chalked up her reticence to the strain that had been building over the past few weeks. "So, tell us about yourself. I understand you worked undercover for quite a while?"

"Yes, ma'am, I did. I was deep undercover for several years on a case that hasn't gone to trial yet. So, I really can't talk about it. But if there's anything else you'd like to know…"

She grunted her understanding. "I get it. Let's cut to the chase then, shall we? Detective Wolfe tells me you're here because of some animal cruelty cases that happened when you were a child. I'd like to hear more about those incidents."

George seemed eager to tell his story, probably because he understood that Kate was the gatekeeper, and if he wanted in, he'd have to go through her. He began his story, and before long, everyone was chuckling at some of the mischief he and his brother Steve and a couple other boys had gotten into when they were kids.

George was quite the storyteller, and I enjoyed the spin he put on their antics. Having a gift for bullshit was common among undercover cops. They can talk your ear off on just about any topic, and you'll never know whether they're telling the truth or jerking your chain.

Kate watched him with a bemused look that told me she was just as familiar with undercover personalities as I was and didn't fully believe everything he said.

When he came to the part about the fires, George sobered, and it became immediately apparent he was telling the truth as he remembered it. "It was like my brother, Steve, and I told Detective Wolfe. When he and I were about seven, in first grade, a few pets in the neighborhood started to go missing. You have to understand, it was a lower-middle-class neighborhood, and people, at least the adults, didn't pay too much attention when pets disappeared. After a while, a dead cat showed up here, or what was left of a dog showed up there. They'd been burned, and their carcasses were left in places only the kids would find; you know, like abandoned sheds we commandeered as forts or beneath the old bridge where we used to kick around a soccer ball."

Kate crossed her arms, "You mean to tell me that none of the parents had any idea this was happening? The kids didn't tell their parents?"

George shook his head, "Like I told them," he indicated me with a lift of the chin, "we were a blue-collar neighborhood, and kids didn't go whining to their parents back then. In fact, if Steve or I ever went to our father and cried about something, he'd tell us to man up and quit sniveling."

Kate nodded. "Okay, I get it. Go on with your story."

"Well, Steve and I had a pet rabbit. He disappeared, and a few days later, we found him. We—"

Kate interrupted to ask, "Where?"

Apparently, only Steve could interrupt his brother with impunity because George cocked his head and said, "Does it matter?"

CREDO'S BANDIDOS

Kate didn't just cock her head; she narrowed her eyes, crossed her arms, and began tapping her pen on her bicep, a sure sign of mounting irritation.

George stared at the tapping pen and seemed to understand the implications. He sighed, "It was an old building. Actually, it was a hotel that had closed down, jeez, years before we were born. All the doors were off their hinges, and the city should've boarded it up. Anyway, Steve and I were playing war games with some friends, and everybody was dodging in and out of the rooms. One kid called out that he'd found a dead animal, and when we found him, we saw that it was a rabbit. Who knows if it was our rabbit, but both Steve and I were pretty sure it was."

He stopped to see if Kate had any questions. She didn't, so he continued, "He'd been burned like the others, but what was really upsetting—" he caught and held Kate's gaze, "and this is what made me come here, and what drew our attention to your cases—when we found him, someone had taken out his eyes and set them in the corner of the room. They weren't burned or anything; they'd been very carefully set off to the side. He'd actually cleaned off a spot on the floor just for the eyeballs; all the dirt had been brushed away as though they were significant somehow."

Captain Smith's head popped up at that, and he murmured, "Good God."

Kate, who'd already heard this part of the story, nodded. "I wasn't clear on where you got the information about the eyes in our cases. You said that the reason you came here was because of the eyes. That information hasn't been released to the press or the general public. I want to know how you and your brother found out about that particular piece of information."

"We really didn't know anything for sure until Detective Wolfe confirmed it when we met yesterday."

"You knew something, or you wouldn't have traveled all the way from L.A. to follow my detective all over the city and interfere with ongoing investigations by talking to people she'd interviewed."

George looked slightly chagrined. "Yeah, sorry about that. But we honestly didn't know for sure whether this guy was removing the eyeballs or not. Steve was sitting at a table, and—"

Kate interrupted, "Where?" Her tone was all business, and the word came out sharp and clipped.

George blinked several times while trying to gauge her mood.

Kate tilted her head and waited.

"Did I say something to upset you?" He sounded genuinely confused.

"I'm trying to decide whether I want to work with you or not, or rather whether I want you to work with us. I need someone who's going to be straight with me, and I want to know whether you're that man."

George nodded, "Fair enough. Steve was sitting in a coffee shop. I don't remember which one and two people he thought were journalists were talking about writing a story on the Coward and the fires. One of them asked if the other had heard a rumor about the eyeballs. The other one said no, they hadn't, and the first one decided not to run the story because they hadn't been able to corroborate the information. So, in other words, you have a leak. But it's not an open faucet. I'd say it's just a drip somewhere."

Kate uncrossed her arms and motioned for Captain Smith to follow her a short distance away.

George looked at me and raised his eyebrows. "I don't think I'd like to get on her bad side."

"You definitely don't want to get on her bad side. She's a badass with a ponytail. When you deal with her, you need to be completely straight and honest and cut out any extraneous crap that might muddy the waters." I marveled at the fact that these words were coming out of *my* mouth.

"Crap?"

"Crap. U.C. guys can spin yarns with the best of them, and ninety percent of what they say is just that. Crap."

"Maybe not ninety percent. More like fifty."

"Well, when you're dealing with Kate, it better be zero percent, or she'll send you packing."

Kate and the captain started back our way, and George whispered, "Roger that."

"Mr. Ogilvie, if you'd like to work with us on our case, there are some things that need to happen first. Chief Sepe from our department spoke with Sheriff Harrison of the Pima County Sheriff's Department earlier today. If you're willing, The sheriff authorized Captain Smith to deputize you into their department. TPD doesn't have that capability. This is a temporary move, but it will protect both you and us should anything happen during the investigation."

George raised his eyebrows and looked over at me.

I shrugged because I had no idea this was going to happen.

Kate waited a minute and finally asked, "So, Mr. Ogilvie, is that something you'd be willing to do?"

"Yes, but what about my brother, Steve?"

"Honestly, you're my main concern. Your activities will be more police-related than his. For example, when you helped Detective Wolfe follow our victim and set up surveillance, that's more boots on the ground than sitting in a library doing research. Both activities could be a liability if something happens and you aren't working directly under a member agency."

George scratched the back of his head. "Makes sense. You

need to cover your butts if I end up having to take police action to stop this guy."

"Exactly. Not to mention the fact that you're carrying a concealed weapon." She said the last as a statement, not a question because it was apparent to anyone who knew what to look for that he was packing.

Captain Smith chimed in, "Do you have a concealed carry permit?"

George pulled out his wallet and produced a card. "Yes, sir. I have a federal permit that allows me to carry my weapon in all 50 states."

The captain glanced at the card. "Then let's get this done. I have a meeting I need to get back to at the station. He reached into his pocket, pulled out a folded piece of paper, and smoothed it open. "If you're willing to be deputized, raise your right hand and repeat after me." When George raised his hand, Smith read the oath verbatim.

George repeated it back to him, and when they'd finished, Smith held out his hand. "Then Mr. Ogilvie, I deputize you into the Pima County Sheriff's Department. Congratulations. I'm assigning you to Sgt. Brannigan here. You'll work directly under her, and she'll liaison between you and my department."

After they shook hands, Smith nodded to me and made his way back to Kate's car.

Kate shook his hand also. "We can talk later, but for right now, get back to your surveillance on the house." She pulled out her card and handed it to him. "Here's my number, but I'd prefer you contact me through Detective Wolfe or Detective Bowman first before you call me. Any questions?"

"No, ma'am." For a chatty guy, he kept his words to a minimum around Kate and the brass.

Kate lowered her chin and pinned him with a steady gaze, "Make absolutely sure you stay within the confines of the law,

Mr. Ogilvie, and if you're unsure about what that might be, ask."

George flashed her his most charming smile. "Please, just call me, George."

Kate nodded, "And you can call me, Sgt. Brannigan."

We watched her walk back to her car, and as they drove away, George said, "I don't think she likes me very much."

"She doesn't know you. Besides, the first she heard about you was when I told her you'd been following me and interviewing people. That pissed her off as much as it did me. But we need to stop this guy sooner than later, and she's willing to step outside of her comfort zone to do it." I grinned at him. "So, don't fuck up."

He stuck a thumb in his chest and, in typical U.C. fashion, said, "Me? Never." With that, he headed back to his surveillance tree, and I headed to the library to see whether Kelly and Steve needed anything.

CHAPTER 13

At the library, I walked up the beige carpeted stairs to the second floor. The stairs are part of the open, welcoming design of the building. The first step is a long, curving affair that almost runs the length of the back wall between the children's room on the left and the elevators, restrooms, and a small café on the right. Each successive step is slightly shorter as the stairs curve up and around to the second and third floors.

I entered the study room expecting to find Steve and Kelly hard at work but instead found Steve sitting alone and entering data into an excel file on the computer screen. "How's it going?"

He nearly jumped out of his chair when he heard my voice. He grabbed his chest and laughed, "Jeez, don't do that, Alex. You nearly gave me a heart attack."

"Sorry. If you were a cop, there's no way you'd have your back to the door like that. I would have moved the computer so I could keep an eye on who was coming and going."

He looked from the computer to the door and back to the computer again. "You know, George would have said the exact same thing. Me? All I think about is getting information logged into the computer as fast as possible, so I can begin sifting through the data and making correlations."

I rested my hand on the monitor, "Do you mind if I make you a little safer while you're in here? I kind of feel responsible for your safety."

He picked up a yearbook lying open on the table. "Have at it."

Changing things around was an easy job since all I needed to do was reverse the monitor and wheel his chair around to the other side of the table. "Voila. Now nobody can sneak up on you."

"Who's going to do anything in a library, anyway?"

"You'd be surprised at how many petty thieves target people in places like this." I turned and scanned the tables on the other side of the open door. "A lot of people feel the same way you do. You see the third table down? Some lady left her purse under her chair while she went to get a book. Someone else left their backpack and will be shocked and outraged when he calls us because somebody stole his wallet where he'd put it in the zippered pocket for safe-keeping. Or not just the wallet. Probably the entire backpack."

"Now you really sound like my brother." He set the yearbook back on the table and once more sat at his computer. Pointing a box at his feet that had three books stacked inside, he said, "I got lucky on those three. The high school had already loaded them into an online database. They're doing it as a long-term project so people can go online and check out their classmates. I spoke to the woman in charge of the project. She's a volunteer who relies on other volunteers to scan in the books. It's a slow process, but at least they'd gotten to some of the ones I need and I don't have to enter every single name."

"You're actually making a database of every name in those yearbooks?"

"It's not as daunting as it looks. There's a lot of duplication, and I set the file up so that it lets me know if I begin to enter a duplicate. Plus, I'm impressed with this place. This is a very nice mid-range computer that has dictating capabilities. Watch."

He ran his finger down a list of names in the book. "Okay. Here's one I know I've already entered. He put his fingers to his lips and then said, "Wake up. Thackery, Ran—" The computer dinged, and he said, "Go to sleep." He grinned up at me. "See? I tell the computer to turn on the mic by saying 'wake up,' then I read the name, if it's already in the database, the computer stops me with a ding and automatically erases what I just said."

"Why did you say, 'go to sleep?'"

"Turning the microphone off. As a matter of course, most programs won't automatically erase the unwanted data, but I added a little program that I'll delete once we're finished."

Even though I knew what he'd done was child's play to most programmers, I was still impressed.

"Also, I eliminated all the female teachers and girls, because from what I understand, most arsonists are male?"

"Most of the time, plus I got a good look at the guy from the rear, and I'm almost positive it's a man."

"What do you mean you got a look at him? When? Was there another arson?"

I realized I hadn't filled him in on the Molotov cocktail at my house, so I gave him the bare-bones version of what happened.

"Wow. Thank God you were there to stop the fire when you did. When I was stationed in Livorno, Italy, we had one of those thrown through a plate-glass window of a bar my friend, Eddie, and I were in. Luckily for the bar owner and us, there were six guys from an army fire suppression detail throwing back a few beers, too. Otherwise, that place would have gone up like a Roman candle."

"Damn. I'm glad you were okay. Did you like Italy?"

"I loved it. One aspect of the military I enjoyed was getting to see the world on someone else's dime. And not just see it, either. A lot of soldiers go to a country and rarely leave the base. Me? I went everywhere I could as often as I could. I liked being stationed in a country for a year or more because then I got to know the culture and the people."

"How many countries did you live in?"

Kelly came in as I asked the question. She closed the door behind her and pulled a couple of footlong sandwiches out of her bag. "I didn't know you were gonna be here, Alex, or I would have brought you one, too." Her voice dropped to a conspiratorial whisper. "We're not supposed to have food in here, but when I get my teeth into research, I hate to stop. I'll be happy to split mine with you, though. I can never eat an entire sandwich on my own."

"No, thanks. I'm meeting Casey for lunch in a bit. You go ahead."

She handed Steve a wrapped sub that had "tuna" written on the wrapper. "You were going to tell us where you were stationed around the world. I think that lifestyle is fascinating."

Accepting the proffered sandwich, Steve began listing countries on the fingers of his free hand. "Italy, Germany, Belgium, Nigeria, Korea, Japan, and quite a few others. My friends and family enjoyed it too. I always had people come to visit, and we'd take off and explore the region."

I pointed to the computer screen. "So, I guess it's too early to ask whether you've found anything. How much longer before you can begin the research?"

Both Kelly and Steve chuckled at an inside joke.

197

"What's so funny?"

Kelly swallowed a bit of her sandwich, her bright, blue eyes twinkling with amusement. "We're not just sitting around twiddling our thumbs, Alex. I'm researching people Steve remembers as students who might have ended up in prison instead of college, if you know what I mean. We also have a program running in the background to identify people who might have lived in that neighborhood at the same time as they did. As it comes up with names, I run them through the prison records as well." She tapped the side of her head with a manicured, emerald-green fingernail that perfectly matched the green of her blouse. "It's not all cotton candy up here, ya know."

I returned her smile. "I never doubted it for an instant. I'll leave you to it, then. Call me if you find anything or if you need me to bring you something." I pointed to her sandwich. "I could even smuggle in some dinner, later, if you want me to."

"Oh heavens, no. If anyone's going to break library rules, it had better be me." She waved me out like a farm wife clearing her yard of hens. "Off you go. I'll call if we need you."

As I descended the staircase, a sea of elementary-aged kids swarmed around me as they bounded up the steps.

A middle-aged woman called out from below, "Walk, children. This is a library, not a zoo."

A couple of the kids grinned up at me. One was missing her two front teeth, and when she saw that I'd noticed, she stuck her tongue through the gap and waggled it around. I rolled my eyes at her, which sent her and her friends into fits of laughter. You gotta love kids—as long as they belong to someone else.

I pulled out my phone and called Casey, who answered on the first ring. Without waiting for polite chit chat, she plunged right in, "Hi. Kate said you'd be free. Can you meet me at Mrs. Holloway's house? Kate and I met with Mitch just now, and we realized that since we didn't know about the shovel when we searched the scene, none of us knew we should be looking for one. There's not one in evidence, so Kate wants us to go back and secure it."

I'd reached the underground parking garage and was having a hard time hearing her. "You're breaking up. Did you say we *don't* have the shovel Babe used to bash the guy in the head?"

She spoke slowly like most people do when someone says they have a bad connection. I always wondered about that since talking slower doesn't mean the connection gets any better. "We do not. You and I need to go get it at Mrs. Holloway's house."

"Shit. That's going to cause all kinds of chain of custody issues when the case goes to trial." I pulled out of the garage onto Alameda and then turned south onto Stone Avenue, heading for Mrs. Holloway's house.

"I know. At this point, though, we're more focused on catching and stopping the bastard, so if there's any DNA on it, that'll help. We'll worry about using it as evidence for trial when we get to that point."

She and I pulled up in front of the residence at the same time. The crime scene tape was still up, so hopefully no nice neighbors had gone inside and cleaned up in anticipation of Mrs. Holloway's return. I was surprised to see Casey's girlfriend, Terri Gentry, waiting for us near the front door. Terri usually works uniform patrol on the west side, and Mrs. Holloway lives in Team One on the southside. "I didn't expect to see you here."

Terri seemed distracted when she lifted her chin to greet me. "Hey, Alex. I needed some extra cash, and Team One is having staffing problems. They asked if anyone wanted to work some extra shifts, so here I am." Terri is a muscular woman with short, spiked, honey-blond hair that occasionally falls into her eyes. She shoved her bangs aside and continued, "Anyway, Kate called and said you're missing a shovel? I took a quick look around. I don't see one anywhere."

Casey and I exchanged puzzled looks and Casey started for the front door. "It's gotta be here."

I followed, and Terri fell in behind me.

Casey pulled out a set of keys she must have gotten from Mrs. Holloway. When she put the key in the lock, the door creaked open. She glanced back at Terri with a furrowed brow. "Was the front door unlocked when you got here?"

Terri shook her head, "No, but the backdoor was. I came out the front to wait for you. I thought the backdoor being unlocked was kinda strange, though. Didn't you guys lock up when you left?"

Casey gave her one of those looks married people give their spouses when they say something totally obvious and should have known better. They weren't married, but they'd been living together long enough to have developed the same habits and mannerisms as an old married couple.

Terri ignored the look and asked, "Could Babe have taken it with her without thinking?"

I shook my head. "Of course not." I looked at Casey, "You guys took her straight to the station, didn't you?"

"We took her to the hospital first because she refused to leave Mrs. Holloway until she knew she was going to be okay, but I never saw her with the shovel the whole time we were here."

We went into the living room, and I oriented myself according to what Babe had told Mitch and me during the interview. "Okay, I assume they took the chair he'd tied Mrs. Holloway to for evidence. Can you show me where it was exactly?"

Casey pointed to a spot in the corner. "Over there."

I stepped to where she'd indicated. "So, the suspect must have been standing here, and Babe came up behind him like this. I mimed hitting someone with a shovel. "He had pretty quick reactions because instead of going down, he rammed into her and sent her flying backward. She tripped over a footstool and landed over here?" I looked to Casey for clarification.

"I'm not sure because Babe wouldn't tell us anything. She was too worried about Mrs. Holloway, and then she clammed up until you got to the station. But I do know there was an overturned footstool about here." She stepped to a point near the wall.

We all visually searched the area looking for the shovel. Terri asked, "Kate said it wasn't a big one. More like a smaller, hinged type of thing. I didn't see either kind anywhere."

We turned the place upside down but came away empty-handed. Casey pulled her phone out and muttered, "Kate isn't gonna be happy about this."

Terri and I listened to the one-sided conversation as Casey explained to Kate about the missing shovel and the unlocked backdoor. I heard what sounded like "Duck" coming through the phone and winced right along with Casey. Holding the phone away from her ear, she hit the speaker button so we could all hear what the boss had to say.

Kate continued speaking, "I want you to go over every inch of that house again. Send Terri to search beneath every bush and up every tree in that yard. If you come up empty, I want you and Alex back in the office, understand?"

"Yes, ma'am. We'll go over everything again and call you the second we find it."

"I hope to God you find it. I can't believe someone didn't gather it as evidence yesterday. Who the hell was in charge of the crime scene?"

Casey hesitated, obviously not wanting to get anyone in trouble.

"Never mind. I know exactly who it was." We all winced again when she yelled, "Tony! Get your ass over here, now."

I involuntarily took a step back and whispered, "Thank God it wasn't me."

Kate snarled into the phone, "Just find that damn shovel, Alex."

Casey's home screen popped up when Kate disconnected. Kate was under a lot of pressure from the brass to get this case solved, and the fact that a crucial piece of evidence had gone missing wasn't going to be taken lightly by anyone concerned. The three of us blinked stupidly at each other before Terri headed outside, and Casey and I began to search the home for the second time with renewed determination. We all understood Kate's short temper these days, but it didn't make it any easier to live with.

Unfortunately, we came up empty-handed again, so Casey and I decided to head for the station while Terri locked up the house. She also needed to resecure the garden shed she'd pried open on the off-chance the shovel had somehow ended up put away where it would logically belong. We'd offered to help, but she waved us away, saying, "You guys need to concentrate on catching this coward before he strikes again. This is the least I can do to free up your time."

We'd thanked her and left her to it.

CHAPTER 14

Casey drove straight to the station, but we agreed I'd stop to grab a couple of burgers since we knew with the mood Kate was in, taking a leisurely lunch was out of the question. She would push herself harder than anyone in the brass ever could, and since we had her back—would always have her back—we'd push ourselves just as hard.

I quickly went through the drive through and headed for the station. I pulled into the parking garage, grabbed the bag of burgers and headed for the elevators. When the doors opened, I groaned inwardly. One of my arch-enemies, Lieutenant Paxton, was standing inside next to the call buttons. He and I have a hate-detest relationship. He hates me, I detest him. Pretty straight forward.

I thought about waiting for the next ride but decided I wasn't about to let his presence dictate my actions. I stepped on and moved as far away from him as I could. The third-floor button was already lit, so I leaned against the back wall and waited while the doors closed.

He had a wicked gleam in his eyes when he leaned toward me and said, "I'm waiting for you to screw up on this one,

Wolfe. They want this guy bad, which means Kate wants it bad, which means you'll do anything to make her happy. You're already a dirty cop, so we both know just how far you'll go to please her, don't we? You think you have carte blanche to," he held up two fingers in a quotation mark, "do whatever it takes. Well, you just go right ahead and do what it takes."

His crocodile smile sent chills down my spine, but I remembered Kate's lesson during the narcotics board. I also remembered her warning when she'd spoken to Casey and me the other day.

The doors opened onto the second floor and Chief Sepe stepped in.

When the doors closed, I said, "I think you're the only one on the department, Lieutenant, who wants to catch me out more than you want to catch the arsonist."

Sepe blinked at me, then turned his attention to Paxton, who spluttered, "I have no idea what she's talking about, Sir."

When the doors finally opened on the third floor, I waited for the two of them to get out and then followed. I glared at Paxton's fat back as he licked Chief Sepe's boots as they walked down the hall.

"What's the matter, Alex?"

Kate's voice startled me, and when I turned, a thundercloud still roiled in my gut. "Nothing."

I started for our office, and she pulled me up short. Taking my elbow, she turned me so we were facing each other. "Right now, I need you and all the detectives on their best game. I know you. You'll stew on whatever he said instead of concentrating on the case until you get it off your chest. So, spill."

I pointed in the direction Paxton had gone. "That shithead is more interested in catching me doing something illegal than he is in finding the arsonist."

Her eyes narrowed, "First, don't let me ever hear you call a member of the command staff a shithead."

I growled and rolled my eyes. "Fine."

"And second..." She stopped and raised her eyebrows as though waiting for me to finish the sentence.

I thought a minute and then realized what she meant. I parroted her earlier words back to her. "Second, we stay within the confines of the law, no matter what."

"That's right. You don't need to worry about Lt. Paxton waiting for you to step outside the law because we agreed that wasn't going to happen. The chief knows what kind of a person the lieutenant is, and you don't need to worry about what he's saying about you."

"I don't care what he says about me to anyone. He's not worth the effort."

"Exactly. Did you find the shovel?"

The abrupt change of topic caught me off guard, and I had to regroup a second before I answered. In the meantime, we continued down the hallway to our office. "No. And we looked everywhere."

Someone had propped open the office door, and when Casey saw us, she came to join us. We all took seats inside Kate's cubicle and I handed Casey a burger. I pulled out another one for Kate, who waved it away. "No thanks. I know you must be hungry and—"

"I got this one for you. Mine's still in the bag. I knew you wouldn't eat unless we made you, so take it."

The pleased expression that flitted across her face told me I'd been right. Nobody had thought to buy her lunch, and she wouldn't take the time out to get something. She accepted the burger, set it on her desk, and said, "I'll be right back."

While she was gone, I opened three napkins and set one on the desk close to her chair, one on the corner closest to

Casey, and the third I put in front of me and then poured an equal amount of fries onto each one.

When Kate returned, she had three cans of soda which she also set on her desk.

Casey took one and popped the top. "Thanks, Boss."

I took the other and did the same. It was nice to sit in amiable silence while we ate instead of jumping right into the latest updates about the case. Several years earlier, I'd worked another brutally intense case where a seven-year-old girl had been kidnapped and murdered. In those types of cases, tension builds, and tempers flare, and I found that sometimes you just need to decompress before plunging back into the fray.

Kate had also been on that case, but she hadn't been my sergeant at the time. I remember wishing she had been because she was so knowledgeable about every aspect of working such a high-profile case. I'd learned an enormous amount from her during that time. I was still learning from her to this day.

When she finished eating, Kate rolled up the wrapper and tossed it in the can next to her desk. She pulled in a deep breath and spoke while she exhaled, "Okay. Alex said you guys didn't find the shovel. There are only two possibilities for why it wasn't there. One, it was never there in the first place, and Babe was making the whole thing up about springing to the rescue." She looked from Casey to me to see how that sat with us.

Casey indicated me with a lift of her hand. "Alex has had more contact with her than me."

My first reaction was complete denial, but since Kate had brought it up, I chewed on the idea a minute. "No. I don't think so. I believe her."

Kate also took a moment to think. "And two, someone other than the police took the shovel."

Casey sat forward. "I'm more inclined to go with that because when Terri first got to the house, you know, before we got there, she walked around back to search and found the backdoor unlocked."

Kate's focus sharpened, and Casey held up a hand. "I personally locked that door. I will stand up in court and raise my right hand and swear there is zero chance that back door was unlocked when we left the house."

The implications of that statement flew through my mind and sent a chill down my spine. I didn't want to say what I was thinking, but judging by Kate's stiff posture, I wouldn't have to.

She leaned back in her chair, crossed her arms, and began tapping her bicep. "How would he know we hadn't collected the shovel? Was anything else disturbed that you could see?"

Casey shook her head, "No, ma'am. As far as I could tell, nothing had been disturbed from the way we left it."

"Meaning he went back specifically to grab the shovel. Our leak is getting bigger, and that's beginning to piss me off." Kate rose and headed out of her cubicle. "I need to let the lieutenant know about the latest."

Casey and I exchanged glances. We knew what happened when Kate got pissed and both of us were relieved not to be on the receiving end of her anger. Taking her departure as a dismissal, we returned to our desks to do some administrative follow-up.

The leak bothered me, and I needed to think. When I want to sort through the jumble of facts in my head, my go-to activity is to perform mindless tasks that take up zero mental activity while still accomplishing a job that needs to get done.

I hadn't looked at the random pictures I'd snapped at the crime scene, so I picked up my phone, scrolled through and deleted inadvertent photos of my finger, my shoe, and the pavement. Then I put the rest into a folder and emailed them to myself. I opened my email on the computer and waited for the file to appear. When it did, I downloaded the photos, and as I routinely do with miscellaneous crime scene snapshots, I set them to randomly scroll through on my screensaver.

I happened to glance up to see Burney Macon wander in and head to his desk, which was across the room in the Child Abuse section of our bullpen. Earlier, I'd overheard Kate tell him to research whether there were similar cases from other jurisdictions, so I wandered over to see what he'd discovered. "Hey, Burney, have—"

He looked up from the massive ham and cheese sandwich he'd just unwrapped and interrupted me before I could ask my question. "Hey, Alex." He shoved a quarter of the sandwich into his mouth, closed his eyes, and groaned. It was no secret he enjoyed eating better than anything else in the world. Watching him eat was like watching a bear scratch his back against a tree. He always derives pure pleasure from the experience no matter what the food, no matter what the occasion.

Not wanting to interrupt the apparently orgasmic experience, I waited until his eyes reopened and focused on me. "Whatcha need?"

He started to put the second half in his mouth, but I put my finger on his arm to stop him. "Did you have any luck finding cases with similar MOs to ours?"

"Not yet. I'm still waiting on Interpol, but they said they have at least a three-week backlog, so I'm not holding my breath."

In went the sandwich and since I didn't want to completely destroy his bonding time with the ham and cheese, I thanked him and started back to my desk.

"Oh!" He held up a finger, and I felt guilty that he had to chew quickly in order to tell me what he wanted to say. He picked up a paper and held it out. "This came up when I did a computer search. I have no idea what it says, but maybe you can find somebody who speaks German."

I took the paper and saw what he meant. It appeared to be some kind of article from a German newspaper called, Die Welt. I thought a minute and then called over to Casey. "Hey, Case. I'll be right back."

She was on the phone and raised a hand in acknowledgment.

"Thanks, Burney."

Part of the sandwich had just disappeared. He also raised a hand, only his was a 'you're welcome' instead of an 'okay.'"

I headed out to the hallway where I passed two closed doors before finally coming to the Aggravated Assault unit. I stepped inside and found the secretary, Carla Schmitt squinting at her computer screen. I used to work in Aggravated Assault, and since Carla and I were the only women in the unit, we frequently bonded over drinks after work. She was a second-generation immigrant and had grown up in a German-speaking household. Both sets of grandparents had lived with her growing up, and she spoke the language fluently.

She looked up from her computer when I walked in. "Hey, Alex. Long time no see. We need to catch up once you guys finish up with the Coward case. You any closer to catching him? My mom's moved in with me until you guys find him. She's been nervous being alone ever since my dad died, but now with these Coward cases, she's terrified." Carla had a slight case of what I like to call diarrhea of the mouth. Once she gets started, it's hard to get a word in edgewise.

"We're working overtime on it. In fact, that's why I'm here. Can you tell me what this says?"

She took the paper and held it directly beneath a small lamp sitting on the corner of her desk. She tucked her black curls behind her ear and adjusted the coke bottle glasses perched on the bridge of her nose.

She was practically blind, and I'd once asked her why she'd chosen to be an administrative assistant when a significant portion of her work was reading case files and transcribing interviews. She'd said, "There aren't many jobs out there for people with 20/400 eyesight, Alex. I had to take what I could get. Captain Mueller was a friend of my family, and when he offered me the job, I jumped at the chance."

She angled the paper this way and that until the light shown to the best advantage. After a moment, she began to translate. "Let's see. It's talking about...oh my!" She looked up at me in surprise. "You think this is connected to the Coward?"

"I don't know, I can't read German, so I have no clue what it says." I smiled to take any bite out of my words. "I was hoping you could tell me."

"Well, it says, and I quote 'a hideous crime was committed in Kiel yesterday. Eighty-three-year-old Yetta Goldberg was found deceased in her bed late last night. Police and fire investigators suspect arson was involved, as some type of accelerant was used to burn the body and the surrounding room. Firefighters arrived to contain the blaze but were only able to save part of the house. According to fire Captain Michael Turnbeck, 'The blaze burned hot, hotter than you'd expect to see in this type of fire. We see a pattern where an accelerant was poured around the body and also around the perimeter of the bedroom walls.'"

She stopped speaking but continued to silently read the article. She finished and then took her glasses off and rubbed her tired eyes. "The rest is only talking about how the paper doesn't know any more details and how more information will come in later editions. Would you like me to transcribe this for you? I can have it done in, oh, probably a half an hour."

"Yes, please, that would be great. Where in Germany did you say it happened?" I pulled out my notebook, ready to write down what she told me.

"In Kiel. I believe that's a smaller city in the state of," she returned her glasses to her face and peered down at the paper again. "Schleswig-Holstein. That's up in the northern part of Germany. I believe it's above even Hamburg, but you'd have to check on that."

"And what's the date?"

"Let's see... October 22, 2013."

"Thanks a bunch. This might be really important, and I'd definitely appreciate a transcript."

"I'll move this to the top of the pile."

I thanked her and returned to the office. My mind was churning in a dozen different directions, but one thing was certain. I needed to know if any other countries had had the same type of incidents, and I couldn't wait the three weeks that Interpol said it would take before they could get to it. I pulled out my cell phone and called Kelly.

"Hey Alex, nothing new to report yet."

"Kelly, you have an office somewhere there in the library, don't you?"

"I do."

"Can I meet you there in, say," I lowered my cellphone to check the time, then put it back to my ear. "Twenty minutes? Just you."

"Of course. I'll meet you there."

To my relief, she neither sounded suspicious nor did she question my request. I'd been worried that if she had, Steve might wonder what was going on. To be perfectly honest, I had no idea what was going on. I was simply following up on a lead and had no idea where it would take me. But the little gnome on my shoulder was quietly tugging at my hair, and I'd decided to compartmentalize my investigation. I would get and give out the information on a need-to-know basis, especially since Kate believed someone on the inside was leaking information.

Twenty-five minutes later, I walked into the library and asked the person at the information desk where I might find Kelly's office. The young college-age woman, with jet black hair and dark makeup around her eyes and lips, smiled and said, "She's right over here. C'mon. I'll take you to her. You can't get there on your own." She looked over her shoulder and called out to an elderly gentleman also staffing the desk. "I'll be back in a second, Andrew."

He acknowledged her with a nod and a wave as the girl swished out from behind the counter. There was no better way to describe her walk; her hips swished so far to the right and so far to the left, I was sure she was going to have back problems later in life. She walked through the back hallways snapping her gum so loud the sound echoed off the walls. After several right and left turns and a couple of locked doors, we ended up at the entrance to Kelly's office.

Kelly smiled at my guide, "Thank you so much, Krista."

Krista eagerly looked between Kelly and me, obviously expecting to be invited to wait so that she could lead me back out to the front lobby. I guessed that just about anything would be more interesting to her than staffing the information desk with eighty-year-old Andrew.

Kelly casually walked to her door and rested a hand on the knob, politely sending the hint that she and I needed our privacy. "I can escort Detective Wolfe back to the lobby. Thanks again."

Krista's eyes fastened on me at the word detective. Apparently, she hadn't noticed my badge and gun before now because she said enthusiastically, "Oh! I didn't realize you were a detective." She batted her eyes at Kelly, although what she expected to accomplish with that I had no clue. "That's okay, Mrs. Bruster. I don't mind waiting." She made as though to step into the room, and Kelly stepped forward and swung the door partially closed.

I don't know how Kelly could have been clearer about wanting the other woman to leave, and when Krista hesitated again, Kelly put her hand on her hip and glared.

Krista finally got the idea, and I had to smile at her surprised chirp as Kelly shut the door in her face.

Kelly turned and rolled her eyes. "Krista is an enthusiastic volunteer, and I don't want to discourage her, but on the other hand, she's not one to readily take a hint. Anyway, take a seat, and you can tell me what it is you wanted."

Before I sat, I walked to the door, pulled it open and looked left and right to make sure Krista really had disappeared. Satisfied, I re-closed the door and sat in a surprisingly comfortable, round-backed chair.

Kelly pulled out another one from the corner and sat in that instead of taking the chair behind her desk. She crossed her legs and leaned forward, putting her elbows on her knees and looking at me expectantly.

"What I'm about to ask you to do needs to stay only between us. And I mean you can't tell your husband, you can't tell your friends, and you can't tell Steve. Do you think you can do that?" I knew I didn't need to add that last, but I wanted to emphasize the point, and I also wanted her to buy-in to the secrecy.

"Of course, you know I can, Alex. I understand confidentiality, and if I can do anything that will help catch the Coward, you can count on me."

Out of habit, I pulled out my notebook and held it in my lap. "One of our detectives tried to get the information I need from Interpol, but they have a three-week backlog, and I need the information sooner than that."

"Oh, my goodness, yes, you do. I'm not sure I can get the

kinds of information they have access to, but I'll do what I can." Her brows came down low as though she'd just now registered what I'd previously said. "You said you don't want me to let Steve know. You're talking about the Steve that you have doing research upstairs right now?"

I smiled at her, "Yes, I think that's the only Steve you and I have in common."

Her demeanor turned more serious than I've ever seen before. Her eyebrows descended and she nodded for me to continue.

"I need you to search for a particular set of parameters."

She stood and grabbed a notebook from the top of her desk, and then leaned over, opened the long drawer on the other side and grabbed a pen. She sat back down with her pen poised and ready to take notes. That was something I valued about her. When I ask her to do a specific task, she makes sure she understands the job before proceeding.

"The details I'm about to give you are not for public dissemination. Some of them haven't been released and *cannot be* released to the public. I need you to do a worldwide search for arsons involving people between the ages of sixty and one hundred or older, where an accelerant was used on the body and around the room, and where," I looked into her eyes, "this is a grisly detail. Are you okay with that?"

Without hesitation, she said, "Absolutely, Alex. I meant it when I said I would do anything to help stop this Coward."

"Okay then, arsons where the suspect removes the eyes of the victim and places candles within the eye socket. The candles are used as a delay device to allow the suspect to leave the scene before the fire starts."

To my relief, her brows drew together and, although she started to write that last bit down, she stopped and looked up at me. "I think I won't write down that last part because I know that's the information you haven't released to the public. I would hate to have my notes somehow read by," she flicked her eyes to the door, "enthusiastic volunteers who might not keep their mouths shut."

I looked at this woman who had become one of my most valuable assistants over the last couple of years. "I can't believe you never became a detective. You have an instinct for the work. Did you ever consider becoming a police officer?"

She blushed at the praise and shook her head. "All I ever wanted to be from the moment my mother began reading to me was a librarian. Words opened adventures and new lands and new creatures to me. My dream job has always been to pass along my love of reading to other people." She checked her watch and then stood, "It's about time for us to begin closing down the library. We close at five today, and I need to help make sure everyone is out by then. I also need to let Steve know that we're done for the day, and that he can come back in the morning and start again."

I agreed and followed her down the hall. Just as the two of us stepped from one of the back corridors into the front lobby, a bell dinged, and a recording informed everyone it was time to leave. I stopped her with a tap on her shoulder, "I need to go upstairs to see if Steve needs help packing everything up, so I'll let him know it's closing time. Does he need to take the yearbooks home with him? Or can he leave them here until tomorrow morning?"

"Oh, he's more than welcome to leave them here. I can lock the door and put a sign on it to make sure the janitors don't go in to clean."

I climbed the stairs two at a time and went in to see where Steve was with his research. Various papers were scattered about, and he was taking a moment to gather them into specific piles. He stacked each pile one on top of the other and placed them inside his briefcase. "Kelly said to tell you that you can leave the books here in the box, and she'll lock the door and put a sign on the door to make sure the janitors don't clean."

He nodded amiably. "That'll be great. Yearbooks are damn heavy, and I wasn't looking forward to carting them back and forth every morning and evening. I only have a couple more to go through before I'm finished with this part." He held up a thumb drive. "I put everything on here and then wiped my work from the computer. I don't want anybody having access to what I'm doing, and if it's on the library system, it would be pretty easy to get. They really need to work on their internet security."

I hadn't thought of that, but I'm glad he had. "Did that program you had running give you very many names of people who lived in your neighborhood at the same time you did?"

"Already entered into my database. It was like a walk down memory lane. So many names of people I'd forgotten. There were quite a few friends I'd kinda like to get back together with, you know, chug a few beers for old time's sake."

"And you're going to cross-reference them against..."

"Well, the California Department of Corrections has an excellent database of past and present prisoners. I thought I'd start there and try to figure out a way to access the nationwide databases later. Tonight, when I get home, I'm going to cross-check the two lists to see how many or if any of our old neighbors ended up in prison. If they did, I'm going to check what they were in for. Wouldn't it be great if I found an arsonist among them?"

"If only we could be that lucky..." I pulled out a business card and wrote down my email address. I handed it to him and said, "Would you send that list to me, please? I mean the list with the names of your neighbors. I don't need all of the yearbook names yet. I can have our analyst run the names through NCIC and see if we get a hit."

"NCIC?"

"The National Crime Information Center. It's a computerized index of criminal justice information. It's a database of criminals and crime nationwide. We can run a name through it to see if the person we're holding is a fugitive or a missing person or whether property we have has been stolen from somewhere. There's a whole lot more, but you get the idea."

He almost looked disappointed that I had access to something that could run his names through a nationwide system. I hated to take away his thunder, but I didn't want to waste time waiting for him to figure out how to do it himself.

I called Kelly and told her we were ready to leave. She came upstairs, turned off the lights and locked the door. She'd already written a do not disturb sign which she taped to the door. "There we go. That'll keep anybody out of there who doesn't belong. I know the janitors will enjoy getting a break from having to clean and vacuum the room."

The lights began to flick off as we made our way down the stairs. One of the male librarians was stationed at the front door, letting people out and making sure no one else entered. I turned to Kelly and said, "Thanks for everything, and I'll hopefully see you in the morning." Then I turned to Steve, "Come on, I think we're both parked in the parking garage. I'll walk you out."

When Steve and I were alone in the garage, I casually asked, "I can't remember, were you ever stationed in Germany?"

"Yeah, I taught at the NATO School in Oberammergau. Why?"

"Because my grandfather's family is from there and it's somewhere I've always wanted to go. I guess I'm just jealous of all your travels. Anyway, this is my car. You'll be back in the morning?"

"I'm meeting Kelly at nine."

"I'll see you sometime tomorrow, then."

On the way out of the garage, I called Kate to see if we were pulling another late night.

"No, I think we all need to get a good night's sleep. I'm tempted to put a guard outside your house in case the Coward comes back."

"Don't bother. Megan has already decided to come over, and we're gonna take our sleeping bags up on my roof and sleep up there. It's nice and flat, and there's a short wall that runs around the perimeter to keep us from sliding off. I think if anybody tries to sneak up on us, the dogs will hear it and let us know."

The line was quiet a moment, and then Kate chuckled, "Well, I guess it's a perfect time of year for it. Make sure you bring your phone with you. Good night Alex. Stay safe."

"Good night, boss. You, too."

CHAPTER 15

As soon as I got home, I called Jerry, who answered his phone on the fifth ring. "Alex, can you give me five minutes to call you back?"

"Sure thing, I'll be waiting for your call." I did a lot of doodling and thinking during the fifteen minutes it took for him to call me back. Unfortunately, when he did call back, I'd just popped a piece of toast in my mouth. About all I managed was a muffled, "Hey, there."

"Sorry about that Alex, what can I do for you?"

I swallowed quickly and asked, "What? No foreplay?"

"I've been busy."

"Then I won't take up much of your time. I know you were in the special forces, and I was wondering whether you still have any contacts in the military, maybe among the intelligence community?"

He was quiet a minute before answering. "I do. Why?"

Did I really want to open this can of worms? I was working off a hunch, and I didn't want to start something I couldn't stuff back in the can if it became necessary. "Look, Jerry, this needs to be kept on the down-low. Only between you and me and the person you trust to confidentially give you what I need. The person I'm going to ask you to find information on cannot know that you're looking for the information. Do you think that's possible?"

Again, he didn't answer right away. I appreciated him taking what I'd said seriously enough to think about his answer. If he felt he couldn't do what I was asking, I'd rather he say so now.

"I have a guy in mind. Tell me what you need, and I'll tell you whether it's possible."

"I'm working on nothing more than a hunch right now. No, that's not true. I'm actually grasping at straws. I need to know all of the places Stephen Grate was stationed during his stint in the army."

"Hmm. That might be hard since he was Intel. You peggin' him for the Coward?"

"No. He and his brother are helping with the case, and for reasons I can't tell you right now, I need to know."

"I'll tell you what. I know a guy who's still workin' Intel. Maybe he can get the info without leavin' a paper trail."

Butterflies started in my stomach as it began to dawn on me just how serious a request this might be. "Am I...are we..."

"Violating federal confidentiality laws by asking for the info? I'll find out, and if we are, we won't do it. But I don't think asking where a guy was stationed would violate anything. Leave it to me."

As quickly as he'd begun the conversation, he was gone.

Around seven, Megan showed up with a couple of steaks and a half-gallon of ice cream that went straight into the freezer. I'd recently bought a new grill, and this would be the second time using it. The first time around, I'd burned the burgers, so this time Megan was going to try her hand at it. The grill wasn't a fancy model; it was the kind that still used briquettes. The salesman tried to talk me into the propane model, but I had good memories of my dad fighting with the charcoal, and besides, it seemed easier to add smoky flavored chips to the charcoal than into the propane gas.

I bought one of those metal towers that you put all of your coals in all at once because the guy at the store said it makes it easier to get them going, and he was right. I'd started them about a half-hour before Megan arrived, and the grill was nice and hot. I divided the coals into two separate piles, one on each side of the grill.

Megan pulled a Ziploc bag out of the bigger paper bag and held it up to me. "TaDa! I've been marinating them all day."

"Since when do you know how to marinate?"

She shook the contents back and forth to make sure the juices evenly coated the meat. "Just because all your meals are take-out, Alex doesn't mean the rest of us don't know how to cook."

"I've lived with you my entire life; I know exactly how much you cook. So where did you learn how to marinate, and what did you put in the marinade?"

"Oh, ye of little faith. It was super easy. I added Guinness stout, onions, soy sauce, brown sugar, sesame oil, and minced garlic. Piece of cake." She reached into the bag with two fingers and gingerly pulled out a massive, dripping steak. She lay that on the grill and then pulled out another.

"God, Megs, those are huge. How much did you spend on these things?"

"They were having a half-off sale at that extension center on Campbell. You know the one where they sell meat and stuff? These were a ganga. Besides, didn't your mama teach you it's rude to ask people how much they spent on something?"

Since my mouth was already watering, I didn't argue. "Well, I have some potatoes boiling on the stove, and I bought some asparagus that I thought would go well with this. Do you know how to cook asparagus?"

"Yes, but since the steak costs more than asparagus, I think it'd be better if you ruined the asparagus instead of ruining the steak, don't you?"

"Good point." I went back into the kitchen, where the potato water was boiling over. I wasn't particularly surprised; I was, however, surprised it hadn't put out the flame on the gas burner yet. That tended to happen to me a lot. It was a miracle I didn't have brain damage from all the gas fumes I'd breathed in over the years. I dumped a little bit of the water out so it wouldn't boil over and put it back on the burner.

Then I grabbed my phone and called Casey. "Hey, Case, it's me. Is Terri there?"

"Yeah, just a second, I'll get her."

It wasn't long before Terri came online. "Alex, what's up?"

"Do you know how to cook asparagus?" That was kind of a rhetorical question since Terri was practically a gourmet cook. She could cook anything and make it taste wonderful.

"It's easy, Alex. Even you can do it. Do you have something to write this down? Because well..."

I didn't think cooking asparagus could be that difficult. "Do I really need to write it down?" That kinda worried me because following directions has never been my forte.

She laughed. "No, Alex, I was kidding. Just preheat your frying pan, lightly coat your asparagus spears in olive oil, season with salt and pepper to taste, and then grill them for two to three minutes. Make sure you turn them as they cook. Just roll them back and forth in the pan. That's the easiest recipe I know, and I think even you can do it without messing it up." She put an unnecessary, melodramatic flair in her words, "I have faith in you, Alex. Just don't get distracted like you usually do. If you get distracted and let them cook too long, you'll have a slimy mess."

"Two to three minutes? You gotta be kidding me. You are kidding me, right? It can't be that easy."

"It's easy for the rest of us, Alex; for you, it might be a challenge. Enjoy!"

She ended the call, and I stuck my head out the door and yelled to Megan, "How long's it gonna take you to cook the steaks?"

"Well, since we both like our steaks medium rare, not long."

I went back inside to grab the potatoes, strained them, and mashed them up. I added butter and salt and pepper—another recipe I could handle just fine, thank you very much. Then I grabbed my frying pan, oiled the asparagus, threw in some salt-and-pepper, and went to town. Lo and behold, it was just as easy as Terri said it would be.

Before long, Megan and I were sitting out in my backyard at my little picnic table enjoying a steak dinner with mashed potatoes and asparagus. I swallowed a particularly juicy piece and asked, "Why don't we do this more often? Usually, it's just pizza or chicken or Chinese or hamburger. Believe it or not," I picked up an asparagus stalk and waved it at her, "This was pretty darn easy, and they taste incredible. I could swear Terri was the one who cooked them."

"Shoot, Alex, you know I'd eat steak every night of the week if we could. I brought my sleeping bag. You have yours?"

"Yeah, and as soon as we're finished, we can throw them up on the roof and get ready for bed."

"So, I've been thinking," Megan popped a piece of steak in her mouth and continued talking, "What if the Coward takes down our ladder and then sets the house on fire? I think we'd be up shit's creek then, don't you?"

"I already thought of that. On the way home, I stopped by Jerry's and picked up his portable fire escape ladder." I went over to the side of the house and hefted the oblong roll of ladder rungs that you could pretty much carry under your arm. "See, you just hook this part over the edge and roll the rest down."

"And what if he's standing down there and won't let us down?"

"Then I shoot him."

"Oh yeah! I always forget about that."

We could each only finish half of our steaks, so Megan cut a little bit off hers and used it to train the three dogs in basic obedience commands. Her Labrador retriever, Sugar, was so well-trained she could have given the commands to the other two dogs as easily as Megan. Tessa and Jynx knew the commands pretty well, but they sure did them fast when they found out the steak was the treat.

Megan had brought along a tent, which I didn't think we needed because we don't have dew here in Tucson, but I helped set it up since she'd bothered to bring it. I shouldered the portable fire escape ladder and took it topside. Then she handed me little Jynx, who was easy to carry up and deposit on the roof. Then came Tessa and finally Sugar, who wasn't quite as easy as the other two. She's so intelligent, though, that she kind of climbed the stairs ahead of me, and I just pushed from behind.

I wasn't sure how we'd get her down until Megan disappeared around the front of the house. I walked to that side of the roof, looked down, and watched her open her trunk. She pulled out a large rope with a harness attached. That would certainly make matters easier as far as getting Sugar down and probably Tessa too.

Her hiking boots clanged as she climbed up the ladder, and I was surprised to see the half-gallon of ice cream pop up over the edge before her head made an appearance. Then two bowls clattered onto the roof, and finally, the rest of her clambered over. She held two spoons clutched between her teeth and the rope and harness slung over her shoulder.

As is the case when we're camping, we had very little to entertain ourselves once the sun went down. I hung a portable gas lamp from the tent's center pole, and we played poker and gin rummy until we were both tired enough to sleep.

Sometime around midnight, Megan poked me in the shoulder. "Alex. Wake up."

I came instantly awake, feeling for the Glock I'd left next to my sleeping bag. "What? Did you hear something?" That seemed unlikely since the dogs were sleeping peacefully on top of our sleeping bags.

"I have to go pee."

I blinked at her. "You woke me up because you have to go pee?" Grumbling, I lay back down and pulled the sleeping bag over my head.

"I'm scared to go down by myself. You have to go with me."

I ignored her until I heard, "Fine," and the unzipping of the tent flap.

I sat up just as her hind end disappeared out the opening. "Fine, what?" I didn't trust her "fine."

"I'm gonna do it in the corner of your roof."

There was no doubt in my mind she'd pee, or worse, in the corner, and I shot out of the tent after her. "You can't pee on my roof. What's the matter with you?"

"I told you I have to go, and I don't want to go down by myself, so I'm gonna go right here."

She pulled down her sweatpants, and I pulled them right back up. "You will not." I put my hands on my hips and glared at her before giving in. "Oh, fine. Let's go." Going down a ladder in the dark is a lot different than going down in the daylight. Halfway down, I looked up to see a blob of white, which I knew was Tessa's white head poking over the two-foot wall that ran the entire circumference of my roof. I hurried back up and put my hand on her collar. "Stay here, Tessa. Megan, I can't leave the dogs up here. I'm worried they're gonna jump after us."

"That's okay. I'm done."

"What? How'd you get in the house with the door locked?"

She began climbing up after me. "I didn't."

"You peed in my yard?"

"Don't be so sanctimonious, Alex. The dogs do it all the time. Move."

I climbed over the edge, and she followed. "I don't believe you. You could have just asked for the key, which I have right here, by the way." I jangled the keys in her face.

"It's all good. Go back to sleep." With that, she climbed into the tent and was asleep before I settled into my sleeping bag.

I'm happy to report that other than Megan's peeing in my backyard, the night was completely uneventful. We probably hadn't needed to sleep on the roof. One thing I learned, though, is that the sun is a great alarm clock. We were up and moving around by five AM. Getting the dogs down turned out to be a piece of cake with the rope and harness.

Megan had taught Sugar how to ride in a harness a few years ago because she enjoys hiking, and she wanted Sugar to be able to go with her no matter where she hiked. Once I had Sugar in the harness, I double-checked all of the fastenings and very slowly lowered her down into Megan's waiting arms. I gave her some slack on the rope and called down to her, "Maybe I should get Tessa a harness too."

She set Sugar on the ground and began unfastening the harness. "I'd love for you guys to come hiking with me more often, but you never seem to have time off from work. You're always working this case or that..."

"You're starting to sound like the wives of some of the guys I work with. But when this Coward case is over, let's take a camping trip somewhere. I want to get away from dead bodies and frightened people and just enjoy nature. Life's too short to be spending all my time rounding up assholes only to have two more take their place."

Megan slung the harness over her shoulder and climbed back up to the edge of the roof. "Wow, you're getting pretty philosophical on me. Is this case wearing on you?" She handed me the harness and headed back down the ladder.

I called Tessa over and buckled her in. I spoke quietly to her before lifting her over the edge. She was calmer about the whole experience than I expected. As I slowly lowered her down, I considered what Megan had said, "I think it's wearing on all of us. Every time there's a new victim, I feel like I'm personally responsible because I haven't caught the bastard. I have people coming up to me every day telling me how their parents have moved in with them or how their next-door neighbor is too afraid to even come out of the house, how they're having to do the grocery shopping for them or bring in their mail. So yes, this case is wearing on me more than usual."

Once she'd unbuckled Tessa, I hauled the harness back up on the end of the rope. I could have done it last time, but I think Megan just enjoys climbing ladders. I called down to her, "Come on up. We can roll up our sleeping bags and take down the tent."

The sun had just popped over the edge of the roof, and she shaded her eyes with her hand as she looked up at me. "Oh hell no. I'm coming over here to sleep every night until you catch the bastard. You think I'd let you be here all alone after what he did to you? Just get down here, and when you get home tonight, call me, and I'll come over." She rubbed her backside. "Only this time, I'm bringing my memory foam mattress. It's queen-size, so it's big enough for both of us. Your roof is hard."

"That's a good thing." We ate a leisurely breakfast, and by the time I watched her drive away, it was still only six-thirty. I never have extra time in the mornings. Usually, I wake up at eight-thirty and have to be in the office by nine. I jump in the shower, throw on some clothes, and race to the office.

This was the first morning I'd had a chance to have a nice long shower. It was only seven o'clock by the time I was toweling dry, so I grabbed my clean clothes out of the dryer and ran the iron over them. I put on my chinos and my Tucson Police Department Polo shirt, shut my bedroom door, and admired myself in the full-length mirror attached to the back of the door. Not bad, not bad at all.

The pups were so excited about an early morning walk that I thought I'd try to get them out at this time of the day more often. After a good two miles in the crisp morning air, we slowly ambled our way back to the house. I fed them and settled them in with their toys. Kneeling next to their bed, I watched them a moment. They were so loving, and their beautiful brown eyes so trusting. I ran my fingers through their soft coats and wondered why people couldn't be as uncomplicated and happy as the other members of the animal kingdom.

An unbidden picture of a lioness bringing down her prey played like a movie through my mind. I looked into the eyes of the gazelle and knew that the terror she was feeling mirrored the terror coursing through our city. And I suddenly understood that the difference between the lioness and the Coward is that the lioness doesn't kill because she enjoys the fear she engenders. Not the way the Coward does. I needed to stop seeing the Coward as pure predator.

Natural predators, I understood.

The twisted ones were different. Unnatural. Until I understood *those* differences, felt them, and grappled with the truth of them, I'd be picking up the detritus the Coward leaves behind instead of stalking him as my prey.

CHAPTER 16

I followed Kate into the underground garage and parked next to her. When I got out, she stood next to her car staring at me. I held my hands out to my side. "What?"

She looked at her watch and then back at me. "It's only eight-thirty. What are you doing here? You're usually skidding into the office at nine o'clock sharp. And whose clothes are you wearing?" She came over and tugged on the crease in my chinos.

I shrugged, "I had some extra time this morning because the sun came up at five, and we couldn't sleep anymore, so we got up."

"Oh yeah, how did it go sleeping up on the roof? Any birds leave a present on your forehead?"

I twisted around to stretch my back. "It was really uncomfortable, and the roof was hard. But Megan is bringing a memory foam mattress tonight. That should make it a lot better."

"You're going to do it again tonight? You know you can come sleep with Thom and me until we catch the Coward. We have an extra bedroom, and you'd be welcome."

"Right. You mean along with Tessa and Jynx?"

"Oh yeah, I forgot about them. Do you think maybe Megan could keep them?"

"No, Megan's coming over again tonight. We'll be fine. I kinda like sleeping out except for the hard roof. But it should be better this time. We grilled steaks and had a nice dinner, and we'll probably do something like that again tonight." As we talked, we made our way down the ramp to the elevator. The doors opened, and who do we find standing there? Asshole Paxton again. Just my luck.

Kate turned and gave me a meaningful look before stepping onto the elevator. I followed and moved to the very back, making sure Kate was between me and the asshole.

He was oh so smarmy polite to her. "Rested and ready to tackle the case again today, Kate? I know you've been putting a lot of extra time on this case, and I have every confidence that you and your team," he looked over her head at me and sneered, "will catch the Coward very soon."

Kate tilted her head back to look into his eyes. "I sure hope so." The doors opened, several more people got in, and thankfully, Paxton got out.

I mumbled, "Good riddance to bad rubbish."

Someone at the front said, "Amen to that."

Kate lowered her head and put a hand to her mouth to cover her smile.

The doors opened on the third floor, and everyone but me got out. Kate glanced over her shoulder. "You coming?"

"No, there's someone I need to talk to first. I'll be there in a bit."

She tapped her watch, "Briefing at nine, sharp."

I'd forgotten it was only eight-thirty, and I wasn't sure the person I wanted to see would be in yet. I rode the elevator down to the basement, passed through a set of double doors, and turned right into a long room set in a bullpen setting. A single line of desks ran three-quarters the length of the narrow space, with the fronts of two desks pushed up against each other every ten feet or so. This room housed the burglary unit, but that's not who I'd come to see.

The room was empty except for one lone detective who'd come in early to take care of some paperwork. "Mornin', Alex. You slummin' this morning or what? Coming down to the depths to visit us peons?"

"Hi, Michael. How are the kids?" Michael was another person I used to work with in the Aggravated Assault detail.

Even seated, he looked every inch his six-foot-three-inch frame. He sat back, pushed his curly blonde hair off his forehead, and adjusted the signature round glasses he was inordinately proud of. "They're good. Cecily's off to college, and Carly's playing in a band downtown. The band's pretty good. You should go hear 'em sometime."

"I'd love to after we finish with the Coward. Right now, I have zero free time to do anything much more than sleep. Is the Doc in?"

Doctor Lucille Hampton is the police psychologist who keeps the members of the department relatively sane. Her office sits in its own little alcove at the very end of the room. It's fully enclosed and soundproofed to maintain privacy for the personnel who come to see her. "I'm here, Alex. Come on in." She'd propped open her door with a fifteen-pound kettlebell, which I valiantly tried to move with the toe of my shoe.

I gave up, grabbed the handle, and shifted it to the side. "Hey Doc, how's it goin'?" Doc Hampton is a well-built woman in her early fifties, with skin that always reminds me of creamy chocolate milk and soft green eyes that disguise a sharp, discerning mind.

"I'm fine, Alex. The question is, how are things going with you? I understand the Coward case is taking its toll on quite a few detectives."

"I think it's taking its toll on detectives, officers, sergeants, administrative assistants, crime scene techs, and the community. This guy has slithered into everyone's minds."

I reached back and closed the door, then settled into the comfortable armchair she keeps in front of her desk. "In fact, that's what I'm here to talk about. I know you're not a criminal profiler, but I thought maybe you could help me get inside this guy's head. I need to know why he's doing what he's doing. For example, why is he very carefully taking the eyes out and destroying the body? I know there's that theory that they don't want the victim looking at them while they're doing the crime, but that doesn't seem to fit. I mean, it might fit, but my gut's telling me that's not why he's doing it."

"Does he take them with him?" She saw me eyeing the tin of streusel-topped coffee cake tempting me from the near edge of her desk. "Have some. I baked them early this morning."

I sent her an incredulous look. "This morning? You're kidding, right?"

Sparkling white teeth brightened the room as she smiled, "I'm often up before the sun shows itself over the mountains, and I love to bake, so..." She picked up the edge of the tin and canted it toward me. "Have one." As I peeled a napkin off a stack next to the tin and placed the cinnamon swirled cake on it, she repeated her question, "Does he take the eyes with him?"

I popped a corner of the cake into my mouth and moaned with pleasure. "This is fantastic. Thanks. Yes, he does, and I know the psych theories behind that. That maybe he wants a souvenir from his victims. But are there any other reasons he might be doing it?"

"Don't be so quick to rationalize away his intentions. Your gut may be right, but it might not, and it would be best if you kept an open mind until you've thoroughly examined each possibility. You talk about the ones who want a souvenir. Often, the souvenirs are to help the perpetrator relive the erotic sensations of his violence. Do you have any idea whether or not he's been sexually assaulting the victims prior to death or immediately before burning them?"

"There's no way to tell because the fire burns most of the flesh and muscle from the body. I mean, usually, all that's left is a shriveled, crispy..."

She held up a hand, "I get it. Then I wouldn't completely rule that out. Like I said, keep an open mind. As far as other reasons, there are a few. For instance, back in the 1800s, some scientists and doctors believed in the science of optography. They believed that the last thing a person sees at the moment of death is recorded on the victim's eyeballs."

I thought about that a minute. "So, if this guy believes that, then he's taking the eyeballs so we can't photograph them and identify him through the image recorded on the eyeball." Shaking my head, I said, "This guy seems too organized and possibly too intelligent to believe something like that."

"Organized in what way?" Watching me enjoy the coffee cake proved too much for her, and she took a small piece and set it on an already crumb-filled napkin sitting next to her coffee.

"The victims are always laid out in precisely the same manner, laying on their backs in their bed with their hands crossed over their midsection. He always takes out the eyes and stuffs candles down into the sockets. These act as delaying devices. They allow him to set the stage for what he does next. Things like pouring the accelerant, which he spreads in the exact same pattern every time, except this last time,"

"How did he change this last time?"

"Well, at the previous scenes, he poured the accelerant in

lines away from the body out to the walls. Then he poured it around all four walls of the room. He leaves the bedroom door open, presumably so that the fire will have more oxygen, allowing it to burn hotter and more rapidly. It also allows the fire to spread to the rest of the house. This last time, he spread the lines outward, but he didn't pour the accelerant down each of the four floorboards. And he didn't open the bedroom door because the major damage was confined to the bedroom and didn't extend to the rest of the house. None of the fire reached the rest of the house. In all of the other cases, the fire destroyed the home."

"Do you have any idea why the change?" She sat forward, intensely interested in the fact that he'd changed his MO.

"I don't. And I don't know if it means anything, but there was one other point that interested me. The latest homicide victim was Knox Cailleach. That killer who butchered his wife and five kids. Do you remember him?"

"I remember him well. He entered the system while I was still working for the Bureau of Prisons. He wasn't my patient, but my partner worked with him. He was a violent, evil man. Judge Connor should never have granted him parole."

"Kate has other people working on how he's targeting his people, but I thought it was interesting that he would target someone like Knox Cailleach."

"Very interesting. Is there anything else you can think of?"

"I'm not sure whether you're aware that after his last arson, there was another attempt? There's a young woman who visits older people in their homes. One of her elderly friends called her but didn't say anything. With the Coward cases being front-page news, that worried her enough that she went to the woman's house to check on her. The Coward had the old woman sitting up in a chair with a bag over her head. That's a new piece of information we didn't have before, that he covers their head."

"Interesting. Now, that could be more to incite terror in the victim than to maintain his anonymity since he has every intention of killing them in the end."

"Yeah, Kate mentioned that, too."

"Or—" She thought a moment and lifted a shoulder, "Actually there are so many possibilities for placing a bag over his victim's head that without knowing more about him, any ideas are nothing more than idle speculation. Those are things you won't know until you're able to learn more about his background. Now, I'm only guessing at this, Alex, because you said you wanted my opinion. I would say he's someone who was abused and or terrified as a child by probably..." Her brow furrowed as she looked at me, "...correct me if I'm wrong, but all of the victims have been elderly, 60 and above?"

"Yes."

"Then, my first thought is that he was abused by his grandparents or another important, older person in his life, meaning he possibly lived with his grandparents as a child or spent a good amount of time with them. If you do come up with any suspects, that would be one of the first things I'd check if I were you."

I filed that way in the back of my mind. I brought the cake to my mouth and then paused, "I just remembered something else. The arson guys say the Coward's usually careful when handling his accelerant because it's caustic to the skin. But when this young woman came up behind him and hit him in the head with a shovel, he turned and shoved her into the wall. He grabbed a bag that she'd fallen on, then as he was running away, he dipped down. She thought it was because he was picking something up. Mitch, one of the arson detectives, found a wet spot that he believed to be an accelerant in the general vicinity of where the man reached for something. The young woman said there was a squiggly darker line down his pants, so I'm wondering if he spilled the accelerant down his pants and the accelerant burned him, probably for the first time."

Nodding, she sat back, crossed her arms, and stared at me a minute. "I'm willing to bet that this latest, unfinished incident has rattled his cage. He's going to begin making more and more mistakes. I suppose it could even scare him out of the city, and he may end up laying low for a while to regain his confidence. But the fact that he was caught in the act, that his victim got away, and that somebody may have seen his face..." Her gaze sharpened, "Did she see his face?"

I shook my head, "No. She's very good at silhouettes, so she gave us a silhouette that somewhat gives us an impression of his build. That might prove helpful later on; it might not. I don't know. She had the impression he was short, but when he was running away from my house after he'd —"

"Your house? What do you mean running away from *your house*?"

"Didn't I mention he threw a Molotov cocktail through my kitchen window?"

She chuckled and shook her head. "No, Alex, you didn't. Working with cops is such an interesting experience." She put an innocent look on her face, scratched the side of her forehead, and then comically mimicked what I'd just said. "Oh, by the way, did I forget to mention he threw a Molotov cocktail through my window?"

I smiled sheepishly. "Actually, it scared the shit out of me. But I can't keep obsessing about it because it'll make my job that much harder."

She turned serious again, "I can understand that. Don't underestimate or minimize what happened at your house, Alex. That drastic change in his MO tells me he is seriously unraveling. He's afraid of you. Otherwise, he would've done what he always does. He would have tied you up and burned you in the same way he destroyed his other victims. And I use the word destroyed very specifically. He doesn't just kill his victims. He destroys them. I believe he may be destroying his grandparents over and over and over again. Some serial killers kill in a sexual frenzy or from a need to act out their sexual fantasies. I don't believe that's the case with the Coward. This time, like the coward he is, he chose to burn you from a distance instead of up close and personal. That's significant."

I pulled my lips into a grim smile. "You think we might have him on the ropes? That we might be able to force more mistakes?"

"It's possible. I'd say he has several targets he needs to eliminate before he can move on. You, the woman who stopped him, and the old woman he didn't get the chance to destroy. The three of you will become his obsession because his world has spun out of control, and he needs to pull in the unraveling pieces of his carefully crafted existence."

What she said made sense, and I wondered what expertise she had in working with the criminally insane. I glanced around the room at the many certificates hanging on her walls. I guessed they weren't there from a need to build up her ego, but rather from a need to build up the confidence of those who sat in the very chair in which I now sat. According to the documents on her wall, she held an undergraduate degree in applied psychology with a criminal justice concentration. Her master's degree was in abnormal psychology and her Ph.D. in forensic psychology.

I blinked several times and tilted my head, more out of confusion than any conscious act on my part, "You *are* a forensic psychologist."

Leaning her elbows on her desk, she made a steeple with her fingers. Her green eyes sparkled with amusement, "Forensic psychology is a vast field, Alex. I have two Ph.D.'s.

The first is in the study of the criminal mind as it pertains to psychopathy—"

"Psychopathy?" I'd heard the term bandied about but wasn't clear on the meaning.

"I studied personality disorders, specifically dealing with anti-social behavior and more specifically, with men and women who have limited or no empathy or feelings of guilt."

"Like the Coward, you mean?"

She shook her head, "No. I can't be sure unless I actually work with him, but from the little you've told me, I think guilt may play a very large role in his behavior. Do you remember I said the bag over the victim's head could mean several different things? That it might not simply be a way to terrify his victims?" At my nod, she continued, "It could also mean the opposite. He doesn't want the victim to know what's coming. He might feel guilty for what he's doing to them."

It was obvious to me that Dr. Hampton was a resource the department needed to use to help catch this guy. "Why hasn't the chief asked you to profile him?"

Again, that amused or bemused expression—I couldn't tell them apart with her—flitted across her face. "He did. I recommended they consult a colleague of mine, a specialist whom I trust implicitly."

"Why?"

"Why? Because my second Ph.D. is in the study of Post-Traumatic Stress Syndrome." She pointed to another certificate on the wall behind me. "That's where my heart is. That's why I came to work here and with several other departments around Tucson. I enjoy helping the good guys more than the bad."

"So why didn't you send me to your colleague with my questions?"

"Because one of my detectives needed my help."

I recognized the same affectionate look Kate turned on me every now and again and sat up, startled. "You mean you're shrinking me?" I didn't like the sound of that.

She chuckled at my alarm. "No, I'm not..." She held up her fingers in quotation marks, "...shrinking you. You needed a sounding board to better understand your quarry, and here I am. Granted, I'm probably the most knowledgeable sounding board you could have chosen, but there you have it. I hoped it helped?"

"Absolutely, there's a lot of information jumbled up in my mind. And, I hadn't realized that the bag over the head might mean just the opposite of what I assumed it meant. Thanks for that." The clock on the wall behind her read eight fifty-five, and Kate had said the briefing would start at 9 o'clock sharp. "I need to get back. I don't want to miss Kate's briefing."

"No, that wouldn't be a good idea."

I got up from the chair and pulled down one of the pant legs that had inched up my calf. "Sounds like you know Kate as well as I do."

"I'm sure she's under a lot of pressure since she and Sgt. Longoria are spearheading this investigation."

I pulled open the door, "Thanks again, Doc. I really appreciate your help."

"Any time, Alex. Here, take one for the road." She shook the tin, and I happily obliged.

CHAPTER 17

I had just enough time to make it back upstairs before Kate started her briefing. When I walked in, everyone was gathered around her whiteboard, and she was standing off to the side discussing something quietly with Sgt. Longoria.

Casey leaned against her desk, both arms crossed and waiting for the briefing to begin.

I nodded at her as I walked over and cleared a space where I could sit.

"Make yourself at home."

"Don't mind if I do."

When Sgt. Longoria began the briefing, Kate looked over her shoulder to make sure I'd made it back in time.

I held up what was left of the coffee cake and then took a bite.

She smiled slightly and returned her attention to what Longoria had to say.

He waited for everyone to quiet. "There's not much new this morning. Garlan is in Colorado following up on a previous case there. Burney thinks he may have a line on someone who bought more than one of the ingredients in the accelerant. Kate?"

Kate stepped forward and motioned in my general direction. "As you all know, Alex had a nighttime visit from the Coward night before last. He threw a Molotov cocktail through her kitchen window. It goes without saying we all need to be hyper-vigilant. Watch to make sure you aren't followed home, pay attention when your motion detector lights come on, even if it's windy outside. Talk to your families about being vigilant. We'll catch the bastard, but until we do, keep your eyes and ears open, even during your downtime." The side of her mouth turned up a bit. "There's not much new to report this morning, so I know you'll all be disappointed the briefing is so short."

Everyone was running on lack of sleep, so the response to her comment brought quiet chuckles instead of the usual sarcastic comments about wasted time and boredom.

Kate started for her cubicle. "That's it, folks. Let's get to work."

My phone jangled, but thankfully the meeting was already breaking up. I hadn't expected Kelly to call this early, mainly because the library didn't open until ten.

"Hi, Alex, I have the information you asked for. Do you want me to read it to you over the phone, or would you rather come in to get it?"

"The library isn't open yet, is it?" I wasn't sure how I'd get in since the doors on the underground garage didn't go up until after the library opened for business.

"No, the librarians always come in an hour or two before we open to the public to get everything ready for the day. But I can meet you out front if you'd like. It's still early, and you can probably find a parking space on the street."

"I doubt if I can find a parking spot, but I was gonna walk anyway. It'll only take about ten, maybe fifteen minutes to get there." I didn't think Kate needed me for anything, so I slipped out while she was speaking to Nate and Burney.

As usual, even a bluebird would be jealous of the bright blue, cloudless sky. I used the walk to think over what the doc had said about the Coward's motivation. I'd already guessed he was unraveling; I just hadn't known to what extent. I also hadn't realized that he'd changed his MO when he'd thrown the Molotov cocktail through my kitchen window. I hadn't considered myself one of his victims. I'd just thought he was getting rid of one of the detectives on his case. But now, I wondered why he would target me instead of any of the other detectives. If anyone, I'd think he'd want to go after one of the arson guys, maybe Mitch, for example, since the guy liked playing with fire.

As I'd predicted, it only took about fifteen minutes to get from the police station's doors to the library's, where Kelly waited on the other side of the window that ran the entire length and breadth of the building. She waved the keys to indicate she'd seen me approach.

When she pushed open the door to admit me, a mother with two young children scurried over and shoved in front of me. "We were here first. I don't appreciate you barging in front of us like that."

She turned her angry glower from me to Kelly, who blocked the door with her body and pointed to the library hours. "I'm sorry, but we don't open for another half-hour yet."

The woman sneered down her short, broad nose at me. "*She* gets to come in. Why should she be allowed and not us?"

I didn't want to get involved in this, and I let Kelly do her librarian thing, which she did with the skills of a woman who's had years of practice dealing with pushy, overbearing parents. "Perhaps you'd like to come back in a half-hour when

I'll be more than happy to help you find some books for your daughters?"

"We're not here for the books, as you well know. Wally Wabbit is reading his Whitetail Tales today, and we came early to get front row seats."

One of the little girls proudly displayed a large picture book with a green rabbit adorning the cover.

Kelly leaned down to admire the book, "That's lovely, Sweetheart. I love Wally, too." She straightened and addressed the mother, "I assure you, Detective Wolfe won't be taking your seats at the event. Would you like me to save three seats for you at the reading?" A hint of irritation had crept into her voice.

I was right there with her. I had to admit it was difficult to maintain my passively bored expression while thinking I'd much rather be listening to Wally Wabbit instead of trying to track down a deranged serial killer.

The woman angrily looked my way. "Don't you have something better to do than visit the library during work hours?" She pointedly indicated my badge and gun with laser-focused eyes.

"It would be much easier for me to do my job if you'd stop arguing with Ms. Bruster and step aside."

"This is a public library, and I have as much right to stand here as you do."

I wondered whether the woman would puff her chest out like that if she realized how closely she resembled one of the pigeons strutting about the brick forecourt. I'd just opened my mouth to undoubtedly precipitate a complaint when an officer on foot patrol strode over.

"Having a problem, Detective?"

The woman's chest suddenly deflated. She grabbed the girls' hands and hurried over to the grassy area, sending furtive glances over her shoulder every few seconds.

I smiled at the patrolman. "Curiouser and curiouser as Alice in Wonderland once said."

He nodded, "Yeah, I've dealt with her before. Arrested her once for drunk and disorderly. Maybe I'll go have a chat."

"The kids are waiting to see Wally Wabbit, so try not to ruin their day."

He genially waved at us over his shoulder as he made his way toward the trio.

I stepped inside, and Kelly re-locked the door. With one last look at the patrolman kneeling in front of the little girl to look at her book, I asked, "Does that happen often?"

She slipped her keys into her front pocket. "All the time. Especially for the Children's Hour. Most of the time, the little ones are better behaved than the parents. Anyway, I have the information at my desk."

Even though I'd been to her office the day before, I was still completely turned around by the time we walked through her office door. "This is like a labyrinth down here."

"I know. I often wonder whether the architect had a keen sense of humor when designing the back office space. Here you go." She handed me a stack of papers.

"So many? Or is this just a lot of information on a couple of cases?"

"There are some in there that might or might not be the same MO. I had some difficulty because most of the news articles are written in the language of the country where the crimes were committed. Thank God for translation programs. What would have taken me weeks or perhaps months to research only took me half the night."

"I didn't mean for you to do everything immediately. I mean, you didn't have to stay up all night to do this."

"Half the night, and if it helps catch the Coward, I'll stay up all week if you need me to."

The growl coming from her was so uncharacteristic that I glanced up from scanning the papers. "You okay?"

"Fine. I almost lost it with that woman wasting your time when you're working on the Coward case. If she calls in a complaint, you have Sgt. Brannigan call me. I'll give her an earful."

"I almost hope she calls her because as tired as she is, Kate would take her head off for wasting our time. She's pretty stressed, and I'm trying to stay out of her line of sight."

Kelly gave me a large envelope for the papers and then let me out a side door in the hope the irritating mother wouldn't accost me on the way back to the office. I tucked the envelope under my arm, but before I'd taken more than a few steps, my phone buzzed. I pulled it out to read a text from Jerry. "Parking lot. Front P-station."

I texted back, "OMW," and picked up my pace.

Jerry, who was watching the station's front door, almost hit his head on the roof when I walked up from behind and knocked on his truck's tinted window. He buzzed the window down and grabbed his chest. "Damn, Alex. I thought you'd come out of the building."

I held up Kelly's manila envelope. "I just came from picking up some info from the library." "You got something for me?"

He handed me another envelope. "Not officially, no."

I opened my mouth to ask what he'd found, and the window buzzed back up. At about the halfway point, he bobbed his chin at me, "See ya, Alex."

I said, "See ya," to the back of his truck as he pulled out of the lot. Only a few detectives were working at their desks when I walked in. I stopped at Sharon's desk and pulled down Mr. M&M's arm. Five M&Ms slid out onto the tray, and I scooped them up and popped them into my mouth.

Sharon, our administrative assistant, opened her drawer and pulled out a new bag. "People are eating them faster than I can refill him these days."

"I'll remember to bring you back a bag to re-stock."

"No need. It's one of the ways I get to support you guys. Chocolate is good for the soul, you know."

"Thanks. You're the best."

She harumphed and pulled the candy dispenser closer to refill the big guy's tummy.

Kate wasn't at her desk, and neither was Casey. I nodded hello to Nate Drewery and sat at my desk to study Kelly's material. I was so absorbed in the information she'd compiled that I was completely unaware of my surroundings until I looked up and found Casey hard at work at her computer. "When did you get here?"

"About a half-hour ago. You were so intent on reading your paperwork I didn't want to disturb you."

"Yeah, thanks." I studied the papers laid out on my desktop. The pages were stacked according to case. Some stacks held a single page, while others had several. There were eight in all, and I pulled up a translation program and re-ran some of the information to double and then triple-check Kelly's work.

Then I pulled out Jerry's info, and after skimming through it, felt my blood run cold. Turning to my computer, I ran a search of my own. Without realizing what I was doing, when the information came up, I pushed out of my chair, faced the full-length window behind my desk, and said, "Fuck."

I'm not sure how long I stood there, but when I heard Kate say, "What is it, Alex?" I realized I was standing stock-still with my hand on my forehead, pushing my bangs straight up. She'd come up behind me, and since she hadn't been in the office when I'd come in, it took me a moment to orient myself to her presence.

"Huh?" I turned to face her and tried to look as unconcerned as possible. "Oh, nothing." Several detectives had also returned while I'd been lost in the files, and for some reason, they were all looking my way. I quickly shoved the stacks into one pile and threw everything back into a manilla envelope.

Kate watched me a moment and then motioned for me to follow her. "Come on."

I watched her walk toward the lieutenant's office and then said, "Actually, Boss, I'm running a little late. Can I catch you when I get back?" Not waiting for an answer, I grabbed the envelope and headed toward the door.

That is until I heard "No," spoken in no uncertain terms.

Sighing, I slowly pivoted and returned to my computer. I pulled up the last screen I'd looked at and hit the print button. When the printer whirred to life, I walked over and grabbed the two sheets that emerged.

Kate watched me and then pushed the lieutenant's door open as I approached.

As usual, the LT was at some administrative meeting or other, so I wouldn't have to embarrass myself by presenting a half-assed theory with him present. "It's just an idea I've been working on, Kate. It's nothing, yet."

She'd already shut the door and had hiked her hip onto the corner of the lieutenant's desk. At my words, she cocked her head and crossed her arms. "I'm waiting."

"Look, it's a theory. That's all, and if I'm wrong, I could screw up somebody's life for no reason."

"Well then, tell me, and I'll be the one to screw up their life instead of you."

"I just need time to—"

She held up a hand, stopping me mid-sentence. "I don't have time for this, Alex."

Sighing again, I sat in the chair and pulled out the papers. "Well, it all began with a conversation I had with Steve. I asked him where he'd served, and one of the places was Germany." I stopped to gather my thoughts. "Let me back up a second. Before I talked to him, Burney found a case similar to ours that happened in Kiel, Germany and Carla translated it for me. On a whim, I asked Steve if he'd ever been to Germany, and he said he had."

Nodding, Kate said, "I see what you mean about screwing up someone's life. That's a pretty flimsy tie-in."

I toyed with the idea of agreeing with her and leaving it at that but abandoned the notion just as quickly. "Yeah, well, then I had Kelly look for other cases worldwide with the same MO. I held up her paperwork. I also had—" My tongue froze in time to stop me from blurting out Jerry's name, "—somebody find out where Steve had been stationed during his career."

"Somebody meaning Jerry."

I blinked. How the hell did she know that?

At her tired smile, I realized she hadn't known, but my response confirmed her suspicions. "And?"

"And I didn't have a lot of time to study the data, but—"

She interrupted me, "You've been studying those papers for the last hour."

"No way."

She nodded. "Way."

I handed everything over to her with a sigh. "There's a correlation. But it could still be a coincidence."

Kate sat behind the lieutenant's desk, spread out the papers, and began to read.

"Look, Kate—"

She held up a hand without looking up.

I got up and paced two steps to the door, then did a one-eighty and paced four steps past my chair to the window.

After three such trips, Kate pointed at my chair and growled, "Sit." It took another twenty minutes, but when she

249

finished, she sat back and tapped her pen on her leg. "That's too much of a coincidence, Alex. We need to bring him in."

"No, not yet. It's too soon. I don't believe it's him. My gut is telling me it's not him. That's why I didn't want to bring it to you yet. I don't think someone could pull the wool over both Casey's and my eyes."

"He was in at least five different countries at the same time similar arson/murders happened in those countries. And now he turns up in Tucson, and they start again? And there's a leak somewhere. I assume he's been privy to some of the details of the case?"

That hadn't occurred to me, and I begrudgingly conceded the point. "Well, yeah. But he didn't just turn up in Tucson. He lives here. He's lived here for a while. Why did the arsons just now start? Well, start in the last few months anyway."

Kate stood and walked to the door. "Take Casey and bring him in. Be as low-key as possible, so we don't alert the media. If you're right and it's not him, I don't want to ruin his reputation."

There was no use arguing, so I stood and nodded. "Yes, ma'am."

Before she opened the door, she held up a finger. "But remember, if Steve is the Coward, he is extremely dangerous. Watch yourself."

Casey's desk butts up to mine, and the ends of both of them are shoved up against the LT's wall. As Kate and I came through the door, heads turned our way. Kate must have given them the "there's nothing to see here" look because to a person, they immediately averted their gaze, with several of them swiveling their seats around so their backs were to us.

I leaned close to Casey's ear and said, "No questions. Just get your gear and come with me." I grabbed my briefcase, not because I needed anything in it, but because I wanted to look as normal as possible when I exited the building. Some reporters had taken to standing outside the open garage doors and shouting questions whenever anyone exited the elevator.

Casey closed out whatever she was working on at the computer and took her cue from me. She silently picked up her briefcase and followed me down the hall to the elevators. "Your jaw's working overtime."

I wiggled my jaw back and forth to relax it, and by the time we stepped off the elevator, she'd managed to make me laugh by describing the antics of one of her baby goats. It worked. The reporters clustered around the opening saw us laughing and turned away to pull smoke into their lungs or bite off a piece of their burger.

We drove out of the garage, and as soon as we were well away from prying ears, she turned to me and asked, "Okay, what are we doing, and why the secrecy?"

I pulled into the community center parking lot and parked beneath one of the trees. It took a minute to gather my thoughts, and thankfully Casey knew enough to remain silent. "I... well, Kelly and Jerry came up with some information. I mean, I asked them to, and now I'm not sure I should have."

"Alex. It's me. Just tell me what you found."

I raked the fingers of both hands through my hair and blew out a deep breath. "There are similar cases around the world. Similar arson/murder combinations where candles were put into the eye sockets, and the eyes were taken. Steve was in the army and was stationed in the countries where the arsons took place at the same time they happened."

"In the same cities?"

"No. But he once told me that he loved traveling around whatever country he was living in at the time. Italy, Germany, Nigeria, Korea, Japan, and some others I'm not sure about. And Kate reminded me that we have a leak somewhere. We told Steve and George more than we probably should have. Anyway, Kate wants us to bring him in quietly, without any fanfare. If I'm wrong, and I think I am, I don't want to ruin his life by saddling him with this kind of accusation."

I'd rolled my window partway down, and I sat listening to the doves and pigeons cooing to each other. Traffic was heavy along Church Avenue, unusually so for this time of day. I glanced over and saw a hearse turning south onto Meyer and realized all the cars had their headlights on and were following the hearse to the cemetery.

Casey also watched the procession, crossed herself, and then said, "That's a few notches above coincidence, Alex. We better get going. Do you know where he is?"

"Yeah. He's at the library doing research for me." I looked over at her and shook my head. "Weird, huh?"

"If it's any consolation, I didn't have a clue either. Nothing. No alarm bells or even an inkling of suspicion. But Kate said to bring him in, and that's what we need to do."

"How do we explain it to him?"

"We just say Kate has some questions for him."

Sounded like a good plan to me.

CHAPTER 18

I started the car and drove the few blocks to the underground garage beneath the library. Steve was up in the little room studying something on his computer screen. He looked up and smiled when we arrived. "Hey, guys. I'm almost done with my initial report. Kelly and I sifted through a lot of information, and I think we've come up with a couple possibilities."

He had a complicated Excel file open on his computer. Graphs and charts were embedded within the file, and he had several tabs open down at the bottom of the page.

I let out a low whistle. "Someday, I'm gonna ask you to teach me how to use Excel better. I can do the basics, but when it comes to formulas and adding those kinds of charts and graphs, I'm completely lost."

He grabbed his mouse and randomly clicked through some of the tabs. "As you can see in these other pages, this file is probably more than you'll ever need. But I'd be happy to show you some of the simple basics that would help you in your everyday work. They've made the program so much easier nowadays. So, what brings you guys here so early this morning?"

I glanced at Casey, who raised her eyebrows and shrugged. Translated that meant, 'This is your dog, you deal with it.' I decided to plunge right in. "Sgt. Branigan wanted us to bring you down to the station. She has some questions she'd like to ask you."

"Sure, let me print out a few of these pages so I can take them with me and explain to her what I've gotten so far." He did some clicking around on the computer. "Kelly says these will print out in her office. Hang on a second, and I'll call her and ask her to bring them up." He whipped out his cell phone and called Kelly. After he'd spoken for a few minutes, he hung up and turned to me. "She said they'd already printed out, and she'd bring them right up."

It didn't take long before Kelly bounced into the room with her usual enthusiasm and energy. She handed the papers to Steve. "Here you go. Do you think you'll be needing anymore because my shift at the information desk starts in just a few minutes?"

Steve answered while absently leafing through the papers, "Nope. I'm heading over to the police station to talk to Sgt. Branigan. I should be back fairly soon after that, and we can enter some of that information you came up with yesterday. Thanks for these, by the way."

I shot Kelly a suspicious glance because I'd asked her specifically not to tell Steve about the information she'd given me this morning.

She understood my concern and smiled. "Have you ever heard about Charles Frederick Albright? He was born in the 1930s, and he grew into a serial killer. They nicknamed him The Eyeball Killer. I did some research on him yesterday, and I assume that's what Steve's talking about?" She raised her eyebrows, and Steve nodded.

She shook her head, "He was one sick man. He killed three women, all of them prostitutes in 1990 and into '91. What caught my eye," she winced slightly and wrinkled her nose, "so to speak, was the fact that he always surgically removed the eyes and took them with him. I was wondering if maybe the Coward was mimicking Albright's cases. And something else made me take notice. He used to kill small animals, which his mother helped stuff. Steve said that if the Coward was living in their neighborhood when they were kids, he also killed small animals and removed their eyes."

Casey rested her hands on her hips. "His mother helped him stuffed them? The apple doesn't fall far from the tree, does it?"

Kelly shrugged, "From what I read, he was interested in taxidermy, and she wanted to encourage his interest."

My phone dinged with an incoming text from Kate. It simply read, "Well?"

I quickly texted back, "We're on our way." I caught Steve's eye, "Sgt. Branigan is wondering where we are. I guess we'd better get going."

Casey walked over and held open the door.

I didn't want Steve to get suspicious, so I walked out and headed for the stairs. Kelly came out after me, and Casey and Steve follow behind. In the front lobby, I turned and headed for the garage door.

Steve asked, "Wouldn't you guys rather walk? It's such a beautiful day outside. Of course, ninety-five percent of the days in Tucson are beautiful. I always try to walk whenever I can."

Casey shook her head, "No, Sgt. Branigan has a busy day, and she asked us to drive down here to pick you up."

Steve barked a laugh, "Whoa, a whole three blocks. What are we gonna save like five minutes or something?"

Casey and I nodded, silently implying our agreement with

him, and then I waved my thanks to Kelly, "I'll see you a bit later, Kelly. Thanks for the information on Albright. I'll definitely look him up."

She smiled over her shoulder as the door to the garage closed behind us.

The reporters began yelling questions as soon as we approached the back ramp that served as the underground garage entrance at the police station.

"Hey, Detective Wolfe, any updates on the Coward case?"

"Is this guy a suspect?"

"Hey detectives, who's that in the backseat?"

"Have there been any new incidents around the city? People are terrified. Can you give us a quote?"

We ignored them and pulled down to the lower-level basement so they wouldn't see us get out and walk to the elevator. When we entered the office, Kate and Sgt. Longoria were sitting in her cubicle discussing something. They came out to meet us, and Kate stopped and addressed Steve, "Thanks for coming in to talk to us, Mr. Grate. This is Sgt. Longoria from the arson detail. He has some questions for you as well. Let's go back into one of the interview rooms where we can have some privacy."

Steve separated the papers he'd brought with him into two sets and handed one set to me. "Here, I printed out two copies. I figured you might want to go over the paperwork while I explain what I have."

When the three of them turned to walk to the interview room, I took a few steps, expecting to follow.

Kate let Stephen and Rick go ahead and then turned back and put her hand on my chest. "This interview is just going to be between Rick and me and Steve. I want you to continue working on the case and see what else you can come up with."

"But—"

"No buts about it. Alex. There's still a lot of work to be

done, and I expect you to do it. Did you have any issues with the reporters at the garage door?"

I shook my head and blinked stupidly, unsure why Kate was excluding me from the interview.

Casey answered instead, "No. As we were driving past, they yelled at us, asking if he was the Coward, but they were grasping at straws. You know how desperate they get when they don't have a current case to fill their quotas. They milk what they have for everything they've got."

Kate nodded, gave me a meaningful glare, and then followed Rick and Steve to the interview room.

I stared after her. It wasn't like her to exclude me from an interview, and I racked my brain trying to understand why she'd done it. It never occurred to me that she wanted to grab the glory for catching the Coward. If anything, she was protecting me from making a false and damaging accusation to someone I'd come to think of as, if not exactly a friend, then someone I'd trusted with the information on our case.

Casey patted me on the back and then gently pushed me towards my desk. She leaned in and spoke quietly in my ear, "Don't worry about it. Alex. You need to trust that she knows what she's doing."

I knew she was right, and after a long sigh, I returned to my desk and thought about my next move. I've worked for Kate long enough to know she has her reasons for everything she does. I just had to accept that and move on. I saw the crinkled business card with the illegible phone number on the edge of my desk and realized I hadn't yet spoken to Babe this morning. I picked up the phone and gave her a call.

She answered with a cheerful lilt in her voice. "Hey, Alex. How's your morning going so far?"

I was pleased to hear that her natural, sunny disposition had returned. "That's my line. Everything going okay?"

"Absolutely! Nathaniel just got back with a tray full of coffee and doughnuts. It doesn't get much better than that."

"Are you guys finding things to do to fill your time? Is Mrs. Holloway doing better?"

"Mrs. Holloway is just as feisty as ever. I absolutely adore her."

I heard a delighted cackle in the background and guessed Mrs. Holloway was sitting close by.

Babe laughed as well, and I pictured her with her arm around the old lady's shoulders, giving them a squeeze. "Nate and I spent a lot of last night playing card games while Mrs. Holloway slept. I wanted to stay up to make sure she was okay after that, you know what, hit her on the back of the head. That's why Nathaniel needed to go out and grab the coffees, so we can maybe stay awake today. We were wondering how long we'll be staying here?"

"You just got there. You getting tired of it already?"

"No, it's a really nice house. There's plenty of room for the three of us. I'm actually having a lot of fun, but I still need to visit my other seniors. Do you think I can go out and do that today?"

I thought about whether Mrs. Holloway would be safe alone with Nathaniel. If Babe left, I'd want George following her, and I needed to figure out whether I wanted to split the three of them up. "Can you give me a little bit of time to think about that? I've got a few things in the works. Maybe after work, I could pick you up, and we could go check your seniors together."

"That'd be a lot of fun. There's a couple of 'em I think you'd like. Well, you'd probably like all of them, but two of the ladies are real spitfires, as my mom likes to say."

"Does Nathaniel have any plans to go out for the rest of the day?"

She yelled to Nathaniel, and judging by her volume, he

must have been in a different room. "Hey, Nate! Alex wants to know if you're going out later today?" The line remained silent while she listened for an answer. After what seemed like more time than necessary for him to give a simple answer, she came back online. "He says we need to do some grocery shopping, but he's had groceries delivered before, so we can do that again if we need to."

"That sounds perfect. Maybe around lunchtime, I can bring you guys something to eat. If not, you can always order out. Talk to you soon, okay?"

"Talk to you soon!" Babe parroted back what I'd just said, only her response was a heck of a lot more upbeat than mine.

As I hung up, I noticed the papers Steve had handed me sitting on the corner of the desk. Curious, I picked them up and leaned back in my chair to study them.

Steve had listed approximately 40 people who'd lived in their neighborhood when they were kids. He'd used color coding to denote where he'd found the information. For instance, blue stood for census records, and green represented a website called "Find a Grave." The names in yellow, on the other hand, came from some genealogical database. There were several additional colors as well, but at this point, I really didn't care where he'd gotten the info—only that he'd gotten it. I scanned the list of names, none of which meant anything to me.

The next page held a listing of all the yearbook files he'd collected and collated. He'd separated the boys from the girls, and since we'd discussed the fact that statistically, most serial killers were men, he'd moved the girls to their own tab, leaving the boys in a file all their own.

Casey and I simultaneously heard a commotion outside the door leading to the outer hallway, and we were both staring at the door when it flew open and banged against the sidewall. In a knee-jerk reaction, I glanced at the interview room, first in the hopes the sound hadn't interrupted the interview and second, vaguely wondering whether the door handle had put a hole in the drywall. The irrational thought that Kate wouldn't be happy about that flitted through the apparently empty corridors of my mind. It only took an instant to realize how ridiculous my reaction had been, and I quickly pulled my attention back to the entry door.

George stormed in with a patrolman who staffed the front desk hot on his heels. He strode up to my desk and slammed his hand down hard enough to make one of my pencils jump. "What the hell do you think you're doing bringing Steve down here and reading him his rights? Is he under arrest or what?"

I stood up, got in his face, and hissed, "Unless you want the whole world to know what we're doing here, I suggest you keep your voice down." I glanced around the office and was relieved to see the only other detectives sitting at their desks were Nate and, of course, Burney Macon. I pulled my attention back to George. "How did you know he was here, anyway?"

George followed my gaze, then turned back to me and poked me in the chest with a stiff finger. At least he lowered his voice so only Casey and I could hear what he was saying. "What the fuck is going on, Detective Wolfe?" He spat out my name as though ridding his mouth of a distasteful fungus.

"I asked you how you found out Steve was here."

He glared at me a moment, and then I guess he realized that if he played nice, he might get some answers. He visibly reigned in his temper, stared at the floor a moment, and then raised his gaze to mine. "Steve was smart enough to call me when they read him his rights. He may not understand a whole lot about law enforcement, but he knows enough to keep his mouth shut if some asshole pulls out a Miranda card."

That made sense. I strode over to where Nate and Burney had their desks pushed up against each other. They both looked up from paperwork they were pretending to read while not listening to our conversation. "None of this leaves this room, got it?"

Nate said, "got it."

Burney nodded, "Don't need to worry about anything coming out of this mouth." Since Burney is a very overweight sugar addict, I knew there was a joke in there somewhere, but this wasn't the time to pursue it.

Kate heard the commotion and stuck her head out of the interview room door. "What's the problem, Alex?"

Before I could answer, George strode down the hall, stepped close to her, and snarled, "I want to see my brother, now."

Kate stepped out into the hall and pulled the door shut behind her. "I'm afraid that's not possible right now, Mr. Ogilvie."

"Why not? Have you arrested him??"

"No. But he's not free to leave, either."

The patrol officer who'd brought George into the office followed me to where George and Kate were having their standoff.

I grabbed George by the arm, "George, come over to my desk and have a seat. You have two of the most respected detectives in the country speaking with your brother right now. Believe me, if you want to help him, let them do their jobs."

He looked at me and then back at Kate. "Do I need to get him an attorney?"

"You're more than welcome to do that, Mr. Ogilvie. But Steve has waived his rights and is giving us a lot of good information. Now, as Detective Wolfe said, I want you to go have a seat and wait for us to finish."

I pulled on George's arm and motioned for him to precede me back to the bullpen.

Casey leaned against the corner of the hallway next to her desk, arms crossed and watching to make sure George calmed down. When she realized all was well, she went to one of the empty detective's desks and co-opted a chair, which she wheeled over and placed next to our workspace.

The patrol officer stepped up beside me, "You want me to take him back downstairs? I brought him up here because he had an ID card saying he was a sheriff's deputy. I didn't know he was gonna go off the rails."

I shook my head. "No thanks, Tom. You did the right thing. We'll keep him up here with us for a while."

"You got it, Alex. Let me know if you need me to come get him and take him back downstairs." After shooting a glaring, silent accusation at George, he lifted his chin in Casey's general direction, "See ya, Case."

CHAPTER 19

I indicated the chair Casey had brought over and said, "You're welcome to sit while you wait, George."

George aggressively put his hands on his hips, probably to stop himself from throttling me. "Just tell me you don't think he's the Coward because that's absolute bullshit. I thought you guys knew your stuff, that you were a professional Police Department. But this shit?"

I rubbed my temple, hoping to stem the headache threatening to pounce on my unsuspecting brain. "Look, George, you're just gonna have to trust us on this one." I made sure he was looking me in the eyes, "You're going to have to trust *me* on this one. I can't explain what's going on yet, but when Kate comes out, I'm sure she'll explain everything. Now please, would you take a seat?"

"There's no way in hell I can sit here while he's in there being interviewed about the Coward case." Growling, he turned and paced to the office door, pivoted, and strode back to our desks, where he repeated the process several times. He reminded me of a tiger pacing behind the steel bars of a zoo.

I sat down, leaned back in my chair, and put my hands

behind my head. I stared at the ceiling, the floor, and then at the screensaver as it flashed crime scene photos randomly across my computer screen. I'd taken several of the inside of the residence, but every now and then, one of the pictures I'd randomly shot of the crowd outside would load.

In one, a group of reporters huddled in a circle, probably exchanging notes about what they'd heard. To the left of them was a bunch of what I like to call looky-loos—people who have nothing better to do than stand around a crime scene gossiping. They huddled just behind the crime scene tape, straining their necks to get a view of the burned-out house and of the body they were ghoulishly hoping to see.

As I studied them, one particular person caught my eye. I leaned forward and pulled my chair closer to get a better look. Another picture loaded, and I quickly grabbed the mouse, wanting to reverse the images somehow to get back to the previous photo. "Shit."

Casey chuckled and mumbled, "I hate when you do that. What's the matter now?"

I frantically clicked around in the computer, trying to get it to do what I wanted. "I need to find the crime scene photos I uploaded earlier. You know, the ones on my screensaver." Everybody knows that's my usual practice, and she should have known what I was talking about. At her lowered eyebrows, I impatiently added, "C'mon. You know, the ones that randomly load and show up on the screen when the computer's asleep? How the hell do I find them?" If I hadn't been so frazzled and in such a hurry, I would've immediately known where to look.

Casey came over and stood behind me. Leaning over my shoulder, she brushed my hand off the mouse, and with a few clicks, opened the folder. "There you go. What are you looking for?"

I grabbed the mouse from her and clicked through the

photos until I found the one I wanted. I hit print, accidentally backed into her with my chair so I could stand, and then hurried over to grab the photo from the printer. I yelled to the front of the office, "George."

He'd just gotten to the end wall and turned to face me.

I hurried over and showed him the photo, pointing to one face in particular. "Do you recognize this guy?"

Acrimony dripped off his every word, "Why, you gonna tell me he's the Coward now?"

His tone, combined with the fact that I needed the answer yesterday, angered me. I growled right back, "This isn't the time, George. Just tell me who the fuck this is." Kate's voice flashed through my head, saying almost the exact same thing on several occasions. Minus the cursing, of course.

If the venom in my voice hadn't given him a clue, the metaphorical daggers shooting from my eyes certainly had. He grudgingly looked at the picture again. "That's Eddie. Eddie Gordon. Why?"

"He was in the bar with you the other night playing pool, right?"

"Yeah. Again, why?" He was starting to get pissy again.

I thought I'd recognized the man. He'd been the one wearing the green seersucker suit who'd left when Jerry had walked over wanting to get into the game. I grabbed my hair and pulled, a technique that often helped me focus when my brain was set on auto-spin. "I'm trying to remember. I think Steve once told me that Eddie visited him somewhere when he was in the Army. Somewhere in Europe maybe?"

George shrugged, communicating his lack of interest in anything I had to say. "Yeah, so what?"

"So, do you know what country?" I barely kept myself from baring my teeth at the guy.

He paused before grudgingly answering the question. "Eddie visited Steve in every country he was ever stationed in. The three of us have been best friends since elementary school. Why? What does that have to do with anything?"

When he said, 'every country,' my adrenaline spiked. I grabbed him and pulled him over next to my desk. The two of us were going to have a Come to Jesus talk. In my mounting panic, I spoke more sharply than I should have. In point of fact, I probably snarled just a little bit. "Look, George, I need you to take off your pissy wounded brother pants and put on your big boy cop pants."

He stiffened at that, but I didn't have time to mince words. I grabbed the research Kelly and Jerry had given me and began going through each finding, one at a time. "Steve was in Italy. Arson, murder, same MO, same timeframe. He was in Germany. Arson, murder, same MO, same timeframe. Yugoslavia, Arson, murder, same MO, same timeframe. There are others. And now you're telling me Eddie visited him in every country he was in?" I shook the papers at him. "There are more. Do I need to go on? And I'll bet you guys have been talking to him about the case, too. There's our leak. And how long has Eddie been visiting here in Tucson?"

George slowly shook his head, either not quite comprehending or not wanting to believe what I meant. "He's been here..." He continued shaking his head, first looking out the window and then back into the room, and then to Sharon's desk where he'd been pacing earlier. There was a bewildered quality to his voice when he spoke. "He's been staying with Steve for about three months now. I've been coming down periodically visiting when I could."

He pulled in a quick breath. "Oh my God." He looked at me with near panic in his eyes. "Eddie knows what I've been doing yesterday and today. He knows where, and he knows that I came down here because of Steve..."

"So not only does he know where Babe and Mrs. Holloway are staying, but he also knows they're not being watched right now?" I grabbed him by the collar and shook him, more out of frustration than anger. "Damnit, George!" I took off running and yelled over my shoulder, "Casey!"

What I love about our partnership is Casey didn't even hesitate. Without being privy to my entire conversation with George, she leapt up from her chair and came running. We sprinted to the elevators, and when I saw two people waiting for the elevator to arrive, I took an immediate right, ran a few steps down a short hallway, and shouldered open the stairway door. I took the stairs three at a time.

I hadn't realized George was following until we reached the basement, and I saw the two of them sprinting with me to the car. I stopped and yelled at Casey, "You take your car. If we need to split up, I want to have both vehicles available."

Again, without any questions, she nodded and ran up the ramp toward her car.

I suddenly remembered she had no idea who Eddie was or what he looked like and shouted in frustration. "Shit!"

As if reading my mind, Casey stopped and looked back. "Please stop saying that, or I'm gonna have to add my ulcer to Kate's by the time we're done with this case."

I was still holding the picture of Eddie standing in the crowd, and I ran up and shoved it under her nose. "I'm ninety-five percent sure this is the Coward. This guy here." I pointed to Eddie's face. "I don't have time to explain why I think it's him, but I believe he's going to go after Nathaniel and Babe and Mrs. Holloway since George isn't there watching them."

She took the picture from me and studied it a moment. "Then I think you're right. We do need to split up. I'll go to Nate's house where they're currently staying, and I'll call for uniform backup. You go to Mrs. Holloway's house. If he's already grabbed them, I think that's where he'll take them."

George and I ran back to my car, and by the time Casey

had pulled her door shut, we were already speeding past on the way out of the garage. It was a good thing the reporters weren't standing in the way because I blasted out of the garage, not caring whether I hit any of them or not.

I pulled out my phone and called Babe. No answer. At the stoplight, I scrolled through my contact list and called Nathaniel. Also, no answer. I suppose they could've left their cell phones in another room for whatever reason, but that seemed improbable since this generation is rarely without their phone.

The stoplight was taking too long. It was a relatively small intersection, and I looked left. No cars. I looked right and saw a little Volkswagen putt-putting its way towards us. I ground my teeth and waited until it passed. I looked left again. The road was empty, and I gunned the engine and sped through the red light.

I was impressed that George simply grabbed his seatbelt and pulled it tighter. He angrily pounded the dashboard. "I should've known. I should have fucking known!"

"How the hell could you have known? You didn't know about those other cases, the ones in Europe and Eastern Europe and South America and Asia."

"South America and Asia too?"

"I can't be sure about the one in Korea. All I know is when Kelly put in the search for cases that matched ours, there was one that came up in Korean. The translation program didn't do that well, so I can't be sure exactly what it said, but what I do know is the search engine flagged the article during her search."

George pulled out a cell phone. "Do you think I should call him? Eddie, I mean. Maybe he'll listen to me."

"Absolutely not. Eddie's been using you and your brother as steppingstones to these murders. I mean, he had the nerve to kill your pet rabbit and left the eyes for you guys to find. What kind of a friend is that?"

George must've felt the need to protect the small boy Eddie had been because he said, "He was only seven or eight at the time." Realization dawned, and he smashed his head back into the headrest. "I can't believe this. Not Eddie."

As we drove, I remembered what Doc Hampton said about what we should look for in the Coward. "Did Eddie live with his parents?"

"What does that have to do with anything?"

Out of exasperation, I barked, "Just answer the question, George."

"Okay, sorry, sorry. Yes. Well, most of the time. His father was in the military, and whenever he came back, they sent Eddie to live with his grandparents because his father was a real bastard."

"And the grandparents? Were they his maternal or paternal grandparents?"

"I think they were paternal." He thought about it and then bobbed his head, "Yeah, yeah, they were his paternal grandparents because I remember his mother's parents were killed in a car crash when we were, oh, we must have been around four, I guess."

One thing I know for sure is that abuse is often passed down through the generations. Not always, but often enough. If Eddie's father was abusive, it's a good bet that either his grandmother or his grandfather had been abusive as well. "Did Eddie like going to his grandparents?"

George massaged the back of his neck as he tried to remember back that far. "I think the first time he was excited to go, you know, to get away from his father. But after that, I remember him getting super upset whenever his dad was rotating back home. After a few years, he seemed to become resigned to it. He'd get moody, and a black cloud would descend, and..."

He didn't finish the sentence, and he didn't have to. I think we both got the idea. I called Babe and Nathaniel again. Neither of them picked up. As we entered Mrs. Holloway's neighborhood, I found Casey's number and hit send. When she answered, I asked, "Anything?"

Her voice was low and quiet when she answered, "I'm looking in the windows now. I don't think they're here. But it doesn't look like anything is out of place. You know, like there was a fight or anything. I'm heading your way now."

Up to this point, I'd been gunning the engine at stop signs and around corners, but now I reduced my speed because I didn't want to alert Eddie to the fact we were coming. I pulled to a stop one block over from Mrs. Holloway's house, and George, who by now knew this neighborhood better than I did, motioned me forward with a flick of his hand. "Pull up a few more houses. That'll get us closer to a pathway we can take that'll get us to the back of her house without being seen."

I did as he suggested. When we got out of the car, we both carefully and quietly closed our doors. He led me between two houses, then behind a row of Pyracantha bushes, and finally behind a row of garbage cans lined up along the curve of the cul-de-sac at the end of Mrs. Holloway's road. We hurried to the backyard of the home of one unfortunate homeowner whose front yard happened to butt up against the garbage cans at the end of the cul-de-sac. From there, it didn't take us long to move to the rear of Mrs. Holloway's house.

Once there, I made my way along the side of her house, looking in the windows. Unfortunately, and probably intentionally, all the blinds were closed. When I came to the front corner, I peered around the edge to see into her front yard.

My breath caught when I saw Mrs. Holloway creeping out from behind a car parked in the neighbor's driveway on the opposite side of the house from where I stood.

She held a piece of rebar over her shoulder like a baseball bat, and her gaze was laser-focused on her front door. The determination on her face impressed me, but I definitely didn't want her involved in whatever was going to happen next. I moved quickly across the front of the house, squatting beneath windows as I went because even though someone had drawn the curtains, I didn't want my shadow alerting Eddie to our presence.

Mrs. Holloway saw me and stopped in her tracks.

I motioned her forward with a wave of my hand.

Already unsteady on her feet, she staggered over the gravel at an agonizingly slow pace. I met her halfway and practically picked her up and brought her back to where we could stand with our backs against the side of the house. Although I didn't want to sound unkind, my whisper came out as a loud hiss because I knew she was hard of hearing, "What are you doing? Where are Babe and Nathaniel?"

Fear replaced the determination, and she blinked back tears that threatened to spill over her already rheumy lower lids. "It's all my fault. When they brought me to the hospital, I didn't have time to get my credit cards. I wanted to pay for the groceries for everybody, and Nathaniel and Babe said we could swing by and pick them up. I didn't know he'd be here."

"They're inside?"

"Yes, they told me to wait in the car, and they were going to go in and find my credit cards. But while I was waiting, somebody crept up just like you did, and I just knew it was the Coward. I knew it was him, I don't know how I knew, but I knew."

She hesitated, and unfortunately, I didn't have the luxury of waiting for her to gather her thoughts. I gently took her arm and made her look in my eyes, "Mrs. Holloway, did he go into the house?"

"Yes." Her answer was just above a whisper. The look of determination returned, and she grasped the rebar so hard her knuckles turned white. "I couldn't just sit in the car and wait for things to happen. I had to help them."

I touched the end of the rebar. "Dang, that's sharp."

She pulled it down off her shoulder and brought it close to her eyes to examine it more closely, "I suppose it is. My neighbor down the way sharpens pieces of these for me because I use them in my gardens, and it helps me push it into the dirt."

George had come up behind me, and he said quietly, "Did he have a gun?"

Good question.

Her brows drew together. "I don't know. He was carrying a bag. I'm sure of that." She dipped her chin to emphasize her point, "He had a bag."

George hiked his thumb over his shoulder, "I tested the front door as I went past. It's locked."

When Casey and I had gathered evidence from the kitchen after the Coward's first attempt to kill Mrs. Holloway, I'd noticed that the back door was made of cheap hollow core construction. I took Mrs. Holloway by both shoulders and said, "Please stay here. George and I will go in and get them. But if we have to worry about you as well—"

She held up a hand to stop me, "I understand. I'll wait here. I forgot to tell you I already called the police. I think they're on the way."

George and I drew our weapons and hurried around to the back. We slid up next to the kitchen door, and I carefully turned the handle.

Locked.

I crouched next to the door and said over my shoulder, "We go in fast and loud. Kick it in."

Without hesitation, George stepped in front of the door and bashed it open with a solid kick.

I shoved around the corner and ran into the kitchen, shouting, "Eddie." The time for quiet and slow was over. I wanted to make as much noise as possible to startle him out of whatever he was in the middle of doing.

It worked. I raced through the kitchen and into the living room, where a startled Eddie turned to face me. He held a long knife in one hand and a pair of handcuffs dangling from the other.

More importantly, the sight of George running up beside me, weapon drawn and pointing at his chest, shocked Eddie into immobility.

Babe and Nathaniel were standing behind him on the other side of the room. They'd put distance between themselves so that Eddie had two targets to deal with instead of one. Either he hadn't had time to secure them, or they weren't the docile victims he'd expected. I holstered my weapon since we were in such close quarters, and I didn't want to accidentally shoot either of them if a fight broke out.

Behind Eddie's back, Babe nodded to Nathaniel, and he nodded back. She grabbed a heavy vase from a side table, and before I could yell, "No!" Nathaniel ran forward and wrapped his arms around Eddie in a bear hug. Babe followed, and with a backhanded straight-arm swing, bashed Eddie in the side of the temple with the vase.

With an angry roar, Eddie thrust his arms straight out, breaking Nathaniel's grip. The bastard turned and slashed, opening a gash across Nathaniel's chest and slicing into one of Babe's arms.

Too late, I lunged forward and managed to grab the wrist

of the hand holding the knife. I wrapped my elbow over Eddie's arm and held on.

George grabbed him around the chest and, with his free hand, took control of Eddie's head. Unfortunately, we were jerking this way and that, and George's fingers ended up too close to Eddie's mouth.

Eddie took advantage of George's misplaced fingers and chomped down, hard, on two of them.

George let out a roar but, to my relief, didn't, or couldn't let go.

Eddie was broad-shouldered but not particularly muscular. He was, however, definitely stronger than I'd pegged him back at the bar. He pushed back with his legs, and all three of us landed in a heap on the floor. With the superhuman strength that comes with panic, he struggled to his feet, and we twirled around the room in a parody of a macabre dance.

Blood from George's fingers streaked Eddie's face, but he still didn't let go.

I had to hang onto the knife arm with both hands, so the only help I could give George was to bash the asshole in the side of the head with my elbow. The grazing blows didn't stop him, but it definitely gave him something to think about.

Eddie repeated his previous move of crouching down and bending forward.

I realized too late he was intentionally moving us backward one shove at a time. Once again, I landed on my back, with both George and Eddie landing on top of me. I felt something break beneath me and realized a wet stain was spreading across my back. Just as that realization struck, the noxious odor of gasoline wafted around me. I'd landed on top of and had broken the jar of gasoline Eddie had brought with him to use as his accelerant.

Exactly the result Eddie had been hoping for.

I vaguely wondered why he was using gasoline instead of

his signature mixture of chemicals, but I didn't have time to worry about it right then.

With a roar, he jammed the point of the knife into the floor, a blade's width from my side. There was no doubt in my mind that he'd meant to impale me if he could.

He always seemed to be one step ahead of me, and before I realized what he was doing, he forced my hands down towards his pocket, where he reached in and pulled out a lighter.

I jerked his hand back, but not before he had a good grip on the thing.

George, who'd managed to retrieve his fingers from Eddie's mouth, rolled off us. He grabbed Eddie by the collar and, with Herculean effort, jerked both Eddie and me to our feet.

Smelling the gasoline and seeing Eddie flicking the lighter galvanized both Nathaniel and Babe into action. I still held onto Eddie's wrist with both hands, and Nathaniel reached in and tried to pry the lighter out of Eddie's grasp.

Babe, who was still holding the vase despite the blood running down her arm, reached above George's head and brought the heavy glass down over his shoulder and onto Eddie's face. She was standing at an awkward angle, though, and unfortunately, she couldn't get enough momentum behind her strike to do any real damage.

Eddie was still fighting like a crazed animal. I felt him bunch his legs just like he'd done on the two other previous occasions. When he sprang backward, he launched himself, George, and I straight through the living room window.

The momentum of our fall jerked Eddie's hand out of Nathaniel's grasp, and I watched Nathaniel's face receding from view as the rest of us sailed through the window and landed heavily in the dirt front yard. This time, instead of feeling wetness on my back, I felt sharp jabs of broken glass as I slid across tiny decorative rocks on my shoulder and face.

The ratcheting of the lighter's steel roller continued unabated as Eddie continued with his crazed obsession of engulfing the three of us in flames. Continued, that is until a piece of sharpened rebar came out of nowhere and impaled Eddie's hand in the dirt.

Eddie let out a bloodcurdling scream. He finally released his death grip on the knife and reached over to grab the rebar, trying unsuccessfully to jerk it out of his punctured hand.

Not only had I landed on the bottom of the pile with Eddie on top of me and George on top of him, but I'd also landed on my head with my face pushed down into the dirt. I flinched away from the blood that streamed out from the end of the rebar, which had been driven entirely through Eddie's flesh and bone.

Babe and Nathaniel came running out of the house. Babe grabbed the lighter lying in the rocks next to my face while Nathaniel helped Mrs. Holloway push down on the rebar to make sure the hand stayed securely pinned to the ground.

George wrestled Eddie's free arm up behind his back.

Eddie was still screaming his head off, and I had to yell loud enough so George could hear me over the screams. "Let me up, George. I can't get up."

George jerked Eddie up enough for me to get out from under him.

I threw myself across Eddie's legs to keep him from using his feet as leverage to get away from George. Not that he was going very far with his hand pinned to the dirt, but you know, just in case.

Sirens wailed in the distance, and the sound of several cars careening around the corner sounded like a chorus of angels to me. Car doors opened and slammed shut, and a patrolman ran up and knelt beside me. "I've got him, Alex."

My bell must've been rung harder than I realized because I lay there a few seconds trying to figure out what he meant. A hand grabbed the back of my collar, and Kate said, "You can get up now, Alex. We've got it."

I rolled off Eddie's feet and unsteadily pushed to my knees.

"Don't move around so much." Kate's hand hovered over my cheek, and the concerned look in her eyes told me that it hadn't just been my back and shoulder that had slid across the broken glass.

Casey came running up and, always being the master of the understatement, said, "Ouch."

I looked over my shoulder and saw several patrol officers swarming Eddie.

Steve helped George to his feet while George held his bloody fingers pressed beneath his armpit. He was trying, unsuccessfully, to reassure Steve that he was fine.

Babe, Nathaniel, and Mrs. Holloway stood off to one side. Babe was checking Mrs. Holloway for injuries.

Nathaniel was patting her on the back, congratulating her for keeping Eddie from flicking the lighter.

For her part, Mrs. Holloway dabbed at Nathaniel's bloody chest with a cloth, and I vaguely wondered when she'd had time to grab it during the melee.

I blinked several times at Kate, and with a raspy voice, said, "We figured out who it was."

Casey, who'd been a paramedic in another life, carefully picked glass and stones out of my cheek, "Yeah, I wasn't exactly sure about the how or what your proof was, but after I hung up from you, I called Kate to tell her what was happening."

I shook my head, trying to clear the cobwebs, and asked

Kate, "How did you get here so fast?" I gasped when someone doused my back with cold water from a hose. I jerked around and saw Mitch Johnson holding the hose on me with a worried expression on his face.

He stepped forward, knelt, and smelled the back of my shirt. "Thank God it's only gasoline. If it had been accelerant, the chemicals would be burning through the skin on your back right about now."

Kate stood to get away from the spray of water. "To answer your question, after Casey called us, Mitch, Steve, and I commandeered Arnie Keswick and his patrol car, and he got us here in record time. He'd just pulled into the station when we came running out. We drove around the corner in time to see you flying through that plate glass window."

Arnie had been the patrolman who'd come and taken over from me. He was just now slapping the cuffs on Eddie's free hand after another officer had pulled the bar out of the dirt. The paramedics had arrived, and I overheard them telling the second officer to leave the bar in the hand so the doctors at the hospital could take it out the right way.

Sgt. Longoria strode over and held out a hand, silently offering to help me to my feet.

I grabbed it and, with a bit of a wobble, pushed to a standing position.

Casey had gone to her car and returned with a clean shirt for me to put on.

I pulled the old one over my head, and all the men turned their backs to me.

Sounding exasperated, Kate growled, "Alex."

"What? It's not as if they've never seen a woman's body before. That damn gasoline burns."

I lifted the new shirt to pull it over my head, but Casey stopped me with a hand on my arm. "Hold on." Taking the hose from Mitch, she thoroughly rinsed my back to make sure there was no residue from the gasoline and also gently rubbed her hand across my skin, checking for shards of glass. "Okay. You can get dressed now."

I pulled my shirt over my head and settled it around my hips instead of tucking it in as I usually would. I had enough road rash that I didn't want anything rubbing against the scrapes on my back.

Kate started issuing orders. "Casey, you and Mitch process the scene. Alex, Nathaniel, Babe, and George, all four of you are heading to the hospital."

Both George and I protested, but Kate was adamant. "George, let me see that hand."

She took his palm gingerly between fingers and thumb. "He bit you?"

George pulled back his hand, "Yeah, it's nothing. I'll take care of it."

Kate shook her head. "No, you agreed to be assigned to my unit, and you'll follow my orders. I expect to see you in the ER when I get there with Alex."

I shook my head, "I'm fine, boss. I can help Casey and Mitch with the scene. All I have is a little road rash. I'm pretty sure Casey got all the glass out."

Kate ignored me and turned to Sgt. Longoria. "Rick, I need to stop by the ER to make sure these two get there. I'm pretty sure Babe and Nathaniel will follow orders, but I doubt these two will unless I'm there to follow up. If you'll head to the hospital and take charge of Eddie there, I'd appreciate it." She held out her hand to me, "Keys."

I stared at her moment, feeling more than a little belligerent. I'd just been in a fight with the Coward and thought I deserved to be able to make up my own mind about whether I wanted to go to the hospital or not. I gave in, reached in my pocket, pulled out the keys, and handed them to her. "I'm not an invalid, you know. I can drive."

"You won't be driving until the doctor signs off on your injuries. Let's go."

There were too many of us to all ride in one car, so as Eddie was safely ensconced in the ambulance, we split up and made our own way to the emergency room.

CHAPTER 20

A month later, I couldn't believe I had to sit on stage in front of a bunch of people I didn't know to receive an award I didn't want. Of course, everybody on the special task force was up there with me, and when I'd had to step forward to receive my award, I know that my face was redder than a baboon's backside. I'd asked the chief if he could just hand me the unit citation in the office and let me pass on the award ceremony. He'd said that was not an option.

I listened as the mayor called George, Steve, Kelly, and, of course, Babe, Mrs. Holloway, and Nathaniel to the front of the stage. I looked out over the crowd where proud husbands and wives and parents watched their loved ones receive an award for catching one of the vilest international serial killers ever to terrorize the state of Arizona.

Everyone except Mrs. Holloway had family there. But when she stepped forward and the mayor placed the ribbon around her neck and handed her the plaque, everyone in the auditorium gave her a standing ovation.

Babe's family, her mother, father, sisters, and brother, who'd flown in for the occasion, all had tears in their eyes and were applauding louder than them all. They had officially adopted Mrs. Holloway as a new addition to their family, and they'd already arranged for her to visit them in Pittsburgh in the next couple of weeks.

When the mayor placed the ribbon around Babe's neck, her mother brought her hand to her mouth and tried to hold back the tears of pride cascading down her cheeks. Her husband smiled and put his arm around her shoulders, and the two of them stared lovingly at their youngest daughter as she received a plaque proclaiming her a hero of the City of Tucson.

When it was Nathaniel's turn, his mother, uncle, sister, grandparents, and friends all beamed from the very first row. They'd gotten there two hours early to make sure they had their places reserved.

George and Steve had their wives and children come up on stage with them as they received the award. Both of them had earned many awards in the past, but each one had told me privately that helping bring the Coward to justice was one of the greatest achievements of their lives. Their self-imposed shame over the fact that he had been one of their closest friends had almost cast a pall over the celebration, but Kate had a long talk with them, and I think they'd come to realize there was no way they could have known or prevented any of the killings.

Mitch, Garlan, and Rick each received a medal of exceptional service for the innumerable hours they'd devoted to catching the Coward over the last several months. Understaffed, they'd worked tirelessly, putting in eighty-hour weeks to apprehend the killer who'd eluded so many police departments and arson investigation units around the world.

Later that day, Kate called a special briefing to fill in everyone involved in the case on what we'd discovered during Eddie's interview, and during the search warrants we'd carried out at various California and Arizona locations. "Several of you have asked me to clear up a few of the loose ends of the case. So, I'm just going to go down the list and give you what information I have. First, did he have a reason for targeting Knox Cailleach? Before we knew who the Coward was, Mitch did some checking at the prison and found out that Knox had had around 15 to 20 visitors over the years. Mitch was in the process of going through that list when we discovered Eddie was the Coward. He cross-referenced the list of visitors and discovered that Eddie had indeed visited Knox while he was in prison."

Kate took a bite of the chocolate croissant she was holding and washed it down with a sip of her coffee. "Eddie, who as you know confessed to everything, said that he'd gone to visit Knox while he was in prison during one of the times Eddie had come to stay with Steve. Knox apparently told him to go stuff himself and told him that if he had any balls, he'd have his own trophies to brag about. That pissed Eddie off, so on one of his subsequent visits, after Knox had gotten out of prison, he murdered and burned him."

She popped the rest of the croissant into her mouth. "Two. Yes, we did find the entrenching tool in a shed behind Steve's house. If you remember, Eddie usually stays with Steve whenever he's in town. It had Eddie's fingerprints all over it as well as Babe's and Mrs. Holloway's. It also had some of Eddie's DNA from when Babe whacked him over the head with it."

A rousing chorus of cheers went up among the detectives for Babe's act of heroism.

Kate held up her hand for silence, "Okay, okay, we're all glad he got his head bashed in. Let's keep going so we can get this over with and head home early. Three. Why did both Babe and Alex say the suspect limped when Eddie doesn't actually have a limp? It turns out that the black streak Babe saw running down the side of Eddie's pants when he ran out of Mrs. Holloway's house was the accelerant, just like Mitch guessed." She looked over at Mitch, and Garlan gave him a congratulatory slap on the back.

Kate continued, "The chemicals burned him rather badly on the side of the leg and must have hurt like a mother whenever he ran. And finally, why did he take the eyeballs? When he was a little boy, he fell in love with one of his grandfather's puppies. To punish him for something he'd done wrong, the grandfather put out the puppy's eyes. So, Eddie said he was keeping the eyes so none of his victims would have to go through what that puppy went through because of something he did." She shook her head. "Doc Hampton said in his twisted mind, that explanation made perfect sense. I guess insanity comes in all shapes and sizes."

She flipped her notebook closed. "All right, does anyone else have any questions?"

George put up his hand about shoulder height, "Yeah, I do. I know you found the eyeballs in some kind of case he carried around, but I never heard exactly how many were in there."

Kate nodded, "Well, there were six sets of eyeballs in that particular case. Four were from the recent cases here in Tucson. Two were from a husband and wife Eddie had murdered in a small town in Colorado. However, we found a second case down in the basement of his home in California, which held close to twenty more pairs of eyeballs. For the time being, we're keeping that out of the media, so do not tell your family or friends or anyone else that piece of information. Understood?"

Everyone nodded their understanding.

When no one else had any questions, Kate crossed her arms and tapped her pen on her bicep. "Every one of you did an excellent job on this case. We worked as a team should, and I couldn't be prouder of every one of you. She caught and held everyone's gaze, and when her gaze settled on me, she smiled slightly and nodded, which made my heart soar.

Casey clapped me on the back as we walked back to our desks. "What time is dinner tonight?"

Casey and Terri were joining Megan and me up on my roof for pizza and Chinese beneath the stars. "Well, it needs to be dark, so how does 8 o'clock sound? You bringing the Mike's?"

"Absolutely, and Megan called and asked us to pick up the Chinese because she's gonna be late helping George show his wife and kids the new tricks she's taught his dog."

Casey grabbed her keys and waved on her way out.

I watched the door quietly click shut behind her. I sat down at my desk and began cleaning up all the paperwork I'd left scattered about. Kate had given everyone the afternoon off, and I was the last one left in the office. I found the plaque I'd been given buried beneath a couple of case files. I picked it up and stared at it a moment. I'd never gotten an award before and wasn't quite sure what to do with it.

To my surprise, Kate came out of the lieutenant's office. I thought she'd gone home, but apparently, she'd been in speaking with him. She came over, took the award out of my hands, and propped it up so that it was displayed prominently on my desktop. "There. That's to remind you that the department really does value you for your skills as a detective." She smiled when I scoffed at her words. "You may be a pain in the ass, Alex, but you're my pain in the ass, and I wouldn't have it any other way." She looked at me and raised her eyebrows. "And if you ever repeat that to anyone, I'll deny it until the day I die." I grinned as she turned and walked out of the office.

ALSO BY ALISON NAOMI HOLT

Mystery

Credo's Hope - Alex Wolfe Mysteries Book 1

Credo's Legacy – Alex Wolfe Mysteries Book 2

Credo's Fire – Alex Wolfe Mysteries Book 3

Credo's Bones - Alex Wolfe Mysteries Book 4

Credo's Betrayal - Alex Wolfe Mysteries Book 5

Credo's Honor - Alex Wolfe Mysteries Book 6

Fantasy Fiction

The Spirit Child – The Seven Realms of Ar'rothi Book 1

Duchess Rising – The Seven Realms of Ar'rothi Book 2

Duchess Rampant - The Seven Realms of Ar'rothi Book 3

Spyder's Web - The Seven Realms of Ar'rothi Book 4

Mage of Merigor

Psychological Thriller

The Door at the Top of the Stairs

ABOUT THE AUTHOR

"A good book is an event in my life." – Stendhal

Alison, who grew up listening to her parents reading her the most wonderful books full of adventure, heroes, ducks and puppy dogs, promotes reading wherever she goes and believes literacy is the key to changing the world for the better.

In her writing, she follows Heinlein's Rules, the first rule being *You Must Write*. To that end, she writes in several genres simply because she enjoys the great variety of characters and settings her over-active fantasy life creates. There's nothing better for her then when a character looks over their shoulder, crooks a finger for her to follow and heads off on an adventure. From medieval castles to a horse farm in Virginia to the police beat in Tucson, Arizona, her characters live exciting lives and she's happy enough to follow them around and report on what she sees.

She has published nine fiction novels and one screenplay. Her first novel, The Door at the Top of the Stairs, is a psychological suspense, which she's also adapted as a screenplay. The Screenplay advanced to the Second Round of the Austin Film Festival Screenplay & Teleplay Competition, making it to the top 15% of the 6,764 entries. The screenplay also made the quarter finalist list in the Cynosure Screenwriting awards.

Alison's previous life as a cop gave her a bizarre sense of humor, a realistic look at life, and an insatiable desire to live life to the fullest. She loves all horses & hounds and some humans...

For more information:
https://alisonholtbooks.com

COPYRIGHT

Credo's Bandidos Written by Alison Naomi Holt

Published by Alison Naomi Holt

Copyright © 2021 Alison Naomi Holt

All rights reserved. No part of this publication may be reproduced, stored in a retrieval system, or transmitted in any form or by any means, electronic, mechanical, recording or otherwise, without the prior written permission of the author.

This ebook is licensed for your personal enjoyment only. This ebook may not be re-sold or given away to other people.

The characters and events in this book are fictitious. Any similarity to real persons, living or dead, is coincidental and not intended by the author.

For more information about the author and her other books visit: http://www.Alisonholtbooks.com

Made in the USA
Monee, IL
23 May 2021